WHAT GOOD IS AN AGENT OF DEATH WHEN THE DEAD WON'T LEAVE?

"A gutsy heroine."
—Nancy Holzner, author of *Bloodstone*

BLACK HOWL

A Black Wings Novel

CHRISTINA HENRY

Author of *Black Night*

ACE
$7.99 U.S.
$8.99 CAN

ISBN 978-1-937007-33-1
9 781937 007331
50799
EAN

PRAISE FOR

BLACK WINGS

"A fun, fast ride through the gritty streets of Chicago, *Black Wings* has it all: a gutsy heroine just coming into her power, badass bad guys, a sexy supernatural love interest and a scrappy gargoyle sidekick. Highly recommended."

—Nancy Holzner, author of *Bloodstone*

"An entertaining urban fantasy starring an intriguing heroine . . . The soul-eater serial-killer mystery adds to an engaging Chicago joyride as courageous Madeline fears this unknown adversary but goes after the lethal beast."

—*Midwest Book Review*

"Fast action, plenty of demons and a hint of mystery surrounding the afterlife make for an entertaining urban fantasy populated by an assortment of interesting characters."

—*Monsters and Critics*

"Henry shows that she is up to the challenge of debuting in a crowded genre. The extensive background of her imaginative world is well integrated with the action-packed plot, and the satisfying conclusion leaves the reader primed for the next installment."

—*Publishers Weekly*

"I love the world-building . . . The take on demons and angels is sufficiently different to separate *Black Wings* from the recent spate of tales in that milieu . . . I do recommend *Black Wings* if just for the unusual world and enjoyable plot and characters."

—*Errant Dreams Reviews*

continued . . .

"Readers will enjoy a fast-paced adventure with an interesting cast, especially Beezle, the gargoyle, and be ready and waiting for a future still yet unwritten. Pick up your copy of *Black Wings* today, and stay tuned for *Black Night*."

—*Romance Reviews Today*

"A fast-paced first novel . . . *Black Wings* is a lot of fun."

—*Fresh Fiction*

"Henry does an excellent job of unveiling the first layers of her unique world and its fascinating inhabitants. There's plenty of kick-butt action and intriguing twists to ensure that this story grabs you from the very first page. One to watch!"

—*RT Book Reviews* (4 stars)

"The story was a nonstop action blast full of smart-alecky gargoyle guardians, devilishly handsome (and enigmatic) love interests, arrogant demons, wicked witches and more jaw-dropping revelations than a Jerry Springer show. I barely had time to catch my breath between chapters."

—*All Things Urban Fantasy*

"Fast-paced, action-packed and hard-core—breathing new life into the vast genre of urban fantasy . . . *Black Wings* is intense, dark and full of surprises."

—*Rex Robot Reviews*

"Amazing . . . Henry's pacing is incredible and keeps you absorbed; plus the characterization is fantastic . . . I strongly urge all you [urban fantasy] fans to get this book!"

—*Read All Over Reviews*

"I finished this book in one sitting and will definitely look out for more by this author." —*Bibliophilic Book Blog*

"A fast-paced book that I had a hard time putting down . . . I can't wait to read *Black Night* and find out where Gabriel, J.B., Antares and Beezle all stand in Maddy's world."

—*A Romance Review*

"*Black Wings* was one of the better beginnings to a series that hit every point that it needed to hit. This is a series that I plan to continue [reading] and will continue to enjoy if Christina Henry maintains this caliber of writing."

—*Books By Their Cover*

"It isn't often that a first book grabs your attention and refuses to let you go. Christina Henry's book was that book for me. I loved every minute of this newest paranormal story about one woman's struggle to figure out her place in the world when everything around her seems to be changing."

—*Fantasy Romance Writers*

"I read *Black Wings* in one day, and I loved spending that time with Madeline (and Beezle). I recommend Christina Henry to readers who enjoy the dark humor of Ilona Andrews's Kate Daniels series and the demon politics of Stacia Kane's Megan Chase series." —*Fantasy Literature*

Ace Books by Christina Henry

BLACK WINGS
BLACK NIGHT
BLACK HOWL

BLACK HOWL

CHRISTINA HENRY

ACE BOOKS, NEW YORK

THE BERKLEY PUBLISHING GROUP
Published by the Penguin Group
Penguin Group (USA) Inc.
375 Hudson Street, New York, New York 10014, USA
Penguin Group (Canada), 90 Eglinton Avenue East, Suite 700, Toronto, Ontario M4P 2Y3, Canada
(a division of Pearson Penguin Canada Inc.)
Penguin Books Ltd., 80 Strand, London WC2R 0RL, England
Penguin Group Ireland, 25 St. Stephen's Green, Dublin 2, Ireland (a division of Penguin Books Ltd.)
Penguin Group (Australia), 250 Camberwell Road, Camberwell, Victoria 3124, Australia
(a division of Pearson Australia Group Pty. Ltd.)
Penguin Books India Pvt. Ltd., 11 Community Centre, Panchsheel Park, New Delhi—110 017, India
Penguin Group (NZ), 67 Apollo Drive, Rosedale, Auckland 0632, New Zealand
(a division of Pearson New Zealand Ltd.)
Penguin Books (South Africa) (Pty.) Ltd., 24 Sturdee Avenue, Rosebank, Johannesburg 2196,
South Africa

Penguin Books Ltd., Registered Offices: 80 Strand, London WC2R 0RL, England

BLACK HOWL

An Ace Book / published by arrangement with the author

PUBLISHING HISTORY
Ace mass-market edition / March 2012

ISBN: 978-1-937007-33-1

ACE
Ace Books are published by The Berkley Publishing Group,
a division of Penguin Group (USA) Inc.,
375 Hudson Street, New York, New York 10014.
ACE and the "A" design are trademarks of Penguin Group (USA) Inc.

PRINTED IN THE UNITED STATES OF AMERICA

10 9 8 7 6 5 4 3 2 1

For Henry, because he never complained
when I was writing this book, even though he didn't see his
mom very much for a few weeks while I was finishing it.

I love you, little bear.

ACKNOWLEDGMENTS

Thanks, as always, to my super-awesome editor, Danielle Stockley, and my equally incredible publicist, Rosanne Romanello.

Thanks to Sarah Kaiser, Faith Park, Anne Posner and Pamela Schneider for moral support when I was trying to finish this book without having a nervous breakdown.

Much gratitude is due to Cynthia, Pedro, Jessie, BJ and all the wonderful staff at Einstein Bros. on Southport (my unofficial office).

Love to all of my family, especially Chris and Henry, who keep me going.

1

"LEGS IN THE AIR, HEELS TOWARD THE CEILING. CRUNCH, quick!"

I lay flat on my back, legs extended up, and started crunching as the instructor counted off reps. After about three movements the atrophied muscles in my abdomen started to scream for mercy. My legs dropped toward the ground.

"Uh-uh-uh. No, no, no," the instructor said to me as he walked around the classroom checking our form. He was a tall, handsome African American man with the demeanor of a drill sergeant. "Keep those legs *up*."

He grabbed my ankles and jerked my legs back into position. I tried to remember why I had made this asinine New Year's resolution to lose weight in the first place. Beezle had laughed for a full half hour when I told him I was going to an aerobics class.

"You should be going with me, too," I'd said. "Except that you'd scare the crap out of all the fit people."

Beezle had patted his round tummy indignantly. "I'll have you know that I am the perfect shape for a gargoyle."

"Yeah, a gargoyle that gets out of breath going to the kitchen for snacks," I'd replied.

"Better to get out of breath in pursuit of chocolate than in pursuit of a fitness you will never achieve," Beezle had said.

I'd sworn then and there to lose thirty pounds by June. In retrospect, this was a stupid thing to say out loud, because if I didn't lose the weight, Beezle would harass me about it for the rest of my life.

"Fifty more!" the instructor shouted.

I groaned and glanced at the clock. Aside from my possibly fruitless pursuit of rock-hard abs, I had a secondary motive for getting up at the ungodly hour of five A.M. and making my way to the local YMCA. I had a soul to pick up, and that soul was Harry Lopardo, presently crunching his way up and down on the mat next to me, scheduled to depart this earth in about eight minutes. Harry was a super-fit middle-aged guy who could easily have been in one of those magazine ads for protein bars. He had that no-body-fat look.

If I knew that I had only eight minutes left on my sand timer, I would definitely be doing something besides crunches. It would probably involve getting Gabriel, the unrequited lust of my life, naked as quickly as possible. Of course, there was a universe of obstacles in the way of that happening.

See, I'm an Agent of death. What that means is that once a week I get a list of names, times and places. The names are souls whose deaths have been foreseen by Agency prophets. My job is to be in the right place at the right time to take the soul to the Door. I'm not sure precisely what's behind the Door, but I know that the soul has a choice of many worlds.

Death is a bureaucracy. It's ordered, and filled with paperwork, and pretty much everyone is on a need-to-know basis. As a lowly Agent (a crappy job I inherited when my mother died) my need-to-know ranking is pretty low.

"Leg lifts, slow, then quick, go!" the instructor shouted.

I looked at the clock again. Two more minutes. Thank the freaking Morningstar, because I wasn't sure if I would be able to bend at the waist ever again if this went on for much longer.

"Fifty more!"

"Fifty more, fifty more . . . Is that all he knows how to say?" I muttered.

Harry looked over at me and grinned. "I know it's tough, but if you stick with it, you'll see results."

"No talking!" the instructor shouted.

I huffed and puffed my way through another few reps, and then Harry's legs dropped to the ground and he clutched his chest. His face turned purple.

Heart attack.

I came to my knees and called out to the instructor. "Hey, you should call nine-one-one! I think this guy is having a heart attack."

Everyone in class turned to look at us. I took Harry's hand. "It's okay, it's okay; just look at me."

People started crowding around. The hip-hop music that blared from the speakers kept running, out of sync with what was happening in the room.

"Clear the way, clear the way; give him some air!" the instructor said.

I dropped Harry's hand and scooted back behind the crowd. This gave me the perfect opportunity to disappear.

I pushed my wings from my back and winked out of sight.

Even though I was invisible I still had to follow the laws of physics. That meant that I had to work around the knot of people surrounding Harry and slip through an opening to get to his body. A second after I knelt beside him again, he breathed his last breath.

His soul came drifting up from the body, attached by a band of ectoplasm. Harry looked down at himself with confusion, then up at me. His eyes widened when he noticed my wings.

"A heart attack? Seriously? I was in great shape," he said. "Are you the grim reaper? Or some kind of angel?"

"A little of both," I said, and this was true. My father was Azazel, a fallen angel, and my mother had been an Agent of death. I was also distantly related to Lucifer, and he loved to remind me of that fact.

Harry watched the class instructor giving his lifeless body CPR. "So I guess if you're here, that means that CPR isn't going to do too much for me."

I shook my head and held out my hand. "Will you come with me?"

You have to give the soul a choice. They have to choose to go with you, or stay and haunt this earth forever. Choosing to be a ghost also creates a lot of annoying paperwork.

Harry put his hand in mine. As he did, he looked me up and down critically. "I meant what I said, you know. If you stick with the class, you will definitely see results."

"I'll keep that in mind," I said. "Got any fitness tips for an overweight gargoyle?"

I dropped Harry off at the Door and made my way toward home. The flight felt a little lonely without Gabriel. He used to be my bodyguard, at the behest of my father, and therefore went everywhere with me except the bathroom. Now he was my thrall, by virtue of my having won him in a magical contest that I was not supposed to survive.

The laws of Lucifer's kingdom said that once you are a thrall, you are always a thrall. You can be passed from owner to owner but you can never, ever be free. I really did not want to be Gabriel's owner. But I didn't want him to belong to someone else who would abuse him, either. So mostly I left him alone and avoided making direct requests of him that he would be forced to follow.

This meant that I spent a lot more time flying solo than I used to, unless Samiel decided to come with me. Samiel was Gabriel's half brother and he'd recently become a part of my household collection of oddities. He frequently came with me on pickups because he had an insatiable curiosity about anything and everything to do with humans, but Beezle had insisted that Samiel stay home this morning and watch a movie with him. The gargoyle had been strangely mysterious about the choice of film, too, so I just hoped that he wasn't making Samiel watch something icky, like a really bloody horror movie.

I was flying lower than I usually do, close to the rooftops, which is why I saw the ghost.

It was walking in circles on the sidewalk, which was odd behavior, even for an apparition. Every once in a while it would walk toward the brick exterior of a building and bounce off, almost as if it didn't know that ghosts could drift through solid objects.

I lowered myself to the ground, so focused on the specter's weird behavior that I bumped into a kid with a hooded sweatshirt and backpack making his way to a nearby bus stop. The kid stopped and looked behind him, alarmed.

Seeing nothing, he continued on, his shoulders tensed as if waiting for an attack.

That was stupid of me. I shook my head and continued on toward the ghost, who was still walking in circles near the newspaper boxes on the corner. As I approached I saw that it was a twentysomething male, and he was talking to himself.

"Got to get to class—can't stop—got to go now—sorry red—have to go—can't stay—don't make me stay—don't make me stay—don't make me stay."

He was dressed in that slouchy, worn-out style that a lot of college students favored. As I got closer his voice rose in a crescendo.

"No, can't stop—can't stay—sorry red—don't make me stay—don't make me stay—DON'T MAKE ME!" He walked into a building, bounced off the wall and walked back, bouncing off again like a record with a skipping needle.

"Hey," I said, putting my hand on his shoulder. "Hey, do you need help?"

He turned on me in terror, his hands raised and his wrists crossed in front of his face as if expecting a blow. "No, can't stop—don't make me!"

I held my own hands up so that he would know that I wasn't going to hurt him. "Hey, it's okay. It's okay. You're safe. Can I help you? Can I bring you somewhere?"

Maybe I could convince this soul to go to the Door. That would probably win me points with J.B., even if he wasn't my direct supervisor anymore. J.B. hated ghosts. He took the presence of every lost soul as a personal affront to his ordered universe.

The ghost had lowered his hands, but when I asked if I could bring him somewhere, he got that panicky, trapped-animal look again. "No, can't stop—got to go—don't make me stay!"

I didn't know if he'd been damaged in life or in death, and I didn't usually intervene in the afterlives of ghosts—once the soul has made their choice to haunt instead of go to the Door, an Agent is pretty much out of it. But this ghost was acting so weird, I couldn't believe that the Agent who had been sent to do his pickup had left him like this. I thought I'd better get him off the streets.

I called an Agent response team and gave them my location.

"Agent Madeline Black, north side, near the bus stop at the corner of Clark and Wellington. Yeah, I've got an unruly ghost here."

I gave the dispatcher some info on the ghost's behavior and he told me to wait until the response team arrived. I tucked my phone in my pocket and settled in to babysit.

They didn't keep me waiting long. A few minutes after I'd called, three burly guys who looked like Navy SEALs came flying in. They all wore black shirts and black cargo pants and had the unsmiling look of military men on duty.

"Agent Black? We'll take it from here."

I stepped back to let them do their thing. The leader of the squad approached the ghost with his hands in the air, indicating that he meant no harm. The ghost had gone back to walking into the wall over and over again.

I felt a tap on my shoulder and turned around. J.B. stood there, glaring.

"What's up with your ghost, Black?"

J.B. had a thing for me, and if I didn't have a whole lot of unsettled lust for Gabriel, I might have had a thing for J.B., too, because he was pretty much as hot as it gets. Six foot plus, body of a runner, green eyes, black hair that sticks up in every direction because he spends a lot of time tugging at it.

Unfortunately, he acts like a stick-in-the-mud most of the time. Also, he was presently pissed at me because his mother had put a spell on him to make him act lovey-dovey toward me—part of her master plan of getting a child from Lucifer's bloodline into her own bloodline. I didn't know why this was my fault, but once the spell was broken, he'd decided to take out his mother issues on me.

"It's not my ghost, Bennett," I said, trying to control my anger. "I found it acting like this."

"This is the fourteenth one this week," he said, his eyes troubled. "I want to know what the hell is going on."

The ghost screamed, and I turned back to see that one of the response team guys had wrapped his arms around the ghost's to restrain him. Another member of the team pulled out a small black device that looked a lot like a remote and pointed it at the ghost's eyes. A laser sight appeared on the bridge of the soul's nose.

The ghost struggled in the Agent's grip, his cries louder and more frantic. "Can't stop—KEEP GOING—SORRY RED—I AM THE SCREAM—I AM THE SCREAM—I AM THE SCREAM!"

The other Agent pressed a button on the remote. It didn't seem like anything had happened, but the ghost abruptly went limp in the Agent's arms. One of the other guys stepped forward with a binding rope.

"How could fourteen ghosts end up like this in one week? Who was supposed to do their pickups?" I wondered aloud.

J.B. was silent behind me. I turned to face him and saw that his jaw was clenched.

"What?" I said.

He looked like he was struggling with some decision; then finally he said, "They weren't scheduled."

"Fourteen unscheduled deaths in one week? And they all ended up like this?" I looked at him with dawning comprehension. "You think it has something to do with the fallen."

"Doesn't it usually?" he said. "Every time something weird and freaky has happened around here in the last few months it's come back to Lucifer. And the weird and the freaky have happened more frequently since you acknowledged your bloodline and came into your powers."

"And so you think I might have something to do with it?" I said. "You know, you accused me of murder once and you looked pretty stupid after when you found out that I hadn't been lying about Ramuell."

"I'm not accusing you of anything. I'm just saying that you are Lucifer's child."

"I'm not Lucifer's child," I said. I could feel my magic pulsing underneath my skin—never a good sign. Even though I had made great leaps and bounds in controlling my powers, I still was at the mercy of my emotions.

"Really?" he said, with a pointed glance at my right hand.

My right palm was covered with what looked like a henna tattoo of an uncoiling snake. Unfortunately, the tattooing had not been voluntary. I'd been branded by Lucifer's sword, and I wasn't happy about it.

I shook my head at J.B. "I'm Azazel's child, and my heritage has nothing to do with this in any case. I don't know what's causing this."

"Maybe I should just have you followed," J.B. said thoughtfully. "You'll probably stumble onto the solution accidentally. That seems to happen a lot."

"I resent the implication that I'm Three-Stooging my way through life. I am the only person who's ever survived the Maze," I snapped. "And may I remind you that you should look to your own backyard before you start making wild accusations."

"You think my mother has something to do with this?" J.B. snorted. "She'd never be able to keep a secret this big from the rest of the faerie court."

"She managed to keep the fact that she wanted a child of Lucifer's bloodline secret," I reminded him.

"What motivation would she have for murdering mortals and leaving them like this?" J.B. said.

"What motivation did she have for trying to have me raped and killed?" I said, and as soon as I said it I was sorry. It hung in the air between us like a living thing.

As if by speaking it aloud, my memories—the ones that I tried so hard to suppress over the last month—came rushing back.

The Maze—a swarm of demons, a giant spider, my demon half brother trying to destroy me utterly.

Nathaniel's face possessed by rage, Nathaniel's hands holding me down.

Gabriel turning away from me in disgust.

"It wasn't real," I muttered to myself. My face was covered in sweat, and a blast of cold January air made me shiver.

"Maddy . . ." J.B. said, and he lifted his hand toward me.

"No," I said, and backed away, trying to get myself under control, trying to forget again. "I'm not doing this with you. You can't be my friend when you feel like it and shout at me the rest of the time. Whatever your mother did, I had nothing to do with it, and I suffered far worse at her hand than you did. You were embarrassed by a love spell. She tried to break me, my heart, my mind, my body."

"But she couldn't," J.B. said, and his eyes were hard to read.

"She couldn't," I agreed. "And I won't let you or anyone else do it, either."

Then I turned and flew away, and he didn't try to follow me.

I came in the back door so I saw the mess in the kitchen first. Apparently Beezle and Samiel had made waffles, because the counter was covered in batter and the sink was full of dirty dishes. The score from a movie swelled in the living room and drifted down the hall to where I stood with my coat in one hand and my gloves in the other.

"Seriously?" I said, and then my voice got louder. I tossed my stuff on a chair and strode down the hall. "Seriously? Beezle, you are way too old for this shit."

I stopped when I got to the living room. Samiel and Beezle were sitting on the couch. Both of them had tears running down their faces.

"Gods above and below. What happened?" I said, rushing to Beezle and picking him up. "Did somebody die?"

He pointed wordlessly at the screen. I glanced at it, then back at Beezle.

"*E.T.*?" I said.

Beezle sniffled, nodding. Samiel blew his nose with a tissue.

"You do know it's make-believe, right?"

Beezle glared up at me. "If you don't cry during *E.T.*, you are a robot. No human could get through this movie without shedding a few tears."

"Far be it from me to point out that neither of you are actually human," I said. "When you've wiped your face you can clean up the mess in the kitchen. I'd like to have breakfast in a batter-free zone."

Samiel looked at me and signed, *He made me do it.*

I signed back, *You don't have to listen to him.*

He threatened to put Grape-Nuts in my bedsheets if I didn't make waffles.

Just make sure he actually does the dishes instead of supervising, I replied. Grape-Nuts in your bed is a pretty diabolical punishment. Those little grainy things would probably get everywhere. How would you ever get them out completely?

"We saved some waffles for you. They're in the fridge," Beezle said.

I looked down at my nonexistent abs and sighed. "I can't have waffles."

Beezle smirked. "Because of your *diet*."

"I am going to lose thirty pounds," I said. "Stop trying to sabotage me by bringing doughnuts into the house."

"No one is making you eat them."

"No, but you are making me buy them," I said. "You could be supportive, you know."

Beezle made a little "pfft" noise.

"And what would you do if I stopped going to the pastry shop for you?" I said.

"You would deny an old gargoyle a few simple pleasures before I turn to stone?" he said, putting on his best I-am-so-adorable-you-can't-resist-me face.

"You act like you're going to turn tomorrow," I said.

"Who knows?" Beezle shrugged. "It could happen very suddenly."

"So could a heart attack from saturated fat overload," I said, and went to the kitchen to make oatmeal. My virtuous breakfast didn't taste nearly as good as Samiel's waffles looked.

After the movie was over they came in the kitchen and

Beezle started washing dishes with a lot of long-suffering sighing. I told them about what had happened with the ghost I'd found, and how J.B. thought it had something to do with the fallen.

"It probably does," Gabriel said from the door.

I turned slowly, my heart beating faster, the way it always did when I heard his voice. He leaned in the doorjamb, hands in the pocket of his ever-present overcoat. His face was implacable as always.

"I didn't hear you come up," I said.

"You gave me permission to come and go as I pleased. I have come for Samiel's morning lesson," he said.

Gabriel was teaching Samiel to channel his powers in a more productive way. Samiel had been raised by a monstrous nephilim and a psychotic angel who'd drilled vengeance into him from the moment of his first breath, and thus mostly knew how to use his powers for destruction. I was very interested in keeping Samiel alive and under the radar of the Grigori, so Gabriel had undertaken the task of making Samiel a more productive member of supernatural society.

"Have your orders changed, mistress?"

"Don't start with the 'mistress' crap," I said angrily. "I've already gotten enough passive-aggressive BS from my other not-a-boyfriend this morning."

Gabriel nodded stiffly. "As you wish."

"And my name's not Buttercup, either."

I sighed. I didn't know how much longer the two of us could go on this way. It seemed Gabriel resented me more because I refused to act like his owner. Since I'd already thrown down with J.B., I wasn't in the mood for another confrontation with Gabriel, especially with Beezle and Samiel watching us like we were the best reality TV ever.

"Why do you think the ghosts have something to do with the fallen? Their own accords state that they aren't supposed to harm mortals."

"And you have witnessed for yourself just how well some of Lord Lucifer's minions follow those accords," Gabriel replied.

"Not very well at all," I said, thinking of Focalor and his bid for power.

My darling great-grandfather had told me that Focalor would be punished for his actions at Amarantha's court. I hadn't heard what that punishment was, but I was certain it had been swift and severe. Lucifer had to make sure that his other courts understood that treason would not be tolerated.

Samiel rapped his knuckles on the counter so we would all look at him. *But to murder mortals and leave their souls in such a state—that law is one that even the most rogue of Lucifer's court would not break. Lucifer is not interested in the death of mortals.*

"No," Beezle agreed. "He wants to collect them."

"Because every creature on his side increases his base of power," I said. "All he's really interested in is lording his strength over the other supernatural communities."

"Which is why he is so interested in you, Madeline," Gabriel said. "You have strength and power that you have not yet begun to imagine, and Lord Lucifer knows this. It is also why you have become such an interesting target for the other courts."

"Yeah, moving on," I said. I didn't like to think too closely about my value to Lucifer and my consequent dead-or-alive value to his enemies. That way lay indigestion and sleepless nights. "Look, the last two times there were deaths outside of the natural order it was because of Lucifer's sons, so I can see why you and J.B. would think it would have something to do with him again. But really—how many more sons could he have floating around?"

Beezle arched his brow at me pointedly. "Lucifer has been alive for millennia."

And therefore would have had millennia to reap and sow, as it were, I thought. Was I really going to have to go through this again—stumbling onto more secrets in Lucifer's kingdom, hunting down another of his children? How many innocents would die before I figured things out?

We all stood silently, each of us brooding on our thoughts. The doorbell rang. Beezle fluttered up and away from the sink, clearly thrilled to have a reason to leave the dishes.

"I'd better see who it is," he said, speeding toward the window.

"You have to finish the washing when you come back!" I shouted after him.

"With any luck, it will be something horrible and you'll be distracted for the next several hours," Beezle snapped back over his shoulder.

I looked at Gabriel, who gave me a sad little half smile. Beezle was probably right. My doorbell rang only when bad things were about to happen. Maybe I should tear the stupid thing off.

Beezle zipped back in through the kitchen window, pulling it shut behind him. "It's cold out there. It's Jude at the door."

I frowned. Jude was a werewolf that I had met about a month ago. I was friendly with Wade, Jude's alpha, but Jude himself didn't think very much of me. He hated anyone related to Lucifer.

I trooped downstairs to see what Jude wanted. My household entourage followed me, Gabriel and Samiel crowding on the stairs and Beezle plunking himself on my shoulder.

"Hasn't anyone in this house ever heard of privacy?" I muttered.

"No," Beezle said. "Your business is my business, and you're only going to tell the other two anyway."

And if Jude was there to claw me to death, Gabriel and Samiel could probably intervene before too much bodily damage occurred.

I swung the door open and saw Jude through the exterior door standing outside on the porch with his back to us. This was standard for supernatural creatures—they couldn't cross the threshold of my house without my permission. I pushed open the exterior door and tried not to think about the fact that Gabriel was standing right behind me, the warmth of his body radiating into my skin and making my clothes feel uncomfortably tight.

Jude turned when he heard the door open, and I gasped. His face and hands were covered in blood and his eyes were wild.

"You have to come. Wade's missing."

2

"I KNEW THERE WOULD BE SOME TRAGEDY FOR YOU TO attend to," Beezle said.

"Shush," I said, my stomach knotted. I liked Wade. He was straightforward and compassionate, two traits that were sadly lacking in most supernatural creatures that I met. "What happened, Jude?"

"Perhaps he should come inside," Gabriel said. "Lest we draw the attention of your neighbors."

Jude ran his hands through his shock of red hair. "I don't have time for tea and biscuits. Wade's missing and he told me to get her. So come now."

"I'm not going anywhere until I know what's going on," I said, "and Wade wouldn't want you running off without a plan. So come inside."

Jude looked mutinous, like he might bolt off the porch just to spite me.

"Please," I said, summoning up all my patience. Jude didn't like me, and I didn't think too much of him generally, but I respected Wade. I could be patient for Wade if not for his second-in-command.

Jude looked down at his hands, seeming to realize for the first time that they were covered in gore. "They attacked us in the night. They took so many."

There was a universe of pain in his voice. Something inside me softened toward him. Whatever he might think of me, he obviously cared about his pack.

"Come inside," I said again, and I took him by the arm. It was a mark of how lost he was that he even let me touch him in the first place.

He shook his head as he crossed the threshold, and then he looked down at my hand on his arm. "I'm okay."

I correctly took that to mean that he wanted my hand off him, and I complied. We all climbed the stairs again—Samiel in the lead, followed by Gabriel, Jude, and me, lugging Beezle on my shoulder.

"Do you want to wash your face and hands?" I asked when we got upstairs. I really hoped he would. It was kind of hard to look at his face in its current condition.

"Yeah," he said, and then he unerringly went down the hall to the bathroom and shut the door, like he'd been there before.

"He can probably smell the soap," Beezle said knowingly.

We all sat around my dining room table and waited for Jude to return. A few minutes later he came back in, his hair damp, his face clean and smelling of the citrusy body wash that I used in the shower.

He sat down at the head of the table and looked at me with his eerie blue-gray eyes. Jude's eyes are like a Siberian husky's—pale with a dark rim. The color and his way of staring at you like he could see through to your soul always made me feel vaguely unsettled.

"I think Wade knew that something was going to happen to him. He told me several times that if anything went wrong, I was to go straight to you," Jude said without preamble.

I stared at him blankly. "Well, I don't know why he would do that. He never said anything to me."

"Maybe because we were attacked by demons?" Jude said, his eyes furious. "I told Wade over and over that we should have no truck with Lucifer or his minions, but he insisted on trying to negotiate a new agreement with the old bastard."

"Hold on a second," I said, completely confused. "Can you just start at the beginning? I didn't even know that Wade was trying to negotiate an agreement with Lucifer."

Jude made a visible effort to calm down and collect his thoughts.

"Start at the beginning. Which beginning?" he muttered. "Okay, so after Wade jeopardized our negotiations with Amarantha by openly backing you . . ."

"You act like this is my fault."

"It is. You charmed him somehow, made him forget his priorities."

Beezle snorted. "Maddy? Charm someone?"

I smacked the gargoyle on the back of the head, although privately I agreed with him. Charm is not a quality that I possess.

"Anyway . . ." I said, indicating that Jude should continue.

"After we lost the opportunity to renegotiate for our lost lands with the faeries, Wade decided that it was time to reestablish ties with Lucifer's court."

"Why?" I asked. "From what I understand, your pack hasn't bothered to have relations with the fallen for a long time."

"And we were better off that way," Jude said heatedly. "However, Wade seems to think that the incident at Amarantha's court . . ."

"You mean the incident where Amarantha and Focalor tried to have Maddy killed by proxy?" Beezle said loudly. "That incident?"

"Yes, gargoyle, that incident," Jude said. "Wade sensed that something big is coming, that Focalor moving openly against Lucifer means that there is dissent among the fallen."

"Well, sure," I said. "From what I understand there's always dissent among the fallen. But Focalor failed, and he's probably having the skin peeled off him in strips as we speak. Wouldn't that suppress any seditious thoughts the other court leaders might have?"

"Focalor moved outside the realm of the fallen when he made his bid for power, and the fate of Amarantha's court is now tied to his. Other supernatural courts are now moving to ally themselves for or against Lucifer."

I blinked. "What? You mean, everybody is picking sides for a future war?"

Jude nodded. "It's subtle, but it's there. Some courts are choosing to remain neutral."

"Meaning they want to wait and see where the chips fall before they make a choice," Beezle said derisively.

"And Wade was trying to reestablish ties with Lucifer because of this? Was Lucifer receptive?" I asked.

"He seemed to be. He was very pleased with Wade for backing you in Amarantha's court," Jude said, his face growing red with anger. "But then he betrayed us and set a pack of demons on us."

"That doesn't sound like Lucifer," I said. "He wouldn't negotiate with you in good faith and then openly attack you."

"He is the Deceiver," Jude said bitterly. "How do you know what he would or wouldn't do?"

"Because he's the Deceiver," I said patiently. "If he wanted to mess with the wolves, he'd find much more subtle ways of doing it. He'd send an ambassador to spread discord in your pack or something like that. He wouldn't say one thing and then attack you the next day. It shows no style."

"Madeline is right," Gabriel agreed. "The Morningstar, above all, prefers to appear above the fray."

"Then who set those demons on our pack? Who took Wade, and the others? They took our cubs," Jude said, and his face was haunted. "They took our future."

The demons had taken the wolves' children. Anger rose up inside me, pushing at my skin. I did not want to think about what demons would do with those children. Samiel slid his chair a little farther away from mine as electricity arced across my fingertips.

"We'll get them back," I promised. "I'll do whatever I have to do to help you."

"How?" Jude said. "I tried to track them. But it was like they disappeared into thin air. The trail just went cold."

I looked at Gabriel, and I could tell that he was thinking what I was thinking.

"Portal," I said. "The demons came through a portal and returned back through one."

"That is the magic of the fallen," Jude said. "Demons can't make a portal on their own."

I thought back to something that had happened a couple

of months ago, and addressed my question to Beezle. "When Antares and his buddies attacked J.B. on the lawn, they escaped using a portal. How did they do that if they can't make a portal on their own?"

"Most demons carry portal charms from their masters so that they can do the fallen's bidding," Beezle said.

"But they weren't on my lawn at the behest of any of the fallen. They were there because of Antares," I said. "Do they carry around extra charms? That seems like it would give the demons a lot more freedom than the fallen had intended for them."

"What does this have to do with finding Wade and the cubs?" Jude said. "The demons are probably slaughtering them as we speak."

"No," I said. "They're not. If the demons just wanted to kill them, then they wouldn't have gone to the trouble of taking the wolves with them. They want them for some other purpose. The question is whether they're doing it by someone's command or if they have enough wherewithal to pull something like this off without any of the Grigori noticing."

Samiel tapped his fingers so I would look at him. *Focalor was trying to start an uprising. Maybe his demons have orders to continue without him.*

Gabriel shook his head. "I am sure that Focalor's minions are being watched closely."

"Could a large group of demons do such a thing and go unnoticed by their masters?"

"In some courts, yes." Gabriel frowned. "Which may help narrow things down. Not every court is as large as your father's."

"That's assuming that the demons are acting without a master," Jude said. He stood from the table and paced restlessly. "We're not going to get anywhere by sitting around talking. We need to leave now."

"And where do you suggest we go?" I asked. "You said yourself that you tried to follow the demons and your lead disappeared."

"I have to do something!" Jude shouted, and something happened that had occurred the first time I met him. His bones shifted under his skin, and for a second I saw the wolf looking at me. Then he visibly shuddered, pulled himself back under control, and when he looked up again his face was Jude's.

Everyone stared at me expectantly. Apparently, I was supposed to take charge.

"Okay," I said, trying not to think about the cubs. If I thought about them, I would get emotional, and then I would be unable to think clearly. "First things first. We have to see if we can find out who's doing this. Gabriel, do you think you could trace a power signature from the site where the wolves were attacked?"

"Possibly, if there is any residue from the demons' magic."

"Where is the rest of the pack, Jude?" I asked.

"They're in hiding. We have a contingency plan in the event of an attack."

"Are they safe where they are?"

His eyes flickered with some indefinable emotion. "Safe enough. I wouldn't have left them otherwise."

"Okay. Gabriel and Samiel, will you come with me and Jude?" I had to make sure to present the request as such. I refused to have Gabriel throwing it back in my face that I'd "ordered" him to do anything.

Gabriel nodded, his face grave. "Of course. I would not leave cubs in the hands of demons."

I'll do whatever I can to help, Samiel signed.

"I'll come along, too," Beezle said. "You'll probably need me."

"I'll need somebody to complain about how hungry they are and to fall asleep in my pocket just when something horrible is about to happen?"

"You know, I'm starting to feel like my services are underappreciated in this house," Beezle said, landing heavily on my shoulder.

"Don't think I've forgotten about the mess in the kitchen," I said.

"Yeah, yeah. The dishes will still be there when we get back."

"If we get back," I muttered, wondering just what I was getting myself into this time.

We took a portal from the back yard to the place where the wolves had last been seen. It was some woody location in northern Wisconsin. I was a little unnerved by the complete and total lack of man-made noises, and tried not to reach for Lucifer's sword, which I'd slung automatically over my shoulder before we'd left.

I am a city girl. I am accustomed to hearing the sounds of cars on the street, the roar of the El going by, the laughter of drunken Cubs fans. I am decidedly not used to the twitter of birds that are not pigeons, or the crackling of brush as little rodent things run through the forest.

The clearing had obviously been the site of an attack. Impressed in the dirt were the four-toed claw marks of demons and the paw prints of wolves. Broken shrubbery and bits of torn clothing were strewn everywhere. There were splashes of blood on the tree trunks, and the acid-burn streaks that indicated demon ichor.

Everyone in my party gave me the now-what? look. Beezle fluttered off my shoulder and alighted on a tree branch that gave him an overview of the area.

"What are you up to?" I asked.

"Surveying," he said loftily.

"Code word for 'napping,'" I replied. "Gabriel, will you look for any traces of power while the rest of us see what physical clues we can find?"

Gabriel nodded, but Jude gave an impatient huff.

"What do you think you will find that I didn't? I told you, I tracked them as far as I could."

"But you were upset and probably not thinking clearly," I said, trying to be patient. "You may have missed a few things."

"This is a waste of time," he said.

"Fine, then don't help," I snapped. "Just sit there on your ass while we figure out who took Wade."

"Are you implying that I don't care about my pack?" Jude said.

I threw my hands up. "I imply nothing. Just do whatever the hell you want."

I stomped away, sick to death of men and their delicate sensitivities. Samiel followed, tapping me on the shoulder.

"What is it?" I asked, turning on him with a snarl.

Don't take it out on me just because you're pissed at Jude.

I ran my hands through my hair. "Okay, okay. Sorry."

It's okay. I just wanted to stay with you while you searched.

I glanced over at Gabriel, who seemed to be feeling

around the other side of the clearing with his magic, and raised an eyebrow at Samiel. He looked guilty.

I don't need a babysitter, I signed.

Maybe I do, he signed back.

I gave a short laugh at that. *Stay with me if it makes you feel better.*

It does.

Jude had taken off somewhere while I'd been talking to Samiel, and good riddance to him. I didn't need him snorting at me and second-guessing everything I did while I tried to help him find his lost pack mates. Beezle, as expected, was already snoring up in the tree.

Samiel and I started at the center of the clearing. I moved clockwise in a circle and he moved counterclockwise in a slightly larger diameter, each of us carefully checking the ground for anything that would indicate who had sent the demons.

I sent out a little questing thread of power, trying to see if I might stumble upon anything that Gabriel missed. I'd been trying to practice the more subtle forms of magic, to not let my emotions dictate to my abilities. I was getting better at it, but I was still nowhere close to Gabriel's mastery. Plus, I still didn't know how to trace a tiny flare of power to its source the way Gabriel did. But if I found something, I could at least show it to him and let him follow it.

I was getting a little dizzy walking in circles, my gaze completely focused on the dirt under my feet, but I didn't want to accidentally miss anything. That was when I noticed something.

I put one knee on the ground and leaned forward, trying to make out the shape that was pressed into the dirt. It was inside a demon's footprint, and it wasn't perfectly clear, but it seemed to be the shape of a small *V* on top of a circle.

"This looks like a demon's sigil," I said, getting excited. I looked up for Samiel.

I realized that Samiel and Gabriel were gone, too. Beezle snoozed away up on his branch.

I didn't know whether to be worried or annoyed that both of them had disappeared without a word. The last time Gabriel had gone missing, he'd been taken captive by Samiel and traded to Focalor.

I didn't think I had to worry about Samiel's intentions anymore, but maybe some other creature had gotten both of them. Or maybe they had gone off following clues, so absorbed in their search that they didn't think to notify me.

"And standing here speculating is not productive," I muttered to myself. "Beezle!"

He kept rumbling away like a freight train, so I goosed him with my power. He came awake with a snort and a glare.

"What was that for?" he said, flying down to my shoulder.

"Samiel and Gabriel are gone," I said.

"You woke me up for that?"

"Don't you care that more than half our party is missing?"

"They're probably just following leads, the way you asked them to," he said, rolling his head and cracking his neck.

"Yeah, probably," I said unconvincingly.

The forest seemed unnaturally quiet all of a sudden, as if all the little creatures had gone still in the presence of a predator. I stilled, too, listening for any sign of Gabriel or Samiel or Jude moving through the brush. Beezle stopped moving, finally catching on that something was wrong.

We waited a few minutes. His claws tightened on my shoulders. I tried to steady my breath, to control my galloping heart. Something was about to happen. I could feel it.

There was a sudden crash in the woods only a few feet from where we stood. I turned toward the sound, saw the flashes of light that indicated magic, heard the repeated percussion of flesh hitting flesh, followed by grunts of pain.

I started toward the noise, drawing the sword and holding it before me. The snake tattooed on my right palm wriggled underneath my glove like it recognized its former home. Beezle squeezed his claws in warning. "Wait. It could be a trick, or a trap."

"It could also be Samiel or Gabriel getting the sense knocked out of them," I said, and continued toward the sound anyway.

A second later Samiel and Gabriel appeared, Samiel looking proud, Gabriel grim. They each held the shoulder of an unconscious figure they dragged between them. Jude followed behind them, wiping his knuckles on his shirt.

The figure had white wings, and golden hair that covered his face, but I knew who he was even before they tossed him to the ground at my feet.

"Nathaniel," I said. "What is he doing here?"

3

"LOOKS LIKE WE FOUND OUR CULPRIT," JUDE SAID with a satisfied air. "Once he wakes up we can make him tell us where Wade is."

I rubbed the bridge of my nose. This was a complication that I had not foreseen.

"Look, I'll agree that it's suspicious that he's out here in the middle of nowhere at the same time as a demon attack, but that doesn't necessarily mean that he's the mastermind behind it. There could be any number of reasons for his appearance."

"Such as?" Jude challenged.

"I don't know," I said helplessly, looking at Gabriel and Samiel. Samiel shrugged.

"He could be here as an ambassador from Lord Azazel," Gabriel said slowly. "Nathaniel is often sent on such missions for both Lord Azazel and Lord Lucifer. He is a trusted emissary."

"Then why was he sneaking through the woods, trying not be detected?" Jude said. "I followed him for a good distance and he was clearly trying not to make noise."

"Just because he was trying to be circumspect doesn't mean that his actions are suspicious," I said.

"Just because he is your fiancé doesn't mean that he is above suspicion," Jude snapped back. "If anything, his ties to Lucifer make him less credible in my eyes."

"You're letting your prejudice blind you. And Nathaniel is not my fiancé," I shouted.

I wondered why I was trying to defend Nathaniel. He had assaulted me in Amarantha's castle. Even though he had been under the influence of a spell at the time, I still suspected that the seed of jealousy had always been there, and that the spell had only magnified thoughts and impulses that he had buried deep within.

I did not like him, I did not trust him and I certainly didn't want to be married to him. But I also did not want to make assumptions, to miss out on finding the real culprits because we were distracted by Nathaniel.

The subject of this heated conversation groaned, and we all looked down. Nathaniel opened his ice-blue eyes, saw himself surrounded by a bunch of hostile stares, and seemed to calculate in an instant the correct course of action. He held his hands up above his shoulders while still lying prone on the ground, and made no move to sit up.

"What are you doing here, Nathaniel?" I asked.

"Why ask him? He's just going to lie. It's the way of his kind," Jude said.

"Shut *up*, Jude," I said, and looked at Nathaniel expectantly.

He glanced again at Jude, at Samiel, at Gabriel. “May I speak with you alone, Madeline?”

“No,” Gabriel, Jude and Beezle replied, and Samiel shook his head angrily.

I could have told the four of them that I was quite capable of handling Nathaniel. When he had attacked me I’d blasted a hole in him that had taken weeks to heal. But it didn’t seem to be the time to engage in another pointless argument. We had enough of those going around.

Nathaniel sighed. “I was following you.”

Of all the answers he could have given, this was the least expected.

“Why?” I asked blankly. “How?”

He looked away from me, seemingly embarrassed. “I arrived at your home just before you entered the portal. I overheard your conversation and wanted to assist you.”

“Why?” I asked again. I’d indicated pretty clearly to Nathaniel that I would be happy if I never saw him again the last time we’d spoken.

He turned his head back and gave me a very pointed stare. “Do you not know?”

My cheeks heated in embarrassment as the other four looked at me speculatively. “Oh, for crying out loud. Okay, show’s over.”

I reached down and hauled Nathaniel to his feet. I immediately regretted this, first since it required touching him—a thing I was loath to do—and second since he towered over me by about a foot. I definitely felt I’d lost the advantage I’d had when he was on the ground.

All the men bristled as their prisoner brushed the dirt from his clothing. That was Nathaniel—appearance above all. So what if you were surrounded by a bunch of people who hated you? It just wasn't acceptable to have your jacket wrinkled while being beaten to a pulp.

"If you were here to help Maddy, why were you sneaking through the forest?" Jude asked. "You were heading in the opposite direction of the clearing."

Something flickered in Nathaniel's eyes. It was so brief I thought maybe I'd imagined it. Then he looked at me and said, "I was following the demon trail through the woods. I thought perhaps if I found something, I could redeem myself in your eyes."

I wanted to tell him that it would take a lot more than that to redeem him, and that his references to an incident I'd rather forget weren't doing a lot to help his case.

I looked at Jude for verification. "Was he actually on the demon's trail?"

Jude looked mutinous. "Yes," he said through gritted teeth.

"Okay, then. Fine. Nathaniel is here to help, and we can all treat him accordingly."

Nobody looked happy about this except Nathaniel, who seemed to regain some of his usual arrogance.

"If you will all follow me this way, I did in fact discover something interesting," he said.

Then he turned and disappeared into the woods without waiting to see if we would follow.

"Yes, your majesty," I muttered.

Gabriel and Samiel looked at me questioningly. Jude scowled, as usual. I heaved a sigh and went after Nathaniel, and the rest fell in line behind me.

Nobody spoke as we moved through the forest, not even Beezle. I suspected that he was trying to save me some embarrassment by not telling Nathaniel off. Beezle understood better than the others how vulnerable I'd felt since Nathaniel's assault, no matter how big a game I talked.

Jude was obviously still furious because I didn't suspect Nathaniel, Gabriel was being cool and reserved as usual, and Samiel was waiting to see what happened before he passed judgment.

I was trying very hard not to think too much about Nathaniel or my somersaulting stomach, and concentrate instead on moving quietly through the woods. The other four glided over rocks and tree roots like water, but my boots managed to detect every possible obstacle to trip over. I just wasn't born with the sneaky-ninja gene.

After several minutes had passed Nathaniel came to a stop in a small clearing. A large outcropping of rock with visible glacial striations rose along the west side of the clearing. Green moss covered in frost clung weakly to the formation. The weak winter sun shone above the bare branches of red oaks and sugar maples.

"This is the place where the demons' trail ran out when I followed them earlier," Jude said. "So if that's what you've brought us here for, we can just turn around."

Nathaniel didn't even deign to answer Jude. He simply crossed to the bottom of the rock formation and beckoned to me.

"If you would look here," he said, and pointed to a spot about four feet above the ground.

I stepped closer and crouched down, peering into the shadowed notch where Nathaniel had pointed.

"What are we supposed to be looking at?" Beezle asked belligerently.

"Quiet," I said, leaning forward.

I brushed away some dirt and frost with the three

remaining fingers of my left hand. Samiel had cut off the ring and pinkie fingers before we'd come to an understanding. Lucifer had told me the missing digits would grow back but so far I didn't detect anything exciting happening on that front.

"Look." I pointed to the same sigil I'd seen earlier, a circle with a small *V* on top. "I found this in the clearing where the pack was attacked," I said. "It was inside the footprint of a demon."

"I've never seen a demon's mark like that before," Beezle said.

That was saying something. Beezle is pretty much an encyclopedia of things that go bump in the night, and he knows the arcana of the fallen like he knows all the flavors at Dunkin' Donuts. If he didn't recognize the mark, then it was something new. And my recent experience with the fallen had taught me that anything new was something to dread.

Gabriel leaned over my shoulder and I smelled a whiff of cinnamon, the scent that I associated with an angelic being using their powers.

"It is a holding place for a portal," Gabriel announced.

"What is that?" I said, standing up. Gabriel took an immediate step back so that he wouldn't brush up against me. I ignored the little pulse of hurt that accompanied his action and turned around.

"You would think of it, hmm, perhaps like a button to open an elevator?" Gabriel said. "The magic for the portal is embedded inside this symbol. The demons' master would have given them a key that could activate the sigil and open the portal."

Jude pushed forward, shouldering Gabriel and me out of

his way. He glared at the sigil like he could open it with his force of will.

"Are you saying that we just need to open this little thing and we can find Wade and the rest of the pack?" Jude said. "The demons went through here?"

"It is possible that the demons took another portal elsewhere once they exited this one," Nathaniel said. "However, they certainly left the forest this way."

"Then open it," Jude said.

"Gabriel just explained that you need a key, you numbskull," Beezle said. "How are we supposed to get it open without a key?"

Jude turned on us with furious eyes. "I did not prostrate myself before the granddaughter of my enemy so that we could stand around in the forest and stare at the only way I have of getting to my pack."

"Who prostrated?" I mumbled. Jude had come to me reluctantly and his attitude had hardly recommended him. But I was trying to give him a pass because he was obviously in a tremendous amount of distress over the loss of Wade and the cubs.

"Find a way," he said.

"Do not speak to Madeline in that fashion," Nathaniel said. I was a little surprised that he'd stepped forward so readily to defend me. Nathaniel, like Lucifer, generally likes to appear above the fray.

Jude whirled and turned on him, his fists clenched. "I'll speak to her how I please. You're not free and clear on this as far as I'm concerned, so I don't think you're in any position to tell me what to do."

"Nathaniel is the one who found the sigil for us," I pointed out. "We didn't have a clue to go on before that."

"Yes, and isn't it convenient that he managed to discover something so small in a forest this size," Jude sneered.

I glanced at Nathaniel, momentarily unsure. It was true that I didn't think of Nathaniel as trustworthy. I considered him an angel who would always put his own desires first, and those desires were generally not compatible with anyone who wasn't completely and totally preoccupied with status in the courts.

He was shallow and vain and annoyingly pompous, but he didn't seem to have any motivation for harming Wade or the pack, and I told Jude so.

"How do you know what motivations he has?" Jude said, turning back to me with a reddened face. "How can you know the secrets of the hearts of the fallen? Just how stupid can you possibly be?"

Gabriel started to say something to this but I waved him away. I didn't need him to stand in front of me. I could handle Jude.

"You may want to rethink your comment," I said through my teeth. I felt the familiar surge of power that accompanied the rising tide of anger. I'd tried to be patient with Jude, to be sympathetic to his plight. But I didn't have to stand still and let him swipe at me. "Given that your alpha is in negotiations with Lucifer, it would not be politic for you to insult his granddaughter."

"Politics," Jude spat. "Politics mean nothing to me. They are an excuse for Lucifer to find a way to have dominion over all things."

I thought that Jude was probably right, but I wasn't about to give him the satisfaction of agreeing with him.

"The point here is not what Lucifer wants or doesn't want," I said angrily. The snake on my right palm tingled, like it was trying to get my attention. I ignored it. "The point is that we're all here to help you find Wade and the cubs and you've offered nothing more helpful than suspicion and name-calling."

Jude's face was purple with rage. His hands flexed into his fists, and I thought for a minute that he might actually hit me.

My right hand suddenly felt as though it were being squeezed between the fangs of a snake, and I cried out.

"What's the matter with you now?" Beezle asked.

I glared down at the snake tattoo. "There are other ways of getting my attention."

The snake writhed, as if to say, "I tried to be nice, but you weren't listening."

"And now I am," I said. Warmth spread under the skin, starting at the head of the snake, and coursed up my arm. A minute later I knew what I had to do.

"I'm not at all certain that I like having you there," I muttered.

It was very disconcerting to have an independent entity working through my body, especially an entity so closely aligned with Lucifer. But there was no denying that the snake tattoo had helped me get out of a sticky situation or two.

The snake winked at me.

Beezle tapped a claw on my head. "Are you talking to your hand? You look like a crazy person."

I looked up from contemplating my unwanted parasite and found the other four staring at me. Jude's rage seemed to have receded somewhat in the face of my strange behavior.

There was no point in trying to explain, so I just waved them all away from the rock that we were huddled around. "Stand back."

Wonder of wonders, they all listened without asking

why, backing away several feet. Maybe I should act like a nutcase more often.

I held my right hand in front of me so that the snake tattoo faced the sigil carved in the rock. Again, I felt an uncomfortable heat just under the skin, and I realized that the warmth pulsed from my heartstone to my hand.

This, then, was Lucifer's power, so long dormant inside of me. I'd felt it once before, when I had taken Lucifer's sword from Nathaniel, before I'd entered the Maze.

The clearing was lit by an intense yellow light. I knew that my eyes were blazing with the magic of the Morningstar.

The sigil on the rock glowed red in response, and a swirling vortex appeared inside the symbol. The vortex grew, sweeping leaves and branches and other detritus from the clearing inside it. I dropped my hand and beckoned to the others.

"Come on!" I shouted. "We don't know how long it will stay open."

Gabriel stepped in front of me, making sure that he entered the portal before I did. Samiel gave Nathaniel a dirty look when Nathaniel tried to get in front of him. He shouldered Nathaniel out of his way and Jude followed suit.

One by one they disappeared into the portal. It was pretty clear that they all considered Nathaniel a second-class citizen. It was equally clear that none of them considered me capable enough to be the first through the portal. Except, that was, Nathaniel, who knew firsthand just what I was capable of.

"After you, my lady," he said, and sketched a little bow.

"I hate portals," Beezle grumbled as I stepped forward.

I felt a moment of trepidation. We didn't know where the portal went. And we could end up smack in the middle of a demon court, or a world that was toxic to humans, or who knew what else. But the trail for Wade and the cubs ended here, and there were no other leads to follow.

I went into the portal.

There was a tremendous pressure between my ears. My eyeballs felt like they were turning to jelly. Beezle squeezed his claws so hard on my shoulder that I was sure they would leave a mark. I closed my eyes and heard only the relentless, swirling wind of the vortex.

The pressure abruptly ceased as we emerged. I tried for a graceful landing but I've never managed one yet despite some recent practice with this mode of travel.

I barreled right into Gabriel, who stood in front of the portal. He caught me easily around the waist. Gabriel has some experience with my ineptitude with portals.

I sucked in my breath at the feeling of his hands through my coat. The heat of him penetrated through layers of clothing. Stars exploded in his eyes.

"Ahem," said a gravelly voice close to my ear. "Before the two of you head into la-la land, you might want to remember that you have an audience."

Gabriel lowered me to the ground, slowly. I didn't look around but I felt my cheeks heating in embarrassment. I don't like drawing attention to my feelings for Gabriel.

He closed his eyes. When he opened them there was a clean canvas of black, the stars muted by shadow, and he let me go.

Nathaniel emerged from the portal behind me, and I turned around in time to see it closing. Where the portal had been, there was another of the demon sigils carved into rock.

I finally took the time to look around. We were crowded in a low cave formed of a strange white rock that gave off a phosphorescent glow. The air was heavy and humid. Water dripped down the walls of the cave and formed puddles beneath our feet. There was only one exit.

Everyone looked at me expectantly.

"Oh, sure, I can't go through the portal first but I get to be the one who makes the life-or-death decisions," I muttered.

I went to the mouth of the tunnel that led away from the cave. The pale gleam of rock stretched from the cave, seemingly endless, and into dark nothingness.

"I don't like this," I said.

"This is where the trail brought us," Jude said. "We need to go forward."

"Yeah, and if a pack of demons comes from the other direction, we'll all be jammed up in that narrow passage," I said. "There's not a lot of room to fight in there."

"For our enemies, either," Gabriel pointed out.

"That means that there will be just as much useless slaughter for them as for us," I said. "We might take out some of them but we'll suffer stupid losses in the meantime."

"Well, what do you suggest we do?" Jude snapped. "Go back through the portal and go home and wait and hope that the demons give Wade and the cubs back to us?"

"No," I said, frustrated.

I knew that we had to go forward. There was no other way. But when I looked down that tunnel I felt a powerful surge of foreboding.

"Okay," I said. "Here's what we're going to do. I don't want us to get stopped up in that tunnel. So we're going to string out in a formation ten steps apart. Beezle will go first . . ."

"Why me?" Beezle asked. "If you're looking for someone to take stupid chances, you're looking at the wrong gargoyle."

"Because you're the smallest, and you can fly ahead and scout for us with the least risk," I said impatiently. "I'll follow at the head of the column."

"No, you will not," Gabriel said.

Samiel shook his head in agreement.

"You both have to get over this idea that I'm helpless," I said. "Besides, there's a small chance that any demons we encounter will back off if I show them Lucifer's symbol."

"And what if they do not, as you say, 'back off'?" Nathaniel asked.

"Well, it's not as though I'm powerless. We're not arguing about this," I said to Gabriel and Samiel. "I'm going first. Then Gabriel, ten steps behind me. Then Jude, Samiel and Nathaniel."

I ordered them thus because I assumed if we ran into trouble, Nathaniel would turn around and run in the other direction and therefore free up some space in the narrow tunnel. I'd never seen any evidence that he was particularly skilled in hand-to-hand combat, and he seemed to value his own skin above anyone else's.

"If Beezle does run into anything, he'll come back to us and raise the alarm. Don't crowd up on me if it comes to a fight. Stay in your positions. We'll have more room to maneuver and the demons won't be sure how many of us there are if we're spread out."

None of them looked particularly thrilled by my plan, and I have to say that I wasn't overwhelmed by my brilliance, either. But it was the best I could come up with, and none of them had anything better on offer.

"Let's go," I said.

Beezle flew off my shoulder, muttering imprecations at

me for forcing an old gargoyle to do such tedious and difficult work.

"There's a doughnut in it for you if you do your job and stop complaining," I said.

Beezle looked contemplative. "Deal. Of course, I fully expect that we'll all be killed by this idiocy."

And with that he took off down the tunnel. I waited a few moments, and then followed behind him. I very much hoped that Beezle was wrong, and that my half-assed plan wasn't about to get us all killed.

4

I CREPT FORWARD INTO THE PASSAGE. THE CEILING WAS even lower here than in the cave. Since I am shorter than average, the top of the tunnel was an inch or two above my head. I glanced behind me to see the others filing in silently at the proscribed distance. The men were all hunched over. The wings of the angels scraped lightly against the walls and ceilings, and downy feathers drifted in their wake.

The tunnel gleamed with the same strange light as the cave, but it was fainter. I couldn't see Beezle ahead of us. He'd obviously gotten a little overzealous with his scouting duties. My heart beat wildly in my chest and I made a conscious effort to silence the sound of my breath. Several minutes passed, and I felt the frantic build of adrenaline inside me, anticipating the attack that would not come.

I became aware of an insistent pressure at my hip and could hear a faint buzzing sound. It belatedly registered that my phone was ringing. I pulled it from my pocket and read J.B.'s name on the screen before stuffing it away again. There was no way I was answering the call right now. Never mind the fact that we could be attacked at any minute—J.B. was probably only calling to yell at me about something.

The fact that I was picking up a cell signal told me that we were still on the Earth that I knew, and that gave me a little comfort. It meant that we didn't have such a long way to get home. If we got home at all, that was.

Beezle suddenly loomed out of the darkness in front of me and I swallowed a startled scream.

"Are you trying to give me a heart attack?" I hissed.

He landed on my shoulder and whispered in my ear. "You have to see this. Tell the others to stay here."

"Oh, yeah, like they'll go for that," I said.

"Order them to stay if you have to," he said, and his voice dropped even further, until I could barely hear. I knew he was trying to dodge the supernatural hearing of certain members of our party. "You don't want Jude to see until you can prepare him."

My stomach dropped. Beezle must have found the cubs.

I turned and waited for Gabriel to catch up to me and then signaled the others to stop. Gabriel looked terribly uncomfortable hunched over. I waved him closer and indicated he should use his wings to block us from the others. He crouched a little farther down so he could close us in the private circle of his wings.

Beezle's found something, I signed. Gabriel had taught sign language to both Samiel and me, and it was pretty handy just now. Jude's hearing is unbelievable. I was surprised he hadn't heard Beezle.

What is it? Gabriel signed back.

I don't know. I'm going to go ahead with Beezle. I want you to keep the others here until I get back.

Gabriel shook his head.

This is no time for . . . I realized I didn't know the sign for "testosterone," so I just said it aloud. *Beezle wouldn't lead me into harm; you know that.*

I do not like you going by yourself, Gabriel replied.

I won't be by myself. I'll be with Beezle. Please, just stay here and make sure the others do, too. Especially Jude.

Gabriel looked like he wanted to argue some more but I shook my head at him. We didn't have time for this.

He nodded and backed away from me, and Beezle and I went forward. I hoped that Gabriel would actually listen to me and keep the others behind. If the cubs had been slaughtered by the demons, I didn't want Jude to go on a suicidal rampage. I was certain Wade would want Jude to take care of their pack.

Beezle and I went forward into the tunnel. I couldn't see any turnings or junctions, just the same endless expanse of white rock, glowing faintly in the dark. I was reminded uncomfortably of my time in the Maze, the dark unknown stretching out before me, taking my measure, waiting for just the right moment to break my heart.

After several minutes I felt Beezle's claws tighten on my shoulder, a sure sign of his growing tension.

"How much farther?" My voice was hardly louder than my breath, but it still sounded like a scream in the eerie stillness. We had long since passed out of the sight and sound of the others.

"Very soon now," Beezle growled.

The tunnel abruptly turned, and I followed it. Beezle put his beak close to my ear.

"Quietly."

I tiptoed forward, sure that the blood pounding in my body would be loud enough to give us away. At the end of the passage there was a brightly lit opening, and beyond that were the sounds of screams and moans.

Gods above and below, I thought. *I don't want to see this.*

I steeled myself and crept to the edge of the passage.

The tunnel sloped downward into a wide ramp for perhaps ten or fifteen feet, and then emptied into a huge cavern with soaring phosphorescent ceilings. There were large floodlights attached at intervals along the cavern walls. Cables snaked along the ground, attached to a humming generator in the far corner of the room.

The wolf cubs were all in human form. There were about twenty of them, ranging in age from maybe eighteen months to ten years. They were all bound to hard metal chairs and their eyelids had been taped open. In front of each eyelid was a small object that looked like a digital video camera, except that the camera emitted targeted pulses of light at the cubs' eyes.

I didn't know exactly what the cameras were doing to the cubs, but whatever it was couldn't be good. Several of the smaller children were crying, and a couple of them looked like they had fainted, but since their eyes were forced open, the camera continued doing its gruesome work.

On the opposite side of my perch, at the very front of the cavern, were three demons. All three were humanoid-shaped with dark green scales. They all had wickedly sharp-looking claws, large pointed ears and long simian tails. The end of each tail was tipped with a barb. The left cheek of each demon was branded with the same sigil that we had found on the rock that led to the portal.

They seemed like they ought to be supervising the proceedings, but mostly they appeared bored. One demon had a chair tipped back against the wall and appeared to be dozing with half-closed eyes. The other two were playing some kind of game in the dirt with sticks. There was a lot of arguing and punching involved, although that may have had more to do with the personalities of the demons involved than the actual rules of their pastime.

All seemed immune to the distress of the cubs. I didn't see any sign of Wade, but there was another opening in the cavern beyond the demons. He could be held in another part of this place, or he could be in another location entirely. The cubs were before me, and obviously in pain, so they were my priority. Once the cubs were free, I could move on to the Wade problem.

The demons looked like they'd be easy enough to take out. The trouble was that they might make noise and raise an alarm, causing who knew how many demon compatriots to come pouring out of the opening behind them. Plus, I had the additional snag of freeing all the cubs and then herding them back to the others.

"Why did you tell me to come alone?" I hissed at Beezle. "This would be a lot easier with backup."

"I just wanted to give you time to plan. I thought Jude would overreact if he saw the cubs this way."

"And so he has," growled a voice behind me.

I almost jumped out of my skin. Jude was so close that I could feel his breath on my neck. I turned to see the others crowded up behind me.

It was absolutely terrifying that four grown men could sneak up on me in the darkness and I had noticed nothing. I was really starting to wonder about my life expectancy.

I glared at Gabriel. "I asked you to keep them behind."

He shrugged. I was beginning to think that he used this I-am-your-thrall business when it was convenient for him to keep me at arm's length. The rest of the time he ignored me if it suited him. He seemed incapable of leaving me alone in a potentially dangerous situation, whether I ordered him to do so or not.

Jude looked like he was ready to leap over me and tear the guards into tiny demon pieces. I laid a restraining hand on his shoulder and he turned his furious, burning eyes on me.

"What now, Lucifer's spawn?" he said through his teeth, pushing my hand from him.

"Don't go charging in like an idiot," I said, my own temper rising. I was sick of being called "Lucifer's spawn" and having to deal with Jude's rages. "We need a plan."

I deliberately stepped back from the opening and waved them all to me. Nathaniel, Gabriel and Samiel followed, but Jude took another look at the cubs, then glanced at me.

"Don't even think about it," I whispered angrily. "Do you want to save their lives or do you want revenge?"

Jude growled something that sounded like, "Why not both?" but joined the group with obvious reluctance.

I outlined what I thought would be the best course of action given our limited numbers. They all nodded, even Jude.

Samiel stepped forward, to the edge of the precipice, and spread his wings wide. It was a mark of how disengaged the demons were that they didn't notice a tall blond angel ready to take flight right at their doorstep.

I stood behind Samiel, Gabriel at my shoulder. Reaching inside me, I found the flickering candle that was the source of my magic. A blue ball of nightfire appeared, floating above the snake on my right palm. Beside me, Gabriel readied the same spell.

I tapped Samiel once on the shoulder. He took flight, arrowing over the heads of the cubs and straight toward the other entranceway.

The snoozing demon suddenly open his half-closed lids wide and the front legs of the chair slammed into the ground. He never had a chance to cry out. I hit him in the chest with nightfire and he burst into a riot of blue flames.

His equally lazy compatriots tried to rise to their feet, to turn and fight, but Gabriel took out one and I the other. The three of them were nothing but ash by the time Samiel landed in the doorway at the other end. He turned to us and made an "okay" sign with his fingers, indicating that the alarm had not been raised.

The rest of us ran down the ramp to the floor of the cavern and began untying the cubs. The children didn't indicate that they were even aware of our actions.

Some of them slumped in exhaustion as the bonds that held them upright released their limbs, but they all continued to stare into the light pulses as though under a spell, even after we removed the tape from their eyes. None of us could find an off switch for the devices.

Jude gently shook the shoulder of one of the older boys. "Kieran? Wake up. It's Jude."

"Do you think it's safe to just lift them away from the cameras?" I asked Gabriel.

He frowned. "I do not know. They seem to be under some sort of compulsion. I am afraid that if we did such a thing, we might damage their minds."

"We can't stay here," I said, watching Jude grow increasingly frustrated as he approached each child, called him or her by name, and received no response. "I'm sure there are other guards here, and I don't want to try to battle a demon horde while protecting twenty cubs."

"Perhaps if we try to cover their eyes?" suggested Nathaniel. "First one, then the other. Maybe it will break the hold gradually."

"Or maybe," Jude growled, pulling away from another unresponsive child in anger, "we should just break the fucking things."

He kicked the camera that was nearest to him even as I cried out, "No!"

The falling camera knocked over the rest of the machines in the row like a cascade of dominoes. The effect on the cubs was immediate. They all began to scream in unison, high-pitched wails that grew louder and louder.

There was a clatter of noise from beyond the cavern, the sounds of dozens of clawed feet clicking on the surface of rock, the angry, harsh cries of demon curses.

"Great," I said to Jude. "Just great. Come on, let's get them out of here before we're overrun."

Samiel stayed at the door and readied his nightfire. He still preferred to use his fists over his magic but he was a very fast learner. In some ways he was much more adept than I, and I'd had years of practice using my magic as an Agent.

Nathaniel scooped two cubs under his arms. As soon as the children were separated from the pulse of the machines, they went stiff and began screaming.

"Just get them up into the caves!" I shouted. "Nathaniel, you help me collect the kids. Gabriel, you help Samiel hold off the demons."

"I'm going to scope out the action," Beezle said, and flew off in the direction of Samiel. It was a good thing Samiel couldn't hear or else Beezle would probably drive him insane with suggestions for how best to conquer the approaching horde.

Nathaniel and Gabriel headed off on their appointed tasks and I turned to Jude. He stared at the screaming cubs. He looked like he wasn't sure if he was going to be sick or tear somebody's head off.

"Jude, take a couple of cubs and head up into the tunnel. Try to get them to respond to you."

He turned on me with a snarl. "I want to rip the limbs off the demons that did this to our cubs, not play nursemaid."

"Will you stop arguing about every freaking thing?" I shouted. "They know you. We're going to need the older kids to walk if we want to get out of here, so JUST DO WHAT I SAY! Nathaniel and I will fly them up to you."

Jude huffed out an angry breath, then grabbed a couple of kids and bounded up to the tunnel.

I picked up two of the smaller children and they both began to scream. It broke my heart to hear such little ones in so much pain.

"Shh, shh," I tried to soothe as I flew up to the tunnel. "It's going to be all right."

I handed them to Jude, who looked grim. I couldn't blame him. The cubs were all still screaming their heads off. We had a lot of tunnel to cover to return to the portal, and I had no idea how we would do it with almost two dozen damaged kids.

As I flew back to the cavern I heard the sounds of demons crying out, and the air was filled with the smells of ozone and cinnamon. The fine hairs on the back of my neck stood up as the energy of magic filled the cavern.

Samiel and Gabriel were throwing spells faster than I

could see. I didn't want to think about how many demons had to be in that passage beyond the cavern.

I approached the last cubs. Nathaniel was carrying three or four at a go and there were only these two remaining. One of them was perhaps four years old, and the other looked about eight.

As soon as I separated them from the machines the younger child began to scream like the others. The older child, however, got up and walked away from the chair, toward the cavern wall. His eyes were blank and staring but he didn't seem to comprehend what was before him.

"Hey!" I called after him. I was cradling the little one, who had to weigh at least forty pounds, in my right arm. I touched the older child on the shoulder with my free hand and he cried out as if I'd burned him.

"Can't stop—sorry red—gotta go!" he shouted.

I stared at him. The boy walked into the cavern wall face-first, bounced off and walked into it again. Just like the ghost I'd found. Just like all the ghosts that J.B. had told me were popping up all over the city.

"Umm, are you just going to stand there contemplating the mysteries of life or are you going to stop that kid from breaking his nose?" Beezle asked.

I shook my head, coming out of my reverie, and looked around. Nathaniel had gone to help Gabriel and Samiel, and Jude had his hands full with the cubs.

"Get those cameras," I said to Beezle as I stepped forward and lifted the older boy away from the wall.

The younger child in my right arm was screaming in my ear and it made it hard for me to think. I flew the cubs toward Jude.

"Why?" Beezle called after me. "Don't you think you have greater priorities right now?"

"Just do it!" I shouted over my shoulder. "Why does everything I say have to be questioned?"

I handed the last two children to Jude. The older boy was mumbling something under his breath. I leaned closer so I could hear what he said.

"I am the scream—I am the scream—I am the scream . . ."

My eyes widened.

"What is it?" asked Jude.

I shook my head. There was no time to explain. "Start herding the kids toward the portal as best you can. I'm going to see if we can't close off entry to the cave on the other side."

"What about Wade?" Jude asked.

"We don't know for certain that he's here. The cubs have to be our priority."

"He was with the cubs," Jude said stubbornly. "If you close off the entry, how will we find him?"

"We can't let the demons chase us down when we have twenty incapacitated kids," I snapped. "I promise you, we will come back for Wade. Let's just get the cubs to safety."

While I argued with Jude, Beezle had managed to carry several of the camera-things up to the mouth of the tunnel. He looked breathless and out of sorts as he turned back to get another load. I flew next to him for a moment as I crossed the cavern to the others.

"You'd better have a good reason for this," he grumbled.

"Look at it this way—you might actually burn a calorie or two," I said sweetly.

He dipped down to the cavern floor, cursing up a storm, and I continued on to the other entrance. The three angels stood shoulder to shoulder, and all of them looked beleaguered. When I stepped around Nathaniel and peered down the mouth of the tunnel, I could see why.

The tunnel was packed from floor to ceiling with the same kind of green demons that had been monitoring the cubs. They hung from the ceiling, crawled along the walls and ran over the floor of the cave. They were packed so densely that they appeared to be one giant pulsing mass, a many-tentacled monster with a thousand burning eyes.

Gabriel, Samiel and Nathaniel were blasting as many of the demons as they could, and it was keeping the horde back—for the moment. But for every demon that was night-fired into oblivion, it seemed there were three more.

I blasted a few of them myself from underneath Nathaniel's shoulder and then went around to Gabriel.

His face was white with strain and his teeth gritted from the effort of trying to hold back the tide.

"Let's close off the tunnel," I shouted.

He didn't look away from his task, but his left eyebrow quirked upward. I knew he was thinking of Wade. So was I.

"We have to get the cubs away," I said, and threw some nightfire at the approaching horde. "You, Samiel and Nathaniel keep at it while I take down the wall."

He nodded grimly and passed my message down the line. I had been practicing my spellcasting over the last month or so, since it seemed that every time I turned around I had a new enemy. The presence of Lucifer's mark had also awakened some interesting new abilities, although those powers didn't yet come easily to my call.

I took careful aim at a portion of the rock ceiling that was about four feet beyond the leading edge of the demon mass; then I reached inside, to the place where the source of my magic flickered, and pushed it through my heart-stone.

There was a surge in my blood, a painful electricity running through my veins. My body went stiff and I threw my hands out in front of me.

Blue lightning shot from the tips of my fingers and crashed into the target I had aimed at. The effect was immediate. Huge chunks of rock rained down in front of the demons. Cracks spread from the point of impact and more debris fell. The demons hissed angrily and backed away from the falling stones. Several of them were crushed, and my companions continued to blast nightfire at any demons foolish enough or lucky enough to make it past the falling rocks.

The air quickly filled with dust but the fallen rocks only partially blocked the tunnel. I didn't want the demons to come surging over a pile of rock, so I sent another lightning blast at a visible fault line.

The effort of pushing the spell through a second time brought me to my knees. This happens to me a lot. The angelic part of me controls powers that were normally wielded by immortals. The human part of me fatigues in the face of those powers. I could probably be one of the strongest creatures in Lucifer's realm were it not for that tiny beating stain of mortality.

The second lightning blast did the trick. Bigger chunks of rock fell as the whole tunnel became unstable. Gabriel grabbed me under the shoulders and dragged me backward as giant boulders crashed into the mouth of the tunnel. The sight and sound of the demons were completely obscured by the crash of falling rock.

I pushed to my feet, shaking Gabriel away. The four of us stood watching the tunnel disappear. I hoped I'd done the right thing and that I hadn't just buried Wade under a gigantic pile of rubble.

Huge clouds of dust billowed out of the hole where the exit used to be. I approached the rock pile, which still bore the sparkling remnants of electricity from my lightning bolts. Tiny blue arcs shot all over the surface, and far on the other side of the profusion of rock I heard the howls of demons. And I could hear the shifting of stone. I had blocked the tunnel, but it was a temporary measure. The demons would come for us as soon as they cleared the way.

5

"LET'S GET OUT OF HERE BEFORE THAT PILE COMES tumbling down," I said.

I flew toward the upper cavern entrance, the other three following closely behind me. Beezle was huffing up there with the last couple machines. I caught up to him and took the objects out of his claws. He immediately flew up to my shoulder and landed with a grunt.

"You'd better have a reallllly good reason for this," he repeated. "And you owe me doughnuts, big-time."

"Yeah, yeah," I said, landing in the cave.

There was no sign of Jude or the cubs, but I could hear the echoes of the kids screaming from farther down the tunnel. The pile of cameras lay haphazardly stacked close to the place where the ramp tipped down.

I pulled off my overcoat and made a makeshift bag in

which to carry the cameras. My entourage came through the entrance and crowded around me in curiosity.

"Madeline, why are you wasting your time with these devices?" Nathaniel asked.

There was a funny note in his voice, an emotion that I couldn't place that made me glance up at him. I didn't see anything unusual. He was scowling at me, but that was pretty much his default expression when he wasn't trying to make amends with me.

"Whatever is in these cameras—or whatever they are—is behind those weird ghosts that keep popping up all over the city," I said, stuffing the last of the devices in my coat and tying the sleeves together into a handle. I double-knotted it to make sure that it would stay and stood up. "Let's go."

"What ghosts?" Nathaniel asked.

"I'll explain later," I said.

"Yes, you had better," Gabriel said, peering back the way we came from. "Some of the rocks are starting to shift."

"The horde is coming through," I said.

As I ran down the long passageway toward Jude and the cubs, I retracted my wings so that I could maneuver more easily in the narrow space. I glanced behind me to make sure the others followed. They did, but all three were hunched and grimacing. Unlike Agents, angels can't make their wings disappear at will.

We caught up to Jude very quickly. He was red-faced and sweaty and quite obviously at the end of his rope. The cubs still screamed, endlessly. Some of them were getting hoarse.

"If we're lucky, they'll lose their voices," Beezle muttered.

"Hush," I said, though I privately agreed. Nothing seemed

to stop the children from wailing. They were hurting themselves, and, even worse right now, they were broadcasting our location to any monster who cared to find us.

Jude gave me a look that spoke his frustration eloquently. The cubs would not move forward unless herded. If left to their own devices, they would either stand still and scream or else walk into the wall over and over again like malfunctioning wind-ups.

"There are five of you and twenty kids," Beezle said. "What now, genius?"

"We'll carry the littlest ones," I said. "We can herd the older cubs."

From far behind us I heard the ominous crashing of rock.

"Hurry, hurry," I said, scooping up the two smallest cubs.

It wasn't easy juggling the kids and my makeshift bag, especially with Beezle firmly planted on my shoulder. I nudged two kids who looked like first-graders with my knees.

"Walk forward," I said.

Miraculously, they obeyed. They still screamed, but they marched through the tunnel like little automatons. I looked at Beezle, who shrugged.

"Stop screaming," I said loudly.

The cubs stopped abruptly, as if a switch had been thrown. The silence was eerie.

They all looked at me expectantly, except for the ones I had already told to walk forward. They had disappeared into the shadows ahead.

"Jude, go after those other two. You lead the column," I said.

I looked at the cubs, then pointed at five of them in turn. "Walk forward."

They obeyed, proceeding after their companions.

"Gabriel, you stay with them," I said.

I ordered the other cubs forward in small groups with an angel walking behind like a grade-school chaperone. I handed one of the toddlers to Samiel, who nodded gravely at the little boy in his arms.

I shifted the little girl I held to my other arm so that I could carry the bag of cameras with my right hand. It's not comfortable to grip anything for any length of time when you have only three fingers.

Lucifer's sword banged uncomfortably on my back as I took up the rear position behind Samiel. The cub stared off into the distance over my shoulder. The bag of cameras smacked into my thigh and swung out again, over and over. Beezle's weight on my shoulder felt like an anvil, especially when he started to snore.

"Gods above and below," I muttered.

A zillion demons were after us, we were crammed into a tiny space with limited options for defense, we were trying to protect a bunch of helpless children, and my gargoyle goes to sleep right on schedule. No amount of peril would jeopardize Beezle's naptime.

"On the upside, I might have lost a pound or two, what with all the stress and the walking and the not eating for hours." I needed to find an upside before I cracked up completely.

We had just reached the portal entry when we heard the distant whoop of the triumphant demon horde. I pushed to the front of the column to open the portal, only to discover that the cubs in front were still trying to walk forward into the wall.

"Stop walking," I ordered, and they immediately stopped. I frowned at Jude.

"I tried doing what you did, but they wouldn't listen to me," he growled.

That was a complication I didn't want to think about, and in any event there was no time. The demons were coming, and their claws sounded like the approach of thunder.

I held my tattooed hand up to the symbol in the wall, and once more the portal opened. Jude went through first, and then I ordered the cubs through in their chaperoned groups.

Nathaniel approached me before his group was about to enter. He reached for the makeshift bag of cameras. "Let me take this for you. You will need your hands for defense if the demons appear before we are all through."

I handed him the cub instead. "She's heavier, and it's more important that we get all of the kids through."

He nodded, took the cub and disappeared into the portal with the others.

The last feathers of Samiel's wings had just slipped into the portal as the demons emerged over the slope down the tunnel. I leapt into the portal behind the others, one hand holding Beezle to my shoulder—he still wasn't awake—and one hand gripping the knot in my coat. I took a deep breath and tried not to think about the pain that always accompanied portal travel.

A few moments later I crashed on my face into the clearing. The cameras clattered to the ground as the knot came loose. Beezle awoke with a grunt and flew off my shoulder. The portal spun behind me.

Gabriel grasped me by the shoulders and hauled me to my feet.

"You must seal the portal," he said urgently.

"Seal it?" I said blankly.

"You must close it permanently," he said. "The demons

were directly behind us. They will pour forth from that portal if you do not seal it now."

"But . . ." I began, but I didn't need to voice what I was thinking. Wade.

I looked at the cubs, standing in the clearing like broken dolls.

Jude shook his head at me. "No."

"You must close the portal," Gabriel insisted. "We cannot defend the children if the demons come through."

I knew what Wade would want me to do. I turned toward the portal, my right hand outstretched. Lucifer's mark needed no guidance from me.

"No!" Jude shouted.

From the corner of my eye I saw Jude leap toward me. Samiel intercepted him and there was the sound of a scuffle.

Light burst from the palm of my hand, the blazing red light of the heart of the sun. The portal shrank rapidly. I thought for a moment that there might have been the gleam of tooth and fang emerging from the swirling mist, a glint of malicious eyes, but a moment later the portal was closed and the image was gone.

The demon mark in the rock was scorched and blackened. The portal was closed forever. I dropped my hand and turned back to the others.

Samiel was sitting on top of Jude, who was facedown in dead leaves. The angel used his legs to pin Jude's arms to his sides, and the wolf's right cheek pressed into the dirt.

Jude was red-faced with fury. It was a testament to Samiel's exceptional strength that he was able to hold Jude down. Wolves are some of the most physically powerful supernatural creatures around.

Samiel glanced up at me, questioning.

"Let him up," I said.

He looked doubtful.

"It's okay."

Samiel reluctantly released Jude, who leapt to his feet and stalked toward me. His nose had lengthened into a muzzle. His front canines protruded over his mouth. The fingernails of his hands sharpened into claws.

"Bitch!" he shouted, and his voice was the growl of the wolf.

Gabriel tried to step in front of me, but I stopped him with a hand on his shoulder. I would not hide from Jude in his grief. It could be laid directly at my feet.

Samiel moved toward Jude, looking like he intended to tackle the wolf again. I shook my head and stood my ground.

Jude walked right up to me, chest thrust out, breath coming in harsh pants. His right hand was upraised as though he intended to slash my throat open.

He pushed his muzzle into my face. I lifted my chin and held his gaze. I said nothing.

"I should kill you," he breathed. "I should kill you now and rid the world of one more of your kind."

"Killing me won't change anything," I said with a calm that I did not feel. I wasn't sure I could blast Jude fast enough to stop him from ripping me to pieces if he decided the inclination moved him.

"You sealed the portal," he growled. "I always knew the spawn of Lucifer would betray the wolves."

I couldn't hide from this. It was my fault. We had lost our only clue to Wade's whereabouts, and I knew that. I also knew that Jude's heart was breaking. An alpha is everything to his pack, and as his right-hand man, Jude would have been closer than a brother to Wade. But I didn't have to stand there and be insulted for the hundredth time.

"Let me repeat again—I am not the spawn of Lucifer," I said, my temper rising to the surface.

"Lucifer's power runs through you. Lucifer's sword chose you. Lucifer's mark is upon you. Whether by one generation or a thousand, you are his spawn. I see his craft in your face. I see the same black heart."

"His power may run through me," I said softly, "but his heart is not mine. I am sorry about Wade. I am sorry. If you look as closely as you claim to, you will see that."

His ice-blue eyes flickered over my face, confused. His wolf receded, leaving the face of the man. For a moment he hesitated; then he turned his head to the side and spat. I was thankful he didn't decide to spit on me.

"I see only the deception of your kind."

He turned away from me, crossed the clearing and fell to his knees. He raised his face to the sky and howled.

The cubs, who had been standing so still I'd almost forgotten about them, began to howl in unison. Their eyes were still blank and uncomprehending, but their little voices rose in the same grief as Jude's.

Samiel, Gabriel, Nathaniel, Beezle and I stood and waited, outside of the circle of their sadness. Inside my heart, I howled with them.

Once we started moving again we were faced with a different problem. The cubs would follow a direct order, but only if I told them to. They wouldn't listen to anyone else.

"You could make them do anything," Beezle said. "They would all do the Macarena in sync if you asked them to."

"Oh, yeah, because a troop of dancing brainwashed kids would be so helpful right now," I said as we tramped through the woods. Jude was leading us back to the site of the original attack.

"Just trying to lighten the mood," Beezle said. "Everyone is so grim."

"Well, gosh, Beezle, why would we be grim? We've had a swell adventure here in the woods."

"You don't *know* Wade is dead," Beezle said.

"He might as well be. I don't know where that portal went, and now I never will. And we had no other clues to go on."

"Sure you do. The charcarion demons."

I stopped and stared at Beezle, who was perched on my shoulder and looking incredibly smug.

"The charcarion demons," I repeated. "And they are significant . . . why?"

"How many cinnamon rolls will you give me if I tell you?"

"No one in our house needs cinnamon rolls. Especially you."

"*I'm* not the one on a diet. I think I deserve some compensation for information that is obviously important to you."

"Just spill it, Beezle, or I'll replace all your Cheetos with whole-grain crackers."

He puffed himself up indignantly. "You wouldn't dare."

"Try me."

"Okay, okay. Charcarion demons are found in only two courts of the fallen."

"And those are . . ."

"Abezethibod . . ."

"Bless you," I said.

"And Focalor."

"Focalor," I said, somehow not surprised by this information. "What's he up to now? I thought he was being punished by Lucifer."

Beezle shrugged. "I dunno. That's for you to figure out."

"He definitely has an ax to grind with me," I said slowly.

"Yeah, since you publicly humiliated him when you snuffed out his rebellion in front of Amarantha's court."

"Why do you say it like that? Was I supposed to let him tear Lucifer's kingdom apart and endanger millions of innocent people?"

"No, but he definitely wants your head on a stick."

"He's going to have to get in line," I said, thinking of all the scary creatures who wanted to squash me. I shook my head. That was not a productive line of thought.

"And he's always had a grievance with Lucifer—or at least for the last three or four millennia or so."

"Why is that?" I asked.

"Haven't you ever wondered why Focalor looks like a demon even though he's fallen?"

"Well, yeah," I admitted. "I have wondered."

"That was his punishment for defying Lucifer the last time."

"What were they arguing about?"

"Focalor wanted to go home," Beezle said, pointing a claw skyward. "He was gathering a contingent of fallen to ask for forgiveness."

"Why didn't Lucifer just let them go?"

Beezle snorted. "And take half his base of power with them? Lucifer had just established his own kingdom. No one was allowed to have second thoughts."

"So Focalor has a lot of reasons to resent Lucifer," I said thoughtfully. "And not only are the wolves friends to me, but they were negotiating with Lucifer again."

I glanced at Jude, who was silently leading us through the woods. Maybe he was right. Maybe all the wolves' troubles were Lucifer's fault. And mine.

We entered the clearing that was the site of the kidnapping that had started this whole mess. Jude called a halt, and I repeated the order to the cubs. They stopped in their tracks wherever they were, frozen in a long, ragged line.

"I'll take the cubs myself from here," Jude said.

"How?" I asked. "They won't listen to you."

"I am not going to take three of Lucifer's grandchildren into the place where I have hidden the pack," Jude growled.

"Well, you're going to have to take me, or you'll never get them home."

It didn't take a genius to figure out that Jude would have happily ditched me, but even a stubborn wolf must acknowledge the inevitable.

"Fine, but just you. No gargoyle, no entourage."

"No," Gabriel said in that I-am-an-immovable-object way that he has. "How do we know you will not harm Madeline once she is outnumbered by your pack?"

"And what worth is your word when you have taken every opportunity to show just how much you despise Madeline?" Nathaniel challenged.

"Are you questioning *my* honor?" Jude asked, visibly bristling.

"Enough!" I shouted, rubbing my eyes. "Gods above and below. I know too many men. I need to get some girlfriends."

Beezle snorted. "Yeah. I can totally see you drinking cosmos and talking shoes with a bunch of chicks."

Okay. So maybe that *was* absurd. But the fact remained that there was far too much testosterone in my life.

"I am going to go with Jude and bring back the cubs. You," I said, pointing to Nathaniel, "are going to go back to Azazel's court."

Nathaniel looked mutinous. "I would be remiss in my duties as your fiancé if I let you go alone."

"You are no longer my fiancé," I reminded him.

"Azazel has not publicly revoked the engagement," he said stubbornly.

My anger broke. I was tired and pushed to the limit and in no mood to deal with Nathaniel.

"I have told you that I will not marry you, and you know the reason why. Don't make me go into details in front of everyone here, because it will hardly present you in a good light.

"I am not a toy to be manipulated by Azazel. It is not his word that matters in this case, but mine."

As I spoke I became aware that the clearing had filled with light, and that it was coming from me. But I was too angry to care.

"Now, you may not be my fiancé, but you are a member of my father's court. As such, it would be politic for you to go the hell home when I say so," I said.

I could feel a headache building behind my eyes, the pressure of the unreleased magical energy that was burning through me in concert with my temper.

Nathaniel pressed his lips together. "Yes, my lady."

He turned stiffly away, opened a portal and stepped into it without another word. We all watched silently as it closed behind him.

A very small part of me knew that I had behaved badly, that Nathaniel had helped us rescue the cubs, and that he deserved better than to be berated by me in front of everyone. The larger part of me was just mad, and tired of being crossed at every turn by some fractious male who thought he knew better than me.

I turned on Gabriel and Samiel. Samiel's eyes were the size of saucers. He'd never seen me in 100 percent full-on Morningstar mode before. Even when I'd opened the portal with Lucifer's power it had been tempered by my own powers and inclinations.

My eyes didn't always blaze with light, as I'm certain they were doing just then. Ever since I'd been marked by Lucifer's sword this happened occasionally. "Lucifer" does mean "shining one," after all.

"As for you two," I said, pointing at the half brothers. "I want you to go home as well."

"I will not allow you to go into harm alone," Gabriel said.

"Yes, you will. Jude gave his word, and I trust him. He doesn't want all of us there, and I don't trust you not to follow me. So you and Samiel and Beezle are portaling it home before Jude and I take another step."

"Why do I have to miss all the fun?" Beezle complained.

"Because I need you to make sure these two go home and stay home," I said.

"If my lady orders it, then it shall be done," Gabriel said angrily. There were meteors shooting across his black eyes, a sure sign that his own temper was rising.

"Don't even think about giving me that passive-aggressive I-am-your-thrall shit," I said. "I am not in the mood."

"But I am your thrall," Gabriel said tightly.

"Then follow my freaking orders and go home!" I shouted. "And stay there, so that we can have a proper argument about this later!"

Gabriel gave me a stony stare, then wordlessly opened a portal and went through it.

Beezle flew from my shoulder to Samiel's. "Well, you just stepped in a giant pile of dragon dung. Have fun cleaning that up."

I'm so glad that I'm not you, Samiel signed.

"You two are so supportive. I don't know what I'd do

without you," I muttered. I handed the bag of cameras to Samiel. "Take these home and put them in a safe place. Don't let *anyone* mess with them, not even Gabriel or Beezle."

Samiel gave me a two-fingered salute and turned toward the portal.

"And, Beezle, all that waffle stuff had better be cleaned up when I get home!" I shouted.

I saw Beezle's shoulders sag just before the portal closed.

"Told you I wouldn't forget about the dirty dishes," I muttered.

6

THE LIGHT EMANATING FROM MY BODY SLOWLY FADED as my temper cooled. I became aware of how dark it was outside, and just how long it had been since we'd left the house. I'd gotten up at five A.M. to be shouted at by the instructor at the Y and hadn't had a second of downtime since. Plus, that measly bowl of oatmeal was the last thing I'd eaten.

I sighed and faced Jude. He waited, staring at me like I was a circus performer. The cubs hadn't moved a centimeter since I'd told them to stop.

"That's the entertainment for the day. Tune in tomorrow for the exciting conclusion," I said.

Jude said nothing, only turned and moved through the woods again. I told the cubs to follow him and then I fell in at the end of the column.

I don't know how long we tramped through the forest.

I just know that I am not a particularly adept woodswoman even when I can actually see the tree roots. In the darkness my inability to avoid trippable objects was magnified about a thousandfold. I thought I heard Jude snickering a few times.

Jude stopped abruptly. I saw two shadowy figures emerge from behind trees ahead of us. I told the cubs to stop walking while Jude conferred for several minutes with his pack mates. After a while he came back to me, and the other wolves slid back into the trees.

"You can go no farther," he said.

I quirked an eyebrow at him. I could barely make out his features in the starlight, but I knew he could see me as clear as day. Wolves have excellent night vision.

"And just how are you going to get the kids into your camp?" I asked. "This is the same problem that you had before."

"My pack mates are collecting other wolves to help carry them in," Jude said.

"And what will you do after that?" I persisted. "Are you going to pose them like statues? They won't move; they won't even eat unless I say so."

"Do you think it comforts me to know that the children of my pack will respond only to you? Do you think I relish having to face their mothers and explain that we have returned their cubs to them broken? What are you going to do? Live with the pack? Spend your days caring for the cubs?"

"You wouldn't even have the cubs back if it weren't for me. You would never have been able to enter the portal. I am so sick of your attitude. It's like you're reminding yourself to dislike me."

"I don't have to remind myself to dislike anyone who shares blood with the Deceiver."

"Lucifer's not my favorite person, either, you know. Just what the hell did he do to you?"

The woods seemed to go still at my words. The wind stopped moving through the trees. Small animals ceased their scurrying. The cubs were motionless, and Jude stood as though encased in ice.

I thought perhaps that he would not answer me, that I had crossed that invisible line that every person has, the one that says, "This far, and no farther."

But then he spoke, and his voice was like I had never heard it before. It was ragged, and soft, and there was none of the anger that always ran under the surface.

"Do you know how old I am?" he asked.

He looked like a really active man in his mid-forties, but something told me that probably wasn't the right answer.

"A hundred?" I guessed. Wolves are generally pretty long-lived.

"Two thousand and twelve," he said.

I sucked in my breath, shocked to my core. I'd never heard of a wolf so old.

"Do you remember why we count the years of the calendar as we do, why this year is 2011?"

"It's 2011 A.D.," I said automatically.

"And what does 'A.D.' mean?" Jude said patiently.

"Anno Domini," I said. "'In the year of our Lord.'"

I remember weird things. Beezle hates playing Trivial Pursuit with me. He never wins. "Are you trying to tell me that you knew . . ."

I trailed off, all the pieces suddenly coming together. A two-thousand-year-old redhead, and some stories that I remember reading as a child. A kiss, and thirty pieces of silver.

I stared. "You betrayed him."

"I was tricked," Judas said, and that undercurrent of anger was back. "The soldiers told me that he wouldn't be harmed. I thought I was protecting him. There were mobs by then, people who didn't believe, who wanted to kill him. I thought the Romans would protect him. That was what they told me they would do.

"When they came for him in the garden, they threw that money at my feet. I never asked for it. I never betrayed him. But he went to his grave believing I did. And under the helm of the soldier who had thrown the money at me was Lucifer's laughing face. He'd designed it all, from beginning to end, for his own pleasure."

He stopped for a moment, and I was afraid to speak, afraid to break the spell. I held my breath, waiting.

"After they killed him, I went into the wild. I wanted to die. I wanted animals to rip my limbs from me, as it seemed only right. But I was bitten by a wolf, and, rather than die as I wished, I was condemned to walk the Earth forever. I can never escape my memories, and I don't deserve to."

"Was he really who he said he was?" I asked tentatively.

"I don't know," Jude said heavily. "All I know is that he was good, and I loved him, and Lucifer tricked me into giving him up. I swore that I would protect my alpha with everything that I had, that I would never again trust another outsider. And today, I trusted a face with Lucifer hiding behind it again, and now Wade is gone."

"I am not Lucifer," I said fiercely. "We don't know that Wade is dead. I promise you, I will find him."

"Lucifer enjoys making promises he doesn't intend to keep."

"I am not Lucifer," I repeated.

Jude turned away from me. I didn't blame him for not believing me. If I had been immortalized as the most famous traitor the world had ever known because of Lucifer's actions, I wouldn't believe me, either.

But this was a promise I would keep. I would find Wade, and show Jude that I was more than just another face of Lucifer.

The snake on my palm wriggled, as if to say, *Good luck with that.*

I handed the care of the cubs off to Jude and his pack mates, secretly glad not to face the rest of the pack. I didn't want to see the joy on their mothers' faces when they were reunited with their children, only to watch it turn to heartbreak when they realized their kids were damaged beyond repair.

I went a little ways in the woods until I could find a clearing. I had no idea how to make a portal, but after what had happened today I knew that the snake would know what to do.

"Get me home," I whispered.

The snake wriggled in response and a portal opened before me. While it was mostly unnerving to have an entity operating independently of my body, it did occasionally have its benefits. I didn't relish the thought of flying back to Chicago from northern Wisconsin.

Of course, I thought as I stepped into the portal, *this isn't my favorite way to travel, either.*

I landed in my own backyard with a crash, just a few inches away from my back porch. I was lucky I hadn't broken a bone yet.

I stood up, brushed my clothes off and started for the stairs. And stopped when I saw Gabriel there, as still as stone.

My head had been so full of Jude's tale that I'd forgotten about Gabriel, about what I'd said to him before he left.

"Gabriel," I said, unsure of how to proceed. Crow-eating is not my favorite pastime.

"I see you have returned safely, my lady," he said stiffly.

The "my lady" bit set me off again. "Don't start. I am sick of you pulling this crap whenever you want to put distance between us."

"And what 'crap' might that be, my lady?" he asked. Not a muscle twitched as he stood there, but I could hear the heat in his voice.

I stomped forward, ready to have it out about this once and for all. I walked toward him until he was forced to back into the side of the house, and then I left him no room to move without touching me. "This thing that you do where you act like a thrall when it's convenient for you and ignore me when it's not."

"Would my lady prefer that I act more like a thrall should?"

I grabbed his shoulders and gave him a little shake. "I don't want you to act like a thrall *at all*, and you know that."

"I will act however my lady wishes me to act. That is my duty."

"No, that is your choice. You want to hold me away, to make sure that we never face each other as equals."

"We are not equals, Madeline," he said, and his façade cracked. I saw the heat and the anger and the want that he bottled up inside. "I have told you this time and again. Even when I was Azazel's we were not equals. We do not live in a world where it is possible for us."

"It was also impossible that I come back from the dead," I said. "It was impossible for me to defeat a nephilim, or to defy Amarantha in her own court. It was impossible for me to survive the Maze. But I did all of those things."

"It is not the same. You believe you can ignore the dictates of Lucifer's kingdom, to defy the class structure that has been in place for thousands of years?"

"Yes," I said. "Because I don't care about Lucifer's stupid class system."

"It exists whether you care about it or not. Would you condemn my life for your own pleasure?"

I stepped back, stung. "You know that's not what this is about."

"Then what is it about, Madeline?" Gabriel said softly. "What is it that you want from me?"

I put my hand on his cheek, felt the roughness of his stubble. A muscle twitched in his jaw.

"I want the truth from you," I said. "I want you to tell me what is in your heart, not what you think you want me to hear. I want to know what you keep hidden from the world because you have been raised to believe that it's wrong for you. I want to know that you feel what I feel."

For the second time that night it felt like the Earth had stopped spinning on its axis, that all things in the darkness went still and waited.

He covered my hand with his hand, turned my palm toward his mouth and kissed it. His fingers tightened around mine.

"You wish to know the truth."

"Yes," I said, my heart pounding in my chest.

"You wish to know what it is that I feel."

I nodded, unable to speak further, every part of my body focused on the point of contact between us, the touch of his hand on mine.

"You wish to know that I have not had a restful night's

sleep since the first moment that I laid eyes upon you. You wish to know that every time I see your face my only thought is to possess you utterly."

I closed my eyes. "Yes."

"You wish to know that the love that you showed me by fighting the Maze humbled me absolutely. You wish to know that the longing that I feel has brought me to my knees, that I am powerless against it.

"You wish to know that there is no one for me but you in all the ages of the worlds, that I love you so completely that it consumes me, that every day that I cannot have you my heart is torn to pieces inside me."

He moved forward, eliminated that tiny increment of space between us so that I could feel the heat of him pressed against me, my face turned to his like he was the sun.

"That is what I wish to know," I said raggedly. "Now show me."

This time he did not hesitate, and it was like being consumed by a ravaging hurricane. I met his ferocity with my own, the intensity of his longing matched by mine.

"This is what I have wanted," I said as he kissed me, his hands under my coat, under my shirt, sliding over my hips. "This is what I have always wanted."

We fell to our knees, the snow-covered grass warming beneath us, the ice melting in the heat that was quite literally generated between us. Angels are born of the sun, and our meeting was like the collision of two blazing stars in the coldness of space.

I pushed Gabriel to the ground, rolled on top of him, slid my hands beneath his shirt and heard him groan in response.

"Am I interrupting something?" an amused voice said.

I knew that voice, and so did Gabriel. He pulled away

from me, his eyes panicked, but I pressed my hand to his shoulder so he wouldn't dump me on the ground in his haste to stand up. I put my forehead against his, made him meet my eyes.

"This was not a mistake," I said for his ears alone, even though I knew our observer could hear me.

Gabriel shook his head, and I could see everything he had just revealed sinking back inside him, and his regret at showing me in the first place.

"This was not a mistake," I said fiercely. "Don't you dare go back to the way you were before."

His face was stiff as he nodded. I knew I had lost him, again. And that made me angry. I pushed off him, and Gabriel scrambled to his feet, bowing low.

"Lord Lucifer," he said.

I stood up and crossed my arms at my distant relation. "What the hell do you want now?"

I heard Gabriel's sharp intake of breath.

Lucifer chuckled. He seems to find my defiance amusing. It was probably the only thing that kept me from being blasted from the face of the Earth, because I knew for a fact that no one else was allowed to talk to Lucifer this way.

He leaned against the tree that stood in the corner of my backyard, wearing a particularly natty suit and very shiny shoes. His golden hair shone under the light from the streetlamps, and his glossy black wings were folded behind him. He pushed away from the tree and walked toward us. Gabriel stood at parade rest, his hands crossed in front of him, his face revealing nothing.

"Perhaps I just wanted a visit with my grandchildren, immediate and otherwise," he said.

"Or perhaps you've come to ruin my day, as you seem to enjoy doing that," I snapped back.

I never liked seeing Lucifer at the best of times, and I was particularly irritated that he had shown up just in time to drive another wedge between Gabriel and myself.

"I must confess that I do have an ulterior motive for my appearance," he said.

"Color me surprised," I muttered.

Lucifer stopped in front of me and reached toward my hair. He pulled a dead leaf from my no-doubt completely tangled mess and dropped it wordlessly to the ground, his eyebrow raised.

I lifted my chin. I was not going to apologize for breaking the laws of his kingdom when those laws were stupid to begin with. Especially if he wasn't inclined to enforce them at the moment.

"The Grigori are convening in two days' time to try Samiel ap Ramuell for his crimes," Lucifer said.

My arms dropped to my sides. I felt cold. "They can't."

"They most certainly can. Samiel has broken the laws of the kingdom. He released a nephilim from its prison and willfully set it forth to harm."

"His mother forced him to do that, and you know it," I said fiercely.

"Did his mother force him to harm my own blood?" Lucifer said, grabbing my left hand and holding it up. The missing two fingers were like a condemnation.

I yanked my hand away. "*He's* your blood, too. If I don't blame him for that, then it's none of the Grigori's business."

Lucifer looked amused. "You would be surprised, I think, at what the Grigori consider their business."

"I promised Samiel that I would keep him safe," I said.

Lucifer shrugged. "Then it is, I suppose, your duty to keep your promise."

"He's your grandson. Why don't you just call the Grigori off?"

He spread his arms wide. "Even I must cleave to the law if I am to maintain order."

"That's a load of bullshit," I said. "I think you just want to see how it all plays out."

Lucifer smiled like the Cheshire Cat.

"What are you doing delivering the message, anyway?" I asked angrily. "Don't you have some toady to do it for you?"

"You killed my messenger," Lucifer reminded me.

"I'm sure you've replaced him by now," I said tightly.

"One can never replace a child," Lucifer said, and there was a flash of real sorrow in his eyes.

I didn't want to see that emotion, to know that I was responsible for it. Baraqiel had broken the rules of the kingdom, too, and he'd tried his damndest to kill me. "I told you before, I didn't know he was your son."

"And I asked you before, would that have made a difference?"

"No," I said decisively. I wasn't going to quibble or make excuses.

Lucifer gave me his enigmatic smile again. "The court will convene two days hence at noon in the home of Azazel. I trust you know how to get there."

"I think I can figure it out," I said.

"I wonder. Your father tells me he has seen little of you since your visit to Amarantha's court."

I was not going to get drawn into a conversation with Lucifer about my duty to my father. It would have given me great pleasure to never see Azazel again, but no matter how hard I tried to avoid him it seemed I was always drawn back into his orbit. I was certain the location of Samiel's trial was not a coincidence.

"Is there anything else you wanted?" I said.

"Have I managed to ruin your day?" Lucifer asked.

I said nothing, and Lucifer laughed.

"I will see you in two days' time, then," he said. He looked at Gabriel, who bowed low again. "I think you should attend the court as well, thrall."

I narrowed my eyes at Lucifer. "What for? And don't call him that."

"The Grigori respect strength," Lucifer said. "And I will remind you, Madeline, that in my kingdom I will do as I wish. If you desire something different, you may remember my offer to you when last we spoke."

I remembered his offer—his offer to be his right hand, to be the heir to his kingdom. He'd dangled Gabriel's freedom in front of me in exchange.

"And you may remember my answer," I said.

"Things change," Lucifer said. "And I have all the time in the world."

His wings spread out, and he took flight. I watched him until he was gone.

When I turned to Gabriel, I found that he was gone, too.

I stood alone in the dark, and watched the stars winking above me, and thought I heard the echo of Lucifer's laughter in my ears.

I hardly remembered climbing the stairs and making it to my bedroom. I fell asleep immediately and woke the next morning to blazing sunshine in my face and a crabby gargoyle pressing his beak to my nose.

"Are you going to get up and feed me or what?"

I pushed him away from my face and he fluttered into

the air. I sat up and rubbed my eyes, feeling like I hadn't slept at all.

"Are your hands broken? You're more than capable of feeding yourself."

"You promised me cinnamon rolls, and no cinnamon rolls have appeared."

"I did not."

He pressed one claw to his chin like he was thinking. "I seem to recall discussing cinnamon rolls in exchange for information."

"And I seem to recall telling you that if you didn't tell me what you knew, I would get rid of all your cheese puffs," I said, swinging my feet to the ground. I glanced at the clock. It was eleven A.M., and I knew that I had a pickup sometime today, but I'd forgotten exactly when it was supposed to be in the insanity of yesterday.

Most of my life had been defined by my duties as an Agent, but lately it seemed like tending to the souls of the dead was at the bottom of my priority list. Now I spent most of my time trying not to become a dead soul myself.

"C'mon, you know you want a cinnamon roll," Beezle whined.

I stood up, stretched and realized I'd slept in my clothes from the day before. There was probably rock dust all over my sheets.

"I don't have time to make a junk-food run for you today, Beezle," I said, going into the closet to change into my robe. I needed a shower.

"Why? What do you have to do that's so important?"

I stuck my head out and glared at him. "Oh, gee, I don't know. I have to find Wade. I have to figure out what's causing the ghost problem. I've got some fences to mend with

Gabriel and, oh, yeah, Lucifer showed up last night to tell me that Samiel's trial is tomorrow."

Beezle looked alarmed. "What? Why didn't you tell me last night?"

"Why?" I asked. "What's the problem?"

"You don't think that the Grigori are just going to let you saunter into court with Samiel tomorrow, do you?"

Beezle sped out of the room. I hurriedly pulled my robe on and followed him. Beezle was right. I don't know why I hadn't thought of it. To the Grigori, Samiel was a criminal, and he would be treated as such.

Samiel sat on the couch in the front room doing a sudoku puzzle. He wore a white T-shirt and gray sweatpants. His golden hair was rumpled from sleep. He looked just like any college student relaxing on a Saturday morning—that was, except for the wings. He looked up in puzzlement as Beezle landed on his knee.

That was when the light shining through the picture window disappeared. My eyes widened. The biggest angel I had ever seen hung suspended in the air just beyond the glass, his enormous white wings blocking out the sun.

7

THE ANGEL WORE A FULL SUIT OF ARMOR FROM THE neck down, and his eyes blazed with a strange red light.

"Metatrion," Beezle said.

The angel opened his mouth to speak, and his voice shook the walls of the building. Books tumbled from their shelves. Furniture scraped across the floor.

I grabbed the archway between the living room and the dining room for support as dust rained down from the ceiling. Samiel stumbled away from the window to join me. Beezle landed on my shoulder. We all stared at the apparition just beyond the glass.

"Samiel ap Ramuell," Metatrion boomed. "You are called before the court of the Grigori to be charged for your crimes against the laws of Lucifer's kingdom. You will present yourself before me to be brought to holding, or else face the consequences of your defiance."

The building stopped shaking once Metatrion stopped speaking. Samiel looked at me in confusion.

I quickly explained what Lucifer had told me the night before. Metatrion still hung outside the window like a looming portent of doom.

I should go out to him, Samiel signed.

"No way," I said fiercely. "I won't have you brought before the Grigori in chains."

But the trial is going to happen no matter what.

"Yeah, and I'll be the one to bring you. I told you I'd keep you safe, and I will. I won't let the Grigori punish you for your father's crimes."

What about mine? He picked up my left hand.

"Like I told Lucifer, if it doesn't bother me, it shouldn't bother them. Besides, it's supposed to grow back." I glared at the place where the missing digits had been like I could make them grow back with just my force of will. "Anyway, Skippy there can't get in without my permission."

"Ummm, about that . . ." Beezle began.

Metatrion narrowed his eyes like he'd heard me. Then he drew back his fist and punched it through the front picture window—a thing that he should not have been able to do. I could see his hand very clearly cross the border of the building.

I shouted in anger and blasted nightfire as Metatrion pulled the broken shards away from the point of impact. The nightfire bounced harmlessly off Metatrion's armor as he climbed through the window. I took Samiel's hand and tugged him backward as Metatrion stalked toward us.

I tried to blast the angel with the same spell that I'd used in the cave, but again the armor seemed to dissipate its effects. I could only conclude that it was impervious to any kind of magic.

"Cheater," I muttered as we backed through the dining room.

Samiel picked up one of the dining chairs and heaved it at the giant angel. They are oak, and heavy, and have been in my mother's family for generations. Metatrion caught the chair before it hit him and snapped the frame in half as easily as if he were breaking a tree branch.

Lucifer's sword lay on the side table next to the front door with my keys and cell phone. I picked up the sword and pushed Samiel behind me. Metatrion paused, staring at the sword.

I didn't want to think about how absurd I must look. I was about two feet shorter than Metatrion and wearing nothing but a ratty blue terry-cloth robe. But the pointed tip of the sword was just a few inches from Metatrion's unarmored throat, and I bet he'd bleed the same as anyone else if I pressed forward.

"Leave," I said. "You can't have Samiel."

"I am the Grigori's Hound of the Hunt," Metatrion rumbled, and I winced at the close proximity of his voice. It seemed to shake the very cells of my blood. A couple of wineglasses in the cabinet shattered.

"I am charged with returning Samiel ap Ramuell to the court of the Grigori for his trial. No walls can bind me, and no creature can stop me, not even you, Madeline ap Azazel. I will not cease until the hunt is complete."

I stood a little straighter, pushed the blade to his skin. Metatrion's eyes narrowed.

"My name is Madeline Black," I said. "And you cannot have him."

"When you are breathing your last breath, remember that you chose this," Metatrion said, and he closed his hand over the sword. As he did he opened his mouth and gave a primal scream.

I closed my eyes in pain, keeping a tight grip on the sword. Metatrion tried to bend it or pull it from my grasp; I don't know which. I wasn't strong enough on my own to keep my hold on it, but the snake on my palm did not seem to like Metatrion's behavior and held the handle to my skin like it was magnetized there.

There was the crunch of breaking glass again, and I opened my eyes. Two more armored angels were coming in through the side windows in the dining room. Samiel desperately shot nightfire from behind me. I heard Gabriel pound up the back stairs and crash through the back door into the kitchen.

"Madeline!" he called.

I couldn't turn. I couldn't answer. I strained with every muscle in my body to hold the sword, to keep Metatrion from taking it or Samiel.

Metatrion swung his other hand toward me and closed it around my throat.

The other angels crashed into Gabriel and Samiel behind me. There were the sounds of grunts and fists pounding into skin. From the corner of my eye I saw Beezle flutter to the opposite side of the room and pick something up.

My vision started to close as Metatrion squeezed his armored hand around my windpipe. The only thing holding me upright was the sword and the force of will behind it. He would not take Samiel. I'd promised.

There was a tiny movement behind Metatrion, and Beezle smashed a sharp-edged metal bookend into the angel's bare head. It could hardly have hurt him, but it distracted him enough that he loosened his grip just a hair, on both my throat and the sword.

I thrust upward with all my might, and the sword passed cleanly through his neck and to the other side.

Metatrion's eyes widened for a moment before the red light in them blinked out. I put my bare foot on his knee and he toppled backward, the blade pulling free and coated in the blood of the Hound of the Hunt.

I looked up at Beezle, who grinned at me and dropped the bookend to the ground with a clatter.

"*Now* can I have cinnamon rolls?" he asked.

"Totally," I croaked. It hurt to talk.

I realized suddenly that it was far too quiet and spun around. Gabriel's boot was just visible at the end of the hallway. Samiel and the other two angels were nowhere to be seen.

I ran into the kitchen, my heart pounding.

"Gabriel! Samiel!" I shouted, and then coughed violently.

Gabriel lay on the floor in front of the refrigerator, his face covered in blood. Just beyond the back counter of my kitchen was a small covered porch that I used as a breakfast nook. The back wall of the nook looked like it had been blasted through with dynamite. The floor was covered in feathers and spattered blood.

I fell to my knees at Gabriel's side.

"Gabriel? Gabriel?" I said, shaking him. There didn't appear to be any open wounds on him so I assumed it was someone else's blood.

After a few moments he blearily opened his eyes.

"Madeline?" He sat up a little, leaning on his elbows and looking confused.

I threw my arms around him and held him tight. He hugged me briefly before pushing me away to stare at me somberly.

"The soldiers of the Hound took Samiel."

My shoulders drooped. "I failed him."

I was suddenly acutely aware of how Jude must have felt when Wade was taken. I'd made a promise to Samiel that I would keep him safe, and I'd broken that promise.

"We both did," Gabriel said. "There was a third soldier here in the kitchen. He surprised, then restrained, me while the other two removed Samiel."

I stood and surveyed the ruined mess that had been my kitchen. Samiel was gone. My home was vulnerable to attack. I needed to make it safe again before any one of my dozens of enemies construed an open wall as an invitation.

"Lucifer could havc warned me of this," I said dully. "He took the time to tell me of the trial. He could have told me that the Grigori would send Metatrion. Why would he be able to break the barrier that protects the house?"

"He was the Hound of the Hunt," Beezle said, landing on my shoulder. "He was like a super-duper ultimate supernatural bounty hunter. If the magic of an abode could keep him out, then how could he fulfill his charge from the Grigori? Anything he hunted would be able to hide behind the walls of their home. So he, and he alone, possessed the power to break the barrier without punishment."

"Why do you speak of the Hound in past tense?" Gabriel asked warily, rising to his feet.

I glanced away from the broken wall to Gabriel, who had a braced-for-impact look.

"Because I killed him," I said, rubbing my throat.

Gabriel closed his eyes. "Madeline. You did not."

"Yep, she totally did," Beezle said gleefully. "I helped."

"Metatrion has been the Hound of the Hunt since before the Fall. What do you think the Grigori will make of that at Samiel's trial?" Gabriel said angrily. "Do you think that it will dispose them to think more kindly of Samiel?"

"I was trying to save Samiel," I snapped back, my voice little more than a croaky whisper. "And Metatrion would have killed me if he had the chance."

"He was strangling her to death before I dropped a bookend on his head," Beezle said.

Gabriel turned away, rubbing his face. "I fear there will be consequences for this."

"There always are," I said, wrapping my arms around myself. The apartment was freezing in the January cold now that half my windows were open. "What should we do with Metatrion?"

"Call Lord Azazel," Gabriel said. "Perhaps if you explain the incident to your father first, it will go better for you tomorrow."

"Not a chance," I said. "First of all, Azazel will be a lot more annoying about this than the rest of the Grigori. He's always going on about how my actions reflect poorly on him. And he'll try to use this incident as leverage to make me do something he wants me to do, like marry Nathaniel."

"You must contact one of the fallen," Gabriel said. "They will be furious if you do not return Metatrion's body to them."

"I'd sooner call Lucifer than Azazel. At least Lucifer seems to like me."

"Madeline, do not be deceived by Lucifer's affection for you. If he allows you more leverage than others, it is because he desires something of you."

"I'm not stupid, even though you and everyone else insist on acting like I am. I said I'd *sooner* call Lucifer than Azazel, not that I *would*."

"Then what will you do?" Gabriel asked.

I shrugged. "I'm going to Azazel's court tomorrow. I'll bring Metatrion's body with me then."

"I am not certain that would be a wise decision, particularly when you will be arguing for Samiel's life. It might be . . . inflammatory."

"Maybe," I said, thinking of something Lucifer had said the day before. "Or maybe it demonstrates strength. The Grigori respect power."

"As long as it does not conflict with theirs," Gabriel said.

"Look, let's just put Metatrion in the basement for now, okay? We need to get these windows covered before we die of hypothermia."

"I just hope the neighbors don't see us putting a body in the basement," Beezle muttered.

I snorted. "Are you kidding? They haven't noticed demons on the front lawn, decaying dragons in the backyard, crazy shapeshifters committing murder in the alley or any of the other insanity that goes on around here. If I didn't know better, I'd think the house existed in a pocket dimension."

"There's a first time for everything. Demons can be explained away as a hallucination, but no one can ignore a dead body."

"Can we just get through this without hearing one of your premonitions of doom?" I said, walking back to the hallway to Metatrion's prone form.

I picked up the feet of the dead Hound, and Gabriel took the shoulders.

"Fine. Don't listen to me. You'd just better hope that he doesn't start to smell."

Gabriel and I wrestled Metatrion into the basement and covered him with a tarp. It looked totally conspicuous, exactly as if we'd covered a body with a piece of plastic.

"I'm taking a shower," I said.

"Aren't you forgetting something?" Beezle said as he followed me up the stairs.

"I haven't forgotten your reward," I said, wondering just when I was going to get to Ann Sather for cinnamon rolls with everything else I had to do that day. "I'm not going anywhere until I'm clean."

Gabriel walked silently behind. I wondered what he was thinking. Was he thinking of his half brother being taken before the Grigori? Was he thinking that I'd made yet another gigantic faux pas by killing the Hound of the Hunt? Or was he thinking of what had happened before Lucifer had shown up the night before, and what might have happened if the Morningstar hadn't interfered?

I knew we needed to talk about it—*again*—but I had too many other things on my plate at the moment. I wondered how Jude and the pack were managing the cubs. I needed to get those camera things to J.B. They were definitely related to the ghosts that had been appearing all over Chicago. And that reminded me.

"Beezle, do you know where Samiel put those machines that we got from the cave?"

Beezle looked offended. "Of course not. You told Samiel to hide them."

"Please. You are so freaking nosy there's no way you could help yourself from following him."

"He put them in the clothes dryer in the basement," Beezle said without a trace of shame. "I suggested the refrigerator, since we never have any food in it . . ."

"Because someone who shall remain nameless eats everything as soon as I come home from the grocery store . . ."

"But he seemed to think they would be less obvious in the dryer." Beezle sighed, and I knew that he was worried about Samiel. Ever since Samiel had arrived Beezle had treated Samiel like the brother he'd never had.

"I'll get him back from the Grigori," I said.

Beezle nodded and flew to the front room to sit on the mantel over the fire, his favorite brooding spot. Gabriel followed with a broom to sweep up the broken glass. I went to get dressed, and to cry in the shower where neither of them could hear me.

I had just finished braiding my hair into a long plait down my back when the front doorbell rang. Beezle flew into the bedroom a few seconds later.

"It's J.B.," he announced.

"Tell Gabriel to let him in," I said, pulling my dusty black combat boots on and lacing them up over the ankles of my jeans.

"I'm not sure that's a good idea. They have a tendency to act stupid where you're concerned. And J.B. won't like the implications of Gabriel answering the door."

"I really don't care what J.B. likes and doesn't like," I said. "Just tell Gabriel."

"Oookay. Don't say I didn't warn you," Beezle said.

I was sure that J.B. was there to bring bad news in any case, since it just seemed like it was going to be that sort of week.

I finished dressing and walked down the hall to the dining room. J.B. stood in the open front door glaring at Gabriel. Gabriel had his arms crossed and was leaning nonchalantly on the table while giving J.B. death-ray eyes. Beezle sat on the side table, and he turned to raise his eyebrows in an I-told-you-so way as I entered.

Gabriel had covered the windows with plastic so that we weren't getting blasted by cold air, but the room was still freezing. I wore a long-sleeved shirt under a gray wool cabled turtleneck sweater—I am branching out from my usual uniform of black—and I was still chilly. I tucked my hands inside my sleeves.

J.B. broke his staring contest with Gabriel to scowl at me when I entered.

"Do you want to tell me why we intercepted a nine-one-one call this morning reporting a dead body in your basement?"

"Ha!" Beezle shouted, pumping his little fist in the air. "I told you that somebody would notice."

"What do you mean, you intercepted a call?" I asked. "Am I under surveillance?"

"Of course you are," J.B. said in a tone that implied I was an idiot. "It's in the best interests of the Agency to publicly suppress all the weird shit that seems to happen at this address."

"The neighbors do notice, then?"

"They'd have to be either dead or stupid not to. So tell me why it looks like there's been a war in here, and why you've got bruises on your throat."

I summed up the morning's events. J.B.'s eyebrows went up to his hairline when I told him that it was the Hound of the Hunt in the basement.

"I don't know whether to be impressed or depressed," J.B. said.

"I often feel that way around Madeline," Gabriel said, and the two of them shared a look of understanding.

"What's to be depressed about?"

"You're going to have to pay a price for killing Metatrion," J.B. said.

"That happens to me all the time," I said.

"And your enemies, which include my beloved mother, will perceive you as a greater threat since you managed to kill such a powerful being. Which means they will redouble their efforts to kill *you*."

"Well," I said, clapping my hands together, "what's a few extra death threats when you've already got dozens of them? I have something more important to show you, anyway."

I recounted the story of the cubs' kidnapping and what I'd found in the cave as J.B., Gabriel and Beezle followed me into the basement. I pulled the bag of cameras from the dryer.

"That's some security system you've got there," J.B. said sarcastically.

"I don't know if you've noticed, but my house was destroyed this morning and I've hardly had time to think about putting these in a safer place. Besides, now you can take them back to the Agency and put them behind a million layers of lead and steel if you want."

J.B. untangled the knotted sleeves of my coat and pulled one of the machines from the bag, inspecting it. "It looks like a digital camera."

"I know. I can't figure out what they were doing to the cubs, but it definitely damaged their brains. The older cubs were acting exactly like the ghost I found."

"So, is whatever is in this machine killing them? Or is it just damaging them beyond repair and their deaths are unrelated?"

"I can easily see someone dying by accident once they've been exposed to this machine," I said slowly. "They could walk into traffic, or step off a cliff, and never even know where they are."

"But it still doesn't explain why they aren't being tracked by the Agency. We're finding these ghosts by accident, not at the sites of their deaths. If they have souls, then we should know when and how they're going to die. But that's not happening."

"What if the mental damage is affecting the way the Agency perceives these people? They still have souls, but the Agency isn't recognizing them as such because of . . . whatever it is that this machine does."

J.B. looked doubtful. "We've taken the souls of people in many different mental states over the past several millennia. Recognition has never been an issue."

"What else could explain how so many people are disappearing from the Agency's radar?"

"I don't know," J.B. said, obviously frustrated. Then he grinned at me. "But I'm sure that if I wait, you'll find out for me."

"That's nice," I muttered. "Like I don't have enough to do. And somehow I have to make new windows—and a new wall—appear out of thin air."

"I can do that," J.B. said, and pulled his cell phone out of his pocket. He barked a few terse orders at the person on the other end of the line and hung up. "Someone will be here in about an hour to fix everything."

I stared at him. "You know, yesterday morning you were acting like I had a contagious disease. You haven't spoken civilly to me for weeks. Do you have a multiple personality disorder or something?"

He shrugged and looked uncomfortably at Gabriel and Beezle, who were not disguising their interest in the least.

"Don't mind them," I said. "I can't do anything these days without an audience."

"Maybe I thought about some of what you said yesterday, and realized I was being unfair to you."

"Can someone run and check the temperature in Hell, please? Because that sounded a lot like an apology."

"You could just say, 'Thank you for the windows, J.B.,' and stop giving me a hard time."

"Thank you for the windows, J.B.," I parroted.

"And thank you for these," he said, tying the knot of my coat back together and slinging it over his shoulder. "I'll let you know what I find. Don't forget your pickup at two."

"So that's when it is," I said. "You wouldn't, uh, happen to know where it is, would you?"

He rolled his eyes and pulled the piece of paper with the information from his pocket. "I had a feeling."

"I've never missed a pickup before," I said, stung. I might have chaos around me at all times but I'd never failed in my duties as an Agent.

"You've never had a dead body in your basement before," he said, leaning forward to kiss my cheek. I let him, because I do love J.B. Just not the way that I love Gabriel.

Gabriel stiffened and J.B. smiled. "See you around, Black."

It was only after he left that I realized he'd taken my winter coat with him.

I sighed, locked the door and turned to see Beezle fluttering in the air with a hopeful look on his face.

"I don't have time to go to the restaurant before the window guys get here," I said. "I'll make your cinnamon rolls from scratch."

Beezle grinned. "I don't care how I get them, as long as I get what I want."

I thought of Lucifer and the Grigori, and every other creature around me that seemed to stop at nothing until they'd achieved their aims. "Yeah, you and everybody else."

8

BY DINNERTIME I HAD A REPAIRED APARTMENT, A COMpleted soul pickup and a cinnamon-roll-stuffed gargoyle. And I do mean stuffed. He ate enough rolls for a whole family of gargoyles. I didn't say anything, though. When Beezle is upset he eats, and he was really upset about Samiel, even if he didn't say it.

It felt strange to go to bed that night without Samiel in the house. I'd become used to hearing him moving around the apartment, and to the easy company he provided. Samiel was just about the only person in my life who didn't ask anything of me.

Gabriel had returned to his own apartment downstairs after the repairmen had completed their work. I didn't follow him. I honestly wasn't up to another emotional battering.

I hardly slept, even though I desperately needed it. Every time I closed my eyes I imagined the Grigori torturing Samiel for his crimes, and that is hardly conducive to a restful night. At dawn I gave up the pretense and climbed out of bed. Beezle was already awake and digging into the emergency chocolate.

I leaned against the kitchen counter and raised my eyebrow. He ignored me and stuffed a handful of dark chocolate squares into his beak.

"Those are meant to be savored, you know," I said.

"Believe me," Beezle said, through his stuffed mouth, "I am savoring every bite."

I watched Beezle for a few more minutes, and then wandered over to the refrigerator to see if there was anything edible in there. Two eggs, half a carton of milk and one sad-looking stalk of celery in the crisper drawer. I didn't even have condiments on the door. For a person who occasionally freelanced as a food writer my fridge was pretty pathetic.

"So, how are you planning on pulling this one off?" Beezle asked. "You can't get around the fact that Samiel *did* release Ramuell, and Ramuell *did* kill a whole bunch of people. Plus, Samiel kidnapped Gabriel and sold him to Focalor, and I can't even begin to explain to you how many rules of etiquette he broke by doing that."

"Don't you think the murder of dozens of people would rank higher than some infraction of etiquette?"

"The Grigori have been alive for ages untold. They've had plenty of practice being petty."

I stared out the new windows that had been installed the day before in the breakfast nook. They were nicer than the old windows, which had been ancient and drafty and lacking the double-paned fanciness of the new ones.

"I don't think the facts are ultimately that important to

the Grigori. I think if I can demonstrate that I am an adversary to be respected, then I'll win. If I can't, then Samiel . . ."

"Will be beheaded in front of the whole court, no doubt," Beezle said.

"You're such a comfort to me," I said.

"And just how are you going to demonstrate that they should respect you?"

"It's about power," I said slowly. "Not only the power that you wield, but also the power that you command. That's why Lucifer is always trying to collect me."

"You don't have anyone in your pile of chess pieces," Beezle said.

"Maybe not directly. Maybe not the way that Lucifer or Amarantha would. But I do have friends, and allies. And with the fallen, so much is about perception. If they perceive my allies as pawns that I control, then in the eyes of the Grigori I *am* powerful."

"Who are you going to get in the next couple of hours besides that moony-eyed devil that lives downstairs?"

I gave him a look.

"Don't think I don't know what you were doing in the yard the other night."

"Okay, Dad. Anyway, J.B. would come, and Jude, probably."

"Yeah, that'll be great. The son of the woman who tried to help Focalor with his uprising against Lucifer and a wolf who despises anything to do with the fallen. Excellent choices, Maddy."

"It's the best we have," I said, stung. "Besides, we need someone to carry Metatrion, and Jude is the strongest creature I know besides Samiel."

"I almost forgot about Metatrion. This is going to be

awesome. You show up with two crummy allies and the remains of the Hound of the Hunt."

"I have Gabriel, too," I reminded him.

"The half brother of the accused."

"You act like I shouldn't even bother showing up," I said.

"I just don't think you know what you're getting into with the Grigori."

"That's what you said about Amarantha and the faerie court, too."

"Look how well that turned out."

"I think it turned out fine. I defeated Focalor's uprising, suppressed Amarantha's plan to breed a child of Lucifer's bloodline and survived the Maze."

"And now Amarantha and Focalor hate you and want to hunt you to the ends of the Earth."

"I can't worry about the fallout from doing the right thing. Every time I turn around I have another enemy no matter what, just because I'm Azazel's child or Lucifer's descendant. And I don't think that you should underestimate me just because everyone else does."

"I'm not underestimating you," Beezle said. "But if by some miracle you do win Samiel back, what do you think you'll have to give in exchange? 'Free' is not a word in the Grigori's vocabulary."

I didn't say anything. I knew Beezle was right, but there wasn't a lot of point in worrying about it. If I freed Samiel, then I would pay whatever price I had to when the time came.

A little before noon I stood outside the closed doors to Azazel's court. Gabriel, J.B. and Jude stood around me. Of the three, Jude had naturally been the most reluctant to help when I'd called him.

"Why should I care about some court matter of the fallen?" Jude asked. "My pack is dealing with more important matters at the moment, in case you've forgotten."

"In case *you've* forgotten, Samiel risked his life to help return the cubs to you. I think Wade would want you to assist us."

"I don't know what Wade would want, because he's not here," Jude growled.

I sighed and waited in silence. There wasn't a lot I could say to that.

"Fine," Jude said after a few moments. "I will be there."

Jude had arrived at my house wearing his usual worn jeans, flannel shirt and vest. In concession to the frigid cold the vest was down instead of denim and he'd shoved a wool hat over his red hair. He looked like a Bears fan ready for a tailgating party.

Gabriel wore a white dress shirt with black slacks, which was all he ever wore. J.B. had come from work so he was dressed similarly to Gabriel, except his shirt was light blue and his pants were gray.

I'd decided against dressing up. I always feel stupid in a skirt, and pretty much all of my nice clothes seem to end up torn and bloody anyhow. I didn't want to feel any more self-conscious in front of the Grigori than I already did, so on went one of my many long-sleeved black tees and my favorite blue jeans. Beezle just rolled his eyes when I clomped out in my usual uniform, my boots laced up over my ankles.

So we look a little ragtag, I thought, surveying my crew. Beezle snored away on my shoulder. But they were still an impressive collection of power, enough to give the Grigori pause. And if the fallen didn't recognize what was before them because we didn't present an impressive appearance, then that was okay, too. *All the better to underestimate you with, my dear.*

That was, I hoped they would. Lucifer, at least, knew what I was capable of, but who knew if he would bother to enlighten the others? I was certain Lucifer was looking for some advantage from this, but not being privy to every twist of his labyrinthine mind I had no idea what that advantage might be. It was probably best not to worry about Lucifer at all and just hope his wants didn't really conflict with mine.

The doors swung open, and I had a moment of déjà vu when I saw Nathaniel standing there, looking golden and haughty, as he had been the first time I'd arrived at Azazel's court.

"The Grigori are ready for you now," he said, and he gave me a little half smile.

On closer inspection Nathaniel didn't look quite as polished as he usually did. There were dark circles under his eyes, and his hair looked a little more mussed than usual. I wondered if Azazel was blaming Nathaniel for my revocation of the engagement. It would explain why Nathaniel had that slightly hunted look. He was probably getting needled by Azazel day and night.

We went through the open doors, me in front and the other three shoulder to shoulder directly behind me. I paused for a moment when I realized the ballroom had been transformed.

The room was normally an open floor plan the approximate size of half a football field. It was shaped like a rectangle and lined floor to ceiling with windows on the long sides of the rectangle.

Each time I had been here it was like a never-ending

party. Low sofas and chairs lined the walls. Members of Azazel's court would mingle and mill about, while being served champagne and canapés by thralls and demons.

Azazel would hear grievances and conduct court business at the far end, opposite the doors we'd entered. There was a plain wood chair there that nonetheless managed to convey "throne."

Now all of that was gone. The loitering partygoers of the court were nowhere to be seen. The comfy sofas had been removed. There was no one circling with appetizers.

At the far end of the ballroom, two high structures had been put in place. They were long benches that stood about six feet off the ground. The benches were paneled in front so that you could see the creatures that sat upon them only from the waist up, like a judge's seat in a courtroom.

The benches were placed at an angle from a throne that had been positioned in the middle so that the benches made a giant *V*. The throne was at the point of the *V* and the benches were the long sides.

The throne was a resplendent monstrosity of gold leaf and sparkling jewels, and it floated on a little puff of white cloud so that the angel that sat upon it was about half a head higher than everyone else.

Lucifer (for who else would sit on something so ostentatious?) smirked down at me from the throne. The Grigori sat upon the benches—Azazel at Lucifer's right hand, and the others, whom I did not know, arranged down the line according to rank, I presumed.

There was no sign of Samiel, and a whole lot of empty space between us and the scowling members of the court. I raised my chin and strode forward, the heels of my boots ringing loudly on the marble floor.

The others followed silently behind. They were all tall men. Jude outweighed me by at least a hundred pounds and he was carrying Metatrion, but they all managed to walk more quietly than I did. Well, it had been well established that I was a klutz of the first order. Walking gracefully was not one of my strengths.

I came to a halt at a spot in between the benches at the widest point of the *V*. I wanted to be able to see all the faces of the Grigori without twisting my head back and forth.

I had a moment of surprise when I saw Focalor sitting at the far end of one of the benches. I'd thought that he'd be chained up in Lucifer's basement for all eternity for his attempted uprising. But then again, Lucifer had probably devised something completely diabolical that did not involve physical torment. From the sullen look on Focalor's face I had probably guessed right.

I looked up at Lucifer. "You left something at my house."

Jude came forward and flung the body of Metatrion on the floor. Several of the Grigori gasped and muttered angrily.

"Yes, I was wondering where my Hound of the Hunt had gone. His quarry returned without him."

I pointed to the purple bruises on my throat. I'd asked Gabriel not to heal me so that the Grigori could see the evidence of Metatrion's actions. My voice was still pretty raspy, too.

"He tried to give me a present that I had to refuse. And speaking of quarry and returning, you can give Samiel back to me now."

"Samiel is to be tried before this court for his crimes," Azazel said.

I ignored my father. I was getting really good at doing that.

"Tried for his crimes, or for your amusement? Because

I'm pretty sure you could stop this circus with a word," I said to Lucifer.

Lucifer quirked an eyebrow at me, but said nothing. Azazel looked thunderous.

"How dare you speak to Lord Lucifer thus!" he cried, rising to his feet.

"That's nothing. You should hear the way he talks to me," I retorted.

"You will not disrespect this court," Azazel shouted.

"And you will not treat me like a child to be punished for some imagined infraction. I am not on trial. I am here for Samiel, and I will not leave without him."

"You have insulted this court by treating Metatrion with such disrespect."

"And you have insulted me by taking my friend from my home by force and bringing me here for a trial that does not appear to be happening."

Azazel gave me a look that promised retribution later. I was so not worried about this. Once upon a time—only two short months before—I'd been afraid of him. I'd wanted his respect and his love, the two things I'd never had. But that was before he'd tried to marry me to a man I did not know, before he tried to treat me like another pawn in his power struggle with the other courts. One thing I'd learned very quickly about the fallen was that if you did not assert yourself, they would walk all over you.

"Very well," Azazel said. "If it is a trial you wish, then it is a trial you shall have. Bring out the condemned."

Two fallen toadies that I hadn't noticed lurking behind the tall benches went to the front of the room and disappeared into one of the doors there.

"Condemned?" I muttered under my breath to Gabriel. "That sounds like they've already decided."

"They very likely have," he replied in a whisper. "I warned you that the Grigori do not have the same notions of fair play that you do."

I'd expected that, but I hadn't expected them to condemn Samiel before the trial had even begun. It reminded me that my bravado was just that, and that Samiel's life hung in the balance. It was harder to be cavalier when I considered that the Grigori had already made their minds up.

"They're not getting him," I whispered fiercely. "I promised Samiel. I promised."

"Be careful," J.B. said from my other side. "The more you want, the more they will try to take from you. Just like my mother."

Jude stood stiffly on the other side of J.B., glaring up at Lucifer. If looks could kill, the Morningstar would have imploded by now.

Lucifer, for his part, appeared to be doing an admirable job of ignoring Jude entirely. I was certain that he recognized the wolf—how could he not?—but he was no doubt holding his acknowledgment in reserve unless it served his own purpose.

I heard a scuffle behind the tall benches.

A moment later, two guards dressed as Hunt soldiers appeared holding Samiel between them. His hands were bound and he had a few bruises, but those were probably from the incident at my house. He still wore the white T-shirt and gray sweatpants he'd worn the day before. His feet were bare, and this made him look oddly vulnerable.

He gave me a strained smile when he saw us, and then the guards led Samiel past our group to stand in the middle of the room. The guards stepped away from him to take their places at the foot of the benches. Samiel was alone under the glare of the Grigori's judgment.

He lifted his chin and set his shoulders. Good. I was glad that the fallen hadn't broken his will.

Azazel stood again. I noticed Nathaniel had taken his place next to Azazel, and that the angel to Nathaniel's left must be Zerachiel, Nathaniel's father. He looked like he could be Nathaniel's twin. Angels don't seem to age at all after a certain point. I looked older than Lucifer and he had me beat by several thousand years.

"Samiel ap Ramuell, you have been brought before this tribunal to answer for your crimes. Your crimes will be read out to you and you will acknowledge that which you have done. Then sentencing will be passed upon you."

"What about his defense?" I asked loudly.

Azazel turned a glare upon me as several of the Grigori murmured behind their hands. I was sure that Azazel's stature among the other fallen was taking a hit every time I talked out of turn. I don't reflect well on my father's court, as Nathaniel has so often reminded me.

"This is not a human court of law," Azazel said icily. "This is a place of judgment. The Grigori do not hear 'defense.'"

"Forget that," I said. "What did you bring me here for if not to defend Samiel?"

"You were not brought. You came of your own volition," said one of the Grigori halfway down the bench.

"That's Chezaquiel," Beezle whispered. Apparently he'd finished his nap.

"I had no choice but to come. You sent the Hound of the Hunt to break down my walls and take Samiel from my home. If you give Samiel back now, you can have the remains of this loser," I said, nudging Metatrion with the toe of my boot, "and I'll just forget the insult that you gave me by sending soldiers into my home."

"This creature," another Grigori said, "is accused of setting free the nephilim Ramuell so that Ramuell could hunt and kill."

"That's Shamsiel," whispered Beezle.

"How can you tell them apart?" I said out of the corner of my mouth. Shamsiel looked blond and young just like the rest. The only Grigori that stood out were Azazel, who was dark haired and dark eyed like me, and Focalor, trapped forever in his demon's body for defying Lucifer. Lucifer had golden hair and black wings—one of the few angels who did.

"Many innocent lives were lost because of Samiel's actions," Shamsiel continued.

"Please," I scoffed. "Like any of you give a flying faerie about innocent human lives. If it served your purpose, you'd wipe out every last person on the face of the Earth. I, on, the other hand, *do* care about the human lives that were taken. And I punished the creature responsible—Ramuell. Samiel shouldn't be made to pay for the sins of his father."

"He released the monster from the Forbidden Lands," said Zerachiel.

"And those monsters wouldn't even exist if the Grigori had kept it in their pants the first time they saw human women," I said angrily. I have a terrible temper, and I was riding on the edge of it.

"Real smooth," J.B. whispered.

"It is not for you to question the actions of the Grigori," Azazel shouted.

"Why not?" I shot back. "Somebody ought to. It seems to me that the lot of you have had your own way for far too long. You want to talk about wrong? It's wrong of you to condemn an innocent child for the actions of his parents."

This was definitely stretching the truth a little bit, but I continued on.

"Ariell made Samiel release his father from prison. She's the one who set Ramuell on the world. She used Samiel as one uses a key to open a lock."

"Since you speak of the boy's mother, it should be noted that Samiel should not have been allowed to live a moment past birth. We have already made an exception for a nephilim's child," Focalor said silkily.

I went cold. They would not drag Gabriel into this.

I narrowed my eyes at Focalor and felt the familiar buildup of magical energy inside me, the power that seemed to rise with my emotions. Everyone in the room stiffened except Lucifer, who smiled. They could feel the magic coming off me in waves.

"This is not about Gabriel," I said steadily. "And you should remember the last time we met, Focalor. I would keep my mouth shut if I were you."

I was certain that if Focalor were not already bright scarlet, we would see him blushing. He did not like the reminder that the last time he'd competed against me he'd lost—in front of Amarantha's twittering court.

"In addition to his other crimes, Samiel harmed you, the daughter of Azazel and the heir to his court. For that alone he must pay a price," Zerachiel said.

Everyone in the room stared at the place on my left hand where two fingers were missing. I resisted the urge to stick my hand in my pocket and hide the evidence.

"Samiel and I have an understanding about that and I believe his debt to me has been paid. If I don't require a blood price from him, then neither should you."

"The laws of the kingdom state—" another Grigori began.

"Stuff your laws!" I shouted, my temper breaking. "This whole thing is a farce. I don't know why you brought

Samiel here but it has nothing to do with the laws of the kingdom."

"He must pay for his crimes," Azazel said.

"He has committed no crime," I responded.

"We believe otherwise."

"And you've already decided that he'll pay whether he's guilty or not. I think that you just want to get rid of Samiel because he is a reminder of your own failures, your own weaknesses."

Several angry murmurs broke out at this.

"Besides," I continued, "he's Lucifer's grandson. Are you really going to kill your lord's grandson?"

"People died because of his actions," Azazel said, but the rest of the Grigori shifted uncomfortably nonetheless.

It was one thing to view Samiel as a nephilim's child, quite another to think of him as a close and direct descendant of their highest lord.

I just hoped Lucifer didn't decide to remind them that I had already killed two of his children. I glanced up at his face and he gave me a little half smile, like he knew what I was thinking, but he didn't say anything.

"Let Samiel go," I repeated. "I will be responsible for him."

Beezle murmured in my ear, "I hope you understand what you're getting into when you make that promise."

"Yeah, a lifetime of the two of you eating me out of house and home," I replied.

I knew what it meant when I said I would be responsible for Samiel. It meant that if he put even a fingernail over the line, it would be him *and* me standing bound before the Grigori next time—if they even bothered with the pretense of a trial before execution.

Nathaniel leaned over to Azazel and whispered in my

father's ear. All around me the Grigori were speaking behind their hands to one another.

I didn't want it to come to this, but I would blast my way out of here with Samiel if I had to. I would not leave him with the Grigori. I think Jude was secretly hoping for an excuse to lunge at Lucifer.

After several moments in which the Grigori looked like a bunch of kids playing Telephone—"I say kill him; pass it on"—Azazel stood. It seemed he was the voice of the court.

Lucifer had played no role in the decision-making. It appeared that he had acted only as a witness to the proceedings. Still, I knew that something greater than Samiel's guilt was at work here. Lucifer was waiting for something.

"It is the will of this court that Samiel ap Ramuell be remanded into the custody of Lady Madeline Black ap Azazel."

I exhaled the breath I hadn't realized I was holding. I guess the "Lucifer's grandson" argument had carried some weight.

"As Samiel's custodian you will henceforth be responsible for his actions. Should Samiel violate the laws of Lord Lucifer's kingdom, he shall be condemned to immediate death at the hands of the Hound of the Hunt."

I didn't like the part where Samiel would have to live with the threat of execution for the rest of his life, but it was better than the alternative.

"I see one small flaw in this decision," Lucifer said, and the room went unnaturally quiet, like nobody wanted to attract Lucifer's attention to them. "We no longer *have* a Hound of the Hunt."

Metatrion's blank eyes accused me.

"I don't know why I have to keep saying this, but he was trying to kill me at the time," I said.

"And I am sure that it is a comfort to your father as it is a comfort to me that you are so very capable. Still, it does not change the fact that the court has never been without a Hound," Lucifer said.

I shrugged, moving forward to Samiel, who was still bound. I wanted to free his hands and get him out of the court before any of the Grigori thought up an objection. I was sure some of them were already busily crafting one.

"I don't see how this has anything to do with me or Samiel," I said.

"Don't you?" Lucifer said softly. "The Hound of the Hunt is dead at your hand."

I stopped next to Samiel, looking up at Lucifer. Dread washed over me, and I knew that whatever Lucifer had been waiting for had finally arrived.

"As payment for the death of the Hound of the Hunt, you will take over his duties."

The walls were closing around me. Lucifer looked triumphant.

"As you have taken responsibility for the life of Samiel ap Ramuell, so, too, shall you take responsibility for his death should he violate the laws of the kingdom.

"As I am the Morningstar, you shall be my dark star, the hand of my will, my bringer of justice.

"All rise and say hail to my Hound of the Hunt."

The Grigori rose. Over the buzzing in my ears I thought I heard a voice speaking in my head—Lucifer's voice.

"I thought you told me you knew how to play chess."

I'd just been outplayed. Again.

9

"I TOLD YOU THERE WOULD BE A PRICE TO PAY," BEEzle said for the hundredth time since we'd left Azazel's court.

"I know," I groaned, slumping forward to hide my face in my arms. "How many times are you going to say, 'I told you so'?"

"I'm not even close to being done yet," Beezle said. "You think you're so smart. You think you can outwit Lucifer. He's had epochs of practice time."

We sat at the kitchen table—Samiel, Gabriel, Beezle and me—and the mood was positively funereal. You wouldn't think we managed to save Samiel from certain death.

J.B. had shaken his head at me and gone back to work without a word, while Jude had looked at me like I'd contracted some new and contagious disease that involved blisters and boils before returning to his pack.

Samiel rapped on the table so that I would look up at him. *I'm so sorry. This is my fault.*

"No, it isn't," I said heavily. "Lucifer has been looking for an excuse to move me closer to his inner circle, and he took it."

"Yeah, but how could he know that you'd kill the Hound of the Hunt? Nobody has ever managed to before," Beezle said.

I rubbed my eyes. "He didn't know that I would do that. But he did know that I wouldn't let Samiel go without a fight, and I'll bet anything that Lucifer would have found some way to force me to trade myself for Samiel."

"No bet," Beezle said gloomily. "I wouldn't gamble against Lucifer."

We all stared at the table. After a few minutes, Beezle cleared his throat. "I'd just like to point out that it's been several hours since any of us have eaten, and that a pepperoni pizza would not go amiss right now."

I looked up at Gabriel, whose face spread in a rueful smile. Samiel grinned.

I laughed and picked up Beezle and pulled him into a hug. His tiny arms went around my neck as he squeezed me for a moment. Then he leaned back and gave me a serious look, his clawed hands on my cheeks.

"No matter what Lucifer tries to make of you, you are still Maddy Black. Remember that."

"I'll remember," I promised. "And you're right. A pepperoni pizza would not go amiss."

"Yes!" Beezle said, pumping his little fist in the air. "With mozzarella sticks?"

"Don't push your luck," I said, and went to place the order.

I wondered if the Hound of the Hunt was a paying position in Lucifer's court. Probably not. My checking account was dangerously low, as usual. I'd sold a couple of articles in the last month but it can take a long time to get paid for freelance work. Lately, my main source of income was Gabriel's rent checks, and it seemed like a long time until the first of February.

After we'd all stuffed ourselves I said, "We're just going to go on as we were before. If Lucifer thinks I'm going to live at court because of this Hound of the Hunt business, he is out of his tiny mind."

"What of your duties?" Gabriel asked.

"What of them?" I replied. "I'm sure if Lucifer needs me for something, he'll let me know. I still have my Agent commitments."

"And you promised to help J.B. with ghost-hunting. And you still have to find Wade. I don't know that there is enough time in the day for you to do all those things *and* go to the bakery," Beezle said.

"I guess I'll just have to prioritize," I said dryly. "Speaking of duty and priority, I think I have another pickup tonight." I patted my pockets like I was going to find my Agent list there.

"You do, at Addison and Sheffield," Beezle said.

"Close to home; that's nice," I said. "Wait—how do you know?"

"J.B. hung your list on your bedroom mirror yesterday."

"Well, I don't know what he was thinking doing that. I never look in the mirror."

"Yes, we all can tell," Beezle said.

"I will accompany you," Gabriel said.

Me, too, Samiel signed.

"What's with the protectiveness? I think I can go eight blocks from home by myself."

"You made several new enemies today, whether or not you realize it," Gabriel said. "The Grigori do not like to be thwarted."

"That's swell," I grumbled. "I can't even tell most of them apart. How am I supposed to know which one hates me and which one doesn't?"

I looked up at the clock. It was half past six. "What time is my pickup?"

"In fifteen minutes," Beezle said calmly.

I stood abruptly and ran for my shoes. "I would have appreciated a little advance warning."

"What's the big deal? You're only two minutes away by wing. Besides, it's not my fault you never comb your hair."

"I comb my hair . . ."

"Could have fooled me."

"I just don't stare in the mirror while I'm doing it."

I hurriedly pulled on my boots and a blue peacoat that I usually reserved for early autumn. J.B. still had my winter coat, as he'd used it to carry the cameras to the Agency.

By the time I was ready Samiel and Gabriel were already standing at the door like two sentinels. Beezle fluttered to my shoulder.

"Up, up and away, Team Black," I said dryly.

A couple of minutes later we stood at the corner of Addison and Sheffield in front of the statue of Billy Williams. Wrigley Field loomed silently behind us. We were invisible from human eyes.

A steady stream of commuters poured across the intersection as the Red Line stop was only half a block away. Storefronts housed ticket brokers and shops that hawked Cubs merchandise, most of them silent this time of year, when baseball season and the heat of summer seemed like hazy memories.

The bars that liberally dotted the area were quiet tonight, with very few Blackhawks fans willing to brave the freezing temperatures just to drink overpriced beer and watch a game they could just as easily see at home.

I straightened up when I saw him—Cole Stuart Janowik. There's no glowing light, pointing arrow, chorus of hallelujahs or anything like that when I see a marked soul. I just know, like all of my power locks onto that person with a laser sight.

Cole was young, mid-twenties maybe, and he moved with the stream of people that had gotten off the El and walked west on Addison. He talked on an expensive-looking smartphone as he walked, a wireless headset on his head, the phone in his hand.

This was not a dangerous neighborhood, but the guy was totally unaware of his surroundings. A blond kid who had the look of a strung-out junkie pushed Cole just as he reached the curb, then tore the phone from his hand. The thief sprinted across the street toward Wrigley just as the light changed to red.

Cole, intent on retrieving his phone, did not even notice the custom furniture company truck accelerating across Addison on Sheffield.

"Splat," Beezle said.

"That's a little cruel," I said.

I tried not to let death affect me too much. I saw a lot of it, and the weight would be unbearable if I let it. But it seemed so stupid and pointless to die under the wheels of a furniture truck because an addict needed to sell your phone to get a fix.

I told my overprotective entourage to stay back, and went to offer the soul of Cole Stuart Janowik his final choice.

We were flying back home from the Door a short time

later. Everyone seemed to be in a contemplative mood and not inclined for too much conversation. Lucifer's edict had cast a pall over us, and no amount of wisecracking would relieve the heaviness in my heart. Lucifer had cornered me good and proper.

I was flying on autopilot, glancing idly at the scene below, when something caught my eye. I pulled up short so fast that Beezle lost his grip on my shoulder. He fell a few feet, then flew back up, looking irritated. Gabriel and Samiel had paused a little ways ahead, and looked back at me, confused.

"What was that all about?"

"That," I said, and pointed.

Far below us was a semi-industrial area. I knew that some of the larger buildings housed a cable company and the power company.

One of the buildings was coated in a seething mass of energy that looked like green mist. From a distance the feeling of malevolence rising from it was palpable.

"I'm sure that it is not a good idea to do whatever it is you're thinking of doing," Beezle said.

"I think we should check it out," I said. "There's obviously something wrong with that place."

"Like I said, not a good idea," Beezle retorted.

I ignored him and drifted slowly downward. As the ground approached, more features came into view. A short distance away I could see the lights on Addison and Western, the fast food restaurants and the giant structure of Lane Tech High School.

We landed in the parking lot of a plaza that housed the cable company and a large facility that ran kids' soccer programs. The building in question was at the far end of the lot.

As we approached it I felt a wave of nausea rising. Whatever was coming off the structure was making me feel sick, just like that time I was in Amarantha's forest and Nathaniel and I ran into the . . .

"Spider," I gasped.

Samiel and Gabriel looked questioningly at me.

"When I was in Amarantha's forest, I was attacked by a giant spider," I said slowly. It was hard to talk through the sickness rising in my throat. "The spider was surrounded by this same green misty stuff, and it makes me feel like I'm gonna . . ."

I turned away and heaved, Beezle leaving my shoulder.

"What a waste of perfectly good pizza," he said.

Gabriel produced a bottle of water from nowhere and I took it gratefully.

"Better?" he asked after I'd collected myself.

I nodded and looked at the building. "What do you think is in there?"

"A bunch of spiders, obviously," Beezle said. "So do we really want to voluntarily go into a place full of giant arachnids?"

"Want? No." I shuddered. I have a moderate case of arachnophobia, and almost getting eaten by giant spiders twice had done nothing to improve my symptoms. "Should? Yes."

"Why is it our job to check out every freaky thing that happens in Chicago?" Beezle whined.

"Who else is going to do it? The cops wouldn't know what they were getting into."

I approached the building slowly, Gabriel and Samiel moving to either side of me. Both of them seemed unaffected by the miasma, just like Nathaniel in the forest. The mortal half of me was annoyingly susceptible to malignant spells. It was hard to concentrate, to be aware of what was going on around me, when I kept having to stop and fight the urge to boot again.

A small door faced the parking lot. Unlike the rest of the warehouse, which looked like it was in violation of several city codes, the door appeared brand-new and very secure. There was a magnetic strip machine next to the door. You obviously needed a card to enter.

There were no windows on this side of the building, so we flew around it to see if there was another means of entry. Nothing. No windows, no doors, no vents. Nothing. Just the solid blank face of crumbling concrete and that door.

We returned to the starting point.

"I bet Samiel could smash it in," I said.

Samiel nodded and signed, *I'll give it a try.*

Gabriel stopped him with a hand on his brother's shoulder.

"You will certainly set off an alarm."

I rocked back on my heels, annoyed. I don't know why I hadn't thought about an alarm. Of course whatever was in there would be protected by more than just green miasma.

Beezle snapped his fingers. "I don't know why I didn't think of it. Maddy, you can go in."

"What? Why?"

"You can pass through walls. You're the Hound of the Hunt."

"Can I do that even if I'm not on Lucifer's business?" I asked skeptically.

Beezle shrugged. "We might as well try. If it doesn't work, we can go back to staring blankly at the door."

I sighed. "So I get to go into the creepy haunted warehouse all on my own. Hooray."

"You're the one who said we needed to check this out," Beezle reminded me.

Gabriel put his hand on my arm. "I do not like this."

I turned toward him, touched his cheek. "You can't always protect me."

He frowned. "I do not know any other way to be."

I kissed him swiftly and turned away, aware of Beezle and Samiel watching us with unabashed curiosity. One of these days I was going to take Gabriel to a deserted island, far away from prying eyes.

I took a deep breath, trying to quell the nausea that would not leave and the feeling that I was about to do something incredibly stupid. Again.

I put my hand on the wall next to the blinking light of the magnetic strip. Lucifer's sword rattled in its sheath, and the snake on my palm tingled.

"I am the Hound of the Hunt," I said, the words flowing easily, as if I had said them before. "No walls can hide my quarry."

The surface felt suddenly fluid beneath my fingers and my arm slid through it as easily as water. I glanced back at the others. Gabriel looked tense, Samiel worried. Beezle gave me a thumbs-up.

"Draw your sword," Gabriel whispered. "You know not what enemies may await."

I pulled the sword from its scabbard and readied myself.

"I'm going to try and open the door from inside without triggering the alarm. If I can't do that and I'm not back in half an hour, call J.B. and tell him to bring a retrieval unit."

Gabriel nodded. I slipped through the wall, sword at the ready, and shocked the hell out of the charcarion demon sitting at a receptionist's desk.

The demon's mouth dropped open. I took two fast steps forward and threw the sword like a javelin at the demon's head. The sword passed cleanly through the demon's open mouth and pinned him like an insect to the wall behind him.

I had to have had some supernatural help on that one because there was no way that I was that competent a swordswoman. I looked at the snake on my hand and it winked at me. I may never get over the extreme weirdness of having a sentient tattoo.

The demon gurgled and flailed for a moment, then went still. I pulled the sword from its body, the blade coated in green-gray blood.

Now that the immediate threat was over I was able to look around. The interior was surprisingly clean and new-looking. It could have been the reception area of any office downtown—paneled walls, light gray carpet, half-moon reception desk.

The entry door was behind me, and when I turned to look at it I saw a flashing keypad. Chances were good that it was rigged to sound an alarm if it was opened without a code. So if I opened it up and let the others in, then I might as well have let Samiel break down the door in the first place. I guess I was on my own for the moment.

To my right was a long hallway. Several closed doors faced the hall. To my left was another door with a magnetic strip for a key card.

The doors to the right were likely offices. I didn't want to take a chance on disturbing anyone at work who might raise an alarm. Besides, the presence of extra security meant that whatever was interesting in the warehouse was probably behind that door.

I took a deep breath and then a giant step through the

door, my heart pounding in my chest, terrified that some guard on the other side of the door would raise a cry as soon as I went through.

There was no guard on the other side. There was no need.

Three gigantic spiders hung suspended from the ceiling, which was several dozen feet above me. The miasma filled the room so thickly I could hardly breathe. I felt my stomach heave in protest. I swallowed rapidly and breathed through my nose. Puking on the floor would definitely attract the spiders' attention.

Once I got myself under control (and was able to look away from the horror of the spiders), I surveyed the rest of the room. My heart sank.

The room was filled with people, maybe sixty or seventy of them, all sitting bound and silent in plain wooden chairs. Their eyes were taped open and in front of each person was one of those camera things doing an eyeball scan with a laser. Several people were pale and slumped over.

There was nothing for it. I needed help. There was no way I'd be able to free all of these people and herd them out (screaming, no doubt) under the watchful eye of the spiders. The creatures appeared to be dozing right now, which was the only way I'd managed to escape detection.

I was about to step out quietly when a movement about halfway down the room caught my eye.

The familiar silvery wisps that indicated a soul rose from the body of a young woman in her mid-twenties who'd just breathed her last breath. There was no Agent present but me, which meant that this death was not a part of the natural order.

I unfurled my wings and blinked out of sight. I just

hoped the spiders wouldn't be able to see me anyway. I'd learned the hard way that some supernatural creatures can see through the Agent's veil.

I flew over the heads of the other prisoners and touched down softly next to the woman's body. Her soul was emerging much more slowly than a soul usually did, and it was twisting and writhing as it came.

Usually a soul looks just like a mirror image of the living person—except, you know, see-through. But this soul didn't seem to know what it was supposed to look like. The pieces of her face kept scattering and re-forming, and even then the result didn't look quite right, like a digital image missing some pixels.

Despite her indistinct features, I could tell her eyes were wide, staring up, her mouth open in a silent scream. I thought she was reacting to the trauma of the machines, but I realized a second before it landed on my head that she was watching one of the giant spiders descending swiftly and silently. I stumbled away as the spider picked up the dead body and began to wrap it in silk. Her soul struggled in terror, trying to break free of her mortal shell.

Oh, no, I thought.

I hurried forward, praying to the Morningstar that the spider wouldn't detect me. I couldn't let her soul in its already terrified state get stuck inside the silk, still attached to her body as the spider began to eat it.

The stink of the spider's rotten breath and the miasma that poured off it filled my nostrils. I gagged, covered my face with my sleeve and hoped Lucifer's sword would cut through the ectoplasmic cord that held this poor woman's soul to her body.

I usually use magic to cut the soul since my mother's dagger had melted in the flesh of a dragon on my front lawn a couple of months before. But I worried the spider would notice magic being performed under its nonexistent nose, and I didn't have time to do the usual ritual and offer the woman a choice.

I crept closer to the spider busily wrapping up its prey. The soul was struggling, pulling on the cord that bound her to her body. I lifted the sword and struck a clean blow just under the spider's jaws.

The soul broke free, screaming, the incorporeal body dissolving and re-forming in her panic and confusion. The spider immediately dropped the body and made a high-pitched chittering noise. I guess it had noticed something, after all. It didn't seem to see me, because I stood frozen in place less than a foot away from its fangs. But it knew something was wrong, and its chitter had notified the other blood-bloated monsters dangling over my head.

They lowered quickly to their companion, and I saw stars for a moment. I hoped I wouldn't pass out from panic. If you are a moderate arachnophobe, the last place you want to be is in an enclosed space with three spiders the size of CTA buses. Actually, after this I was pretty sure I'd be a full-on arachnophobe. Forget moderation.

The spiders began to click and hiss at one another. Since proximity was making me hyperventilate I backed away slowly, holding the sword in front of me and trying to make my footfalls as soft as possible. It seemed that I might be able to get away and get help.

Until the heel of my boot knocked into the leg of one of the wooden chairs. The person in the chair toppled sideways and, separated from the machine, began to bellow at the top of his lungs.

The first spider screamed and bounded forward in a giant leap to the place where I stood, invisible still.

I didn't have time to run or to think. I saw the spider's huge, hairy body above my head, coming down on me, and I jumped back and pushed the sword into the spider's crazy multifaceted eye as it landed.

The spider jerked, screeched, thrashed its legs on the floor. I set my feet and yanked the sword free, leaving the spider to its death throes. The blade was unharmed, but some acidic goo had run out of the spider's eyes and burned the top of my right hand and the cuff of my coat.

"This is why I can't have anything nice," I muttered. "Including hands."

The other spiders, quite aware that someone was in the warehouse who was not supposed to be, reared up on their silks a few feet—the better to survey the area with, one assumed. I was torn between running to get help and trying to defeat the other two spiders. I worried that a lot of innocent bystanders would be harmed if I stayed and tried to take the spiders out.

Thinking it would be safer for the prisoners if I went out and returned with backup, I resumed my slow backward walk.

The spiders screamed and dropped toward me with frightening rapidity. I didn't know what gave me away until I looked downward and saw my boot prints in the slippery blood pouring from the spider's body.

"Sometimes I wonder if J.B.'s right about me Three-Stooging my way through life," I said out loud.

There was nothing to do now except stand and fight and try to limit collateral damage. The man I knocked over was crying himself hoarse because of his separation from the cameras.

I lifted off from the ground as the spiders landed on the floor near the body of the dead one. I swooped over the head of the nearest eight-legged monster and then arrowed downward with the sword pointed in front of me. I pushed the blade up to the hilt into the spider's body. As I did I shot electricity through the blade and into the spider. I was getting really good at that spell.

There were the smells of flesh cooking and blackened blood, and the spider went still as its insides were fried.

I yanked out the sword and turned toward the other spider, but it was gone.

10

A WHISPER OF MOVEMENT, THE FAINTEST OF CLICKS. I looked up and saw the other spider mere inches from me. I leapt backward off the electrocuted spider. Well, okay, it was a lot more like an awkward motion in which I tumbled ass-over-elbows and landed hard on my side in a big icky pool of spider gore. Lara Croft I am not.

The last spider landed on the body of its compatriot with a triumphant chitter, and then it realized I wasn't there.

I pushed to my feet, discovered the sword had gone flying somewhere and I couldn't see it. I tried to raise my arms to shoot nightfire at the spider and noticed something else. My right arm hurt like hell, and it was hanging at an awkward angle.

"Dislocated shoulder. Awesome," I said through my teeth. It *hurt*.

The spider leapt toward the place where I'd landed in

blood. I shot upward on my wings, threw nightfire at it with my good arm. The nightfire bounced harmlessly off its hairy body. All I was really doing was giving away my position as the spider threw webs and swung closer and closer to the source of the blasts.

Throwing nightfire and flying all over the place like a demented pinball wasn't doing any good. I hung as still as I could, moving my wings only just enough to keep me aloft. The spider paused, suspended on its string, twisting in the air and looking for me. I made barely an eddy in the thick cloud of miasma that blanketed the air.

We were in a far corner of the warehouse, well above the prisoners bound to their chairs below. Glancing down I realized we were above an open space. The closest prisoner was several feet away.

Nightfire didn't work, and the sword was missing. That left something a little know-it-all gargoyle had once told me—*Most things don't like fire.*

I reached down into the place where my magic flickered and pulled on that source of power until it ran in my blood. It passed through my heartstone and was lit by the flame of the sun.

The spider screeched, and I knew it could see me lit from within. It swung toward me, intent on its prey, its blood-stinking jaws wide for the kill.

The flames raced inside my veins, down to the tips of the three fingers of my left hand, and exploded out into a giant fireball that entered the spider's mouth.

The effect was instantaneous. The spider burst into flame and crashed to the ground, screaming the whole way. It thrashed and kicked feebly, smoke pouring from its body. The smell was horrific.

I took a minute to appreciate the fact that I was no longer in immediate danger of being eaten alive by a giant spider. Then I realized the flaming spider had set a nearby table on fire and that the fire was spreading, thereby putting all the captives in danger.

"Because that's what fires do, Maddy," I said to myself. "They spread."

I flew to the ground and looked around for a fire extinguisher. I didn't find any, nor did any internal sprinkler system kick in. This building was definitely not up to code.

It was just possible that I was getting a little hysterical. The room was already growing hotter and the smoke was scorching my throat.

The priority was to get the prisoners out, but I knew from my experience with the wolf cubs that this would not be an easy task. As I crossed the room to the people nearest the source of flame, I heard banging. It seemed like someone was trying to break down the door into the warehouse. I turned toward the pounding, nightfire at the ready.

The door flew open with a crash and J.B. came through, along with dozens of special-forces Agents. The cavalry had arrived.

J.B. took in me, the dead spiders, the prisoners and the flame at a glance.

"Get those people out of here!" he shouted.

The Agents poured forward, cutting the prisoners' bonds and pulling the people from their chairs. The air filled with the sounds of screams.

"Get the cameras, too!" I shouted, running forward to help. I saw something winking in the firelight and stopped to pick up the sword. I shoved it back in its scabbard and began gathering cameras with my working arm.

J.B. reached my side. "Why are you taking these? Get out of here."

"The machines are important. I'm not sure why. But we can't leave them here."

"No, I know they're important. And I'll make sure we collect them all," he shouted over the din of screaming people and crackling flame. "I'm saying you look like garbage and we'll take it from here."

"Oh, right," I said. I was feeling a little light-headed.

J.B. signaled to another Agent, who came and took the cameras I'd collected. Then he gave me a little push. "Go on, get outside."

"There are offices, I think. We might be able to find out who's doing this. On the other side of the wall."

"We'll try to get what we can before the building burns down," J.B. said grimly.

I turned toward the door. The Agents were very efficiently removing the prisoners and cameras. The room had already been mostly emptied.

My boots felt heavy, my arm hurt, and my throat, already sore from Metatrion's ministrations, felt scratchy and irritated from the smoke. My eyes watered and my stomach had never completely settled down despite all the life-in-peril excitement.

Gabriel came through the door, looking worried. I smiled tiredly at him and walked a little faster.

He jogged toward me. I opened my arms to wrap them around his neck.

"Where's Beezle?" I asked.

I was looking into his eyes, and it was only because I was so tired that I didn't realize that his eyes were wrong. By then, the knife had already slid between my ribs.

"Cockroach," I spat, blood bubbling to my lips.

Antares smiled, and the mask of Gabriel fell away, revealing my half brother in all his red-skinned, black-horned demon glory. I hadn't seen him since I'd imprisoned him outside the Maze. Somehow the little insect had managed to escape the cage and all of Azazel's efforts at finding him.

"Maddy!" J.B. cried, and the anguish in his voice broke my heart.

Antares had his hand on my bad shoulder, holding me close as he thrust again with the knife. Hot blood poured from the wounds and I saw stars before my eyes.

Then I heard Gabriel's voice.

"ANTARES!" he shouted, and there was a fury there that I had never heard before.

Antares pulled the knife out and let go of my shoulder. I fell to my knees as he turned to face Gabriel.

Gabriel stood in the doorway, and his face was beautiful and terrible to behold. His black eyes glowed with starlight, his black wings spread wide. The power that pulsed from him seemed to fill up the room, made it hard to breathe. I understood suddenly why the Grigori feared the children of the nephilim. Everyone in the room was frozen and quiet, including the previously screaming prisoners.

"You're too late, thrall," Antares taunted. "Her mortal life is already leaving her."

"Gabriel's not really the type to banter," I slurred.

I knew I was dying. I'd died once before, although that time was a lot quicker. Ramuell had torn my heart out. That was much better than bleeding slowly on a warehouse floor, I can tell you. There's something to be said for efficiency.

I was right—Gabriel didn't respond to Antares. He blasted the demon with a ball of white-hot fire—a power I had never seen wielded by any creature since Ramuell had destroyed the intersection of Clark and Belmont two months before.

Antares produced some kind of talisman that was on a leather bracelet wrapped around his wrist. My half brother has no power of his own, but he is able to wield a wide collection of magical objects left to him by his dead mother.

Gabriel stalked forward and blasted Antares again. This time Antares wasn't fast enough and the white fire hit him square in the chest. I smelled sulfur, and sizzling flesh, and Antares howled with pain. He bounded toward Gabriel, claws extended to tear Gabriel's throat out.

The world suddenly tilted sideways and I toppled forward onto my face. I don't know how long I lay like that, but the next thing I knew J.B. was smacking me in the face.

"Wake *up*, Maddy! You cannot go to sleep!"

"Jeez, no need to be so rough," I said slowly. "I just got stabbed, you know."

He laughed involuntarily and lifted me in his arms like a baby. I raised my head to see what was going on.

The back of the warehouse was completely engulfed in flames. All the Agents and prisoners seemed to have exited the building. Gabriel and Antares faced off in the center of the room like a couple of prizefighters.

Antares sported quite a few burns and bruises. Gabriel looked unharmed but determined.

"I think he's toying with Antares," J.B. said.

"Gabriel's too serious for that," I said. It was hard to talk. My tongue felt thick and heavy in my mouth. "Besides, don't underestimate Antares. He's got more tricks than you can imagine."

Gabriel blasted Antares again, and the demon seemed to have decided enough was enough. He turned on the spot, narrowly avoiding Gabriel's blast, and disappeared into thin air.

"He does that a lot," I said to J.B.

Gabriel gave such an intense cry of rage that the ground trembled.

"COWARD! WRETCH! WHEREVER YOU FLEE, I WILL FIND YOU. YOU WILL PAY FOR WHAT YOU HAVE DONE."

"The cry of a nephilim that has been denied its prey," Lucifer's voice said behind us.

J.B. spun around so fast that I felt my stomach heave. Lucifer stood just behind us, his wings tucked neatly under a black overcoat. He had a speculative look that I did not like, particularly since his speculations seemed to be focused on Gabriel.

The back wall of the warehouse gave an ominous crack.

"The building will come down around our ears at any moment," Lucifer said. "You may give me my granddaughter now, Jacob."

J.B. tightened his hold on me.

"How do I know you're not Antares in disguise?"

"It's him," I said sourly. The magic inside me always seemed to recognize Lucifer.

J.B. still seemed reluctant to give me up.

"Your chivalry is admirable," Lucifer said impatiently. "But you cannot heal her, and I can."

J.B. passed me to Lucifer. I was immediately enveloped in the comforting smell of cinnamon. My limbs filled with warmth, and I knew Lucifer was healing me. I felt cosseted and cared for, and that irritated me. It annoyed me that Lucifer felt more like a father to me than Azazel. I scowled up at him.

"Are you familiar with the term 'bad penny'?" I asked as Lucifer carried me outside, J.B. and Gabriel following behind. Gabriel's anger was coming off him in pulsing waves.

Samiel and Beezle waited for us, looking worried. There was no sign of the Agents or the prisoners, so they must have returned to the Agency. We all gathered in a huddle.

"You can put me down now," I said to Lucifer, and he obliged with a little flourish.

Beezle flew up and hovered in front of me, inspecting me critically. "You have goo in your hair."

"It's spider blood," I said.

"Is there some reason why you feel compelled to burn down everything around you?" he asked.

"You're the one who told me most things don't like fire," I retorted. "Would you rather the spider had eaten me?"

"Speaking of eating . . ." Beezle said.

"Don't even try to tell me you're hungry," I said.

"I was just noticing as we were flying over that there was a Dunkin' Donuts nearby."

Lucifer snapped his fingers next to me. A second later he presented a box of Munchkins to my greedy gargoyle.

Beezle rushed forward and happily accepted the box of doughnut holes from the Prince of Darkness. "Awesome! You need to get him to teach you how to do that."

"Is there some reason you're here besides scoring points with my gargoyle?" I asked.

Lucifer lost the merry look in his eye that had been there when he'd given Beezle the doughnuts. "Gabriel has used the power of the nephilim."

Gabriel suddenly went still.

"What?" I said. "What now? What ridiculous bit of kingdom law have we broken? If you are here to tell me that Gabriel is going to get taken away, you can just forget it."

"The conditions on which Gabriel is allowed to keep his life preclude his using the power of the nephilim," Lucifer said.

"Ramuell was YOUR SON!" I said angrily. I'd had

enough of the fallen to last me a lifetime. "Gabriel is your grandson. He's closer in blood to you than I am. I'm separated from you by thousands of generations. He's not. Do not even try to tell me that you're going to let the Grigori haul him away and kill him."

"No," Lucifer said, looking troubled. "I am supposed to kill him myself."

My magic roared up inside me, hot and angry. The parking lot was suddenly lit by the sun. I was vaguely aware of the massive insult I was doing Lucifer by showing him the full extent of my power, but I was exhausted and sick of angelic politics. Not even Lucifer could take Gabriel from me.

"I will not let you," I said, and my voice did not sound like my own. The ground trembled, and everyone except Lucifer and Samiel covered their ears.

"Do not make the mistake of crossing me, granddaughter. In my kingdom, my word is law."

His voice seemed to come from everywhere. Lucifer grew larger, his wings outspread, his eyes winking pools of starlight, until he looked much like he had in my vision of Evangeline, so long ago.

"You cannot frighten me," I said, and to my surprise it seemed that my power grew to match his own. "You cannot intimidate me. I am not simply a child of your line. I am an Agent of Death, and Death is my dominion."

"Even Death cannot defy the laws of the kingdom."

My body was filling up with power, power that I hadn't even known was inside me. There was too much of it. My skin felt stretched to bursting, and I knew with a sudden surety that if Lucifer tried to fight me in that moment, he would lose.

"I will defy whoever and whatever to keep Gabriel safe. You cannot have him. He belongs to me."

"Belongs?" Lucifer asked, his voice full of innuendo.

"Not as a thrall, but as my equal. I claim him as such, and tell you that he will no longer be a slave of the fallen."

"Very well," Lucifer said suddenly, and shrank back to his normal self.

I was so taken aback that my power receded suddenly like a deflating balloon. I stared at the Morningstar. "Very well?"

"Very well," he said, and the merriment was back in his eyes. "Gabriel, come forth."

Gabriel walked warily to stand in front of Lucifer and beside me.

"Hold out your hands," he instructed.

I held out my right hand, Gabriel his left. We both looked at each other in confusion. The snake on my palm wriggled in anticipation.

"As Madeline has claimed you as her equal, so you shall be," Lucifer said to Gabriel.

He did a little finger wiggle and our hands were suddenly clasped together, palm to palm, bound by golden cord.

"By the laws of my kingdom and by the power of my will, so you, Madeline Black ap Azazel and Gabriel ap Ramuell, are joined now and forever in this life. Henceforth Gabriel will no longer be a thrall, but a husband. As I have proclaimed it, so it shall be."

He clapped his hands together and looked around in delight at the lot of us and the varying expressions of shock on our faces.

"Married?" I said, looking down at the golden cord.

"Married," Lucifer said.

Gabriel fell to his knees, and because we were bound together, so did I.

"My lord," he said, and his voice was full of emotion.

I looked up at Lucifer, who had a surprising expression

of tenderness on his face. It reminded me of something that the faerie queen, Amarantha, had said once—*Everyone knows Lucifer is fanatical about his bloodline.*

"Rise," Lucifer said, "and go forth a free man."

Gabriel bowed his head, and I saw one single tear fall to the pavement. Then he turned to me, and held out his other hand. I placed my free hand in his and we rose, facing each other, the reality and the wonder of it finally dawning on us.

"Kissing is traditional," Lucifer said.

For the first time I felt hesitant. Gabriel and I had done a lot of kissing in secret, but never with everyone I cared about in attendance.

Gabriel, however, felt no hesitance at all. He bent his head to mine, and I had never felt such sweetness from him before, never felt so much love. After a few moments, however, Lucifer cleared his throat.

"Perhaps you want to, as they say in the vernacular, get a room," Lucifer said.

I smiled at Gabriel, and then looked questioningly at the first of the fallen.

"Why? I thought that you, too, were bound by the laws of your own kingdom."

"Nah." Lucifer grinned. "I can pretty much do whatever I want."

He winked, and then disappeared.

"I thought so," I muttered.

The golden cord binding our hands together dissolved. In its place were two beautifully carved golden bands, one on Gabriel's ring finger and one on the ring finger of my right hand (as I was lacking a ring finger on the left). I inspected the ring more closely and saw it was carved with the serpent, the symbol of the house of Lucifer.

"Well, that was a beautiful wedding," Beezle said. "The

bride has spider goo in her hair and the groom smells like sulfur. The parking-lot-in-front-of-the-burning-warehouse location leaves something to be desired, and there was a distinct lack of refreshments, but otherwise, just lovely."

I looked down and realized my coat was slashed and covered in my own blood. I smelled like burned spider. There was the sound of sirens approaching.

"We should get out of here," I said. "The firefighters are coming."

We all took flight, Beezle coming to rest at his usual place on my shoulder. Gabriel held on to my hand like he was afraid I was going to disappear.

J.B. flew east a short distance with us, then turned off to head downtown. I shook free from Gabriel for a moment and followed him.

"J.B.," I said, and when he turned to look at me I didn't know what to say.

"Congratulations," he said, and I could tell he didn't really mean it.

"I'm sorry," I said, and I tried to put a lot of meaning into those two words. I was sorry he was hurting, and that his hurt was caused by my happiness. I was sorry I couldn't feel about him the way he felt about me. I was sorry.

He nodded. "Come to the Agency in the morning. I want to show you something we found with those cameras."

"Okay. I'll be there," I said, and watched him fly away. He seemed very alone.

I turned back to Samiel, Beezle and Gabriel, all waiting for me. Gabriel held out his hand, and I took it.

"I hope the two of you aren't going to be mushy all the time now," Beezle said, resuming his perch on my shoulder. "You were kind of unbearable before, when you couldn't actually touch each other."

"I hope you aren't going to keep up a running commentary on our marriage. Because that might make me lose my motivation for buying snack cakes," I replied.

Samiel tapped me on the shoulder. *So I'm your brother, too, now.*

You already were, I replied. *I wouldn't have fought the Grigori for you otherwise.*

They aren't going to be happy now. Especially Azazel.

"Azazel can suck it," I said fervently. "And so can Nathaniel."

"Ooh, yeah, Nathaniel," Beezle chortled. "I wish I could be there when he finds out about the two of you."

"I'd already told him I wouldn't marry him," I reminded Beezle.

"Yeah, but he thought Azazel's will would prevail."

"It might have with anyone else. But Madeline has the strongest will I have ever known," Gabriel said, and his voice was filled with pride.

"You make it sound like it's a good thing," Beezle said. "Just wait until you have your first argument. Then you'll see how annoying it is."

"It wasn't my will that led to this marriage," I said slowly. "It was Lucifer's."

"Don't examine that thought too closely," Beezle advised. "It'll suck all the joy out of the moment."

"You're right," I said, shaking my head and smiling. "Who cares why Lucifer did what he did? Gabriel is free, we're married, and Azazel and Nathaniel are out of it."

But as we continued home the smile faded from my face. I may have gotten what I wanted, but so did Lucifer. And it was hard not to wonder why it suited him to marry me to Gabriel.

I looked at my husband—my *husband*, I thought, cherishing that word deep down inside me—and wondered just what Lucifer had in store for us.

And I might have imagined it, but Lucifer's merry laugh seemed to follow us home.

11

A COUPLE OF HOURS LATER I WALKED OUT OF THE bathroom, wrapped in my bathrobe with a towel on my head, having finally managed to get all of the spider gunk out of my very long hair. I stopped in the hallway between the bathroom and my bedroom, my heart racing with trepidation.

My husband was waiting for me, and this was unknown territory. What if I disappointed him? My feet felt like they were stuck to the floor.

Samiel and Gabriel had rearranged their possessions while I was in the shower. Gabriel's few things were stacked in the dining room, waiting to be incorporated into my stuff. Samiel had moved his clothes and books downstairs to Gabriel's former abode. Beezle had gone downstairs with Samiel, saying loudly that they were going to watch a really noisy movie with lots of gunfights and car explosions and that they were definitely not going to acknowledge any sounds that might be coming from my—*our*—apartment.

"Madeline," Gabriel said.

He stood in the doorway of my—our—bedroom, wearing nothing but his dress pants. His wings were folded behind him and his feet were bare.

I felt myself staring down the tunnel of the unknown as I had so many times before, and reflected that it was easier to face the prospect of being killed by some horrible monster than to lay myself open, heart and mind and body, before the man I loved.

He was mine. He was all I'd wanted from the first moment I'd met him, and yet I still couldn't bring myself to walk toward him.

"Madeline," he said again, and he held out his hand. "I will not harm you."

I knew he wouldn't. It wasn't about harm. It was about my own fears, my own sense of inadequacy.

I drifted down the hall slowly until I reached him. The air smelled like apple pie baking, the smell I associated with Gabriel. I put my hand in his and smiled shyly up at him.

He kissed me, and it was an easy kiss without expectation. The little rabbit thumping away in my chest calmed.

"Let me comb your hair," he said, and led me into the room.

He'd turned down the sheets. Only the bedside lamp was lit and it gave off a soft glow that left most of the room in shadow. The window was cracked open about half an inch, letting in the frigid January air. I shivered.

Gabriel gave me an apologetic look. "I am often very warm, even in winter."

"It's okay," I said.

The cracked window also let in the sound of thumping bass. One of our neighbors was having a party.

Gabriel led me to the bed and I sat perched on the edge, so tense I was ready to take off. As the moment drew nearer and nearer I felt panic rising again. It was definitely easier to fight monsters.

He knelt behind me and pulled the towel from my hair. The curly mess of it fell over my shoulder and to the middle of my back.

"My hair is too long," I mumbled, just to have something to say.

"I like it just as it is," Gabriel said softly, stroking his fingers through the wet tangles and smoothing them out.

A moment later he began drawing my cheap drugstore brush through the strands. I wished suddenly that I was a vainer person, that I colored away the rapidly multiplying gray hairs or that I had bought a nicer brush. Plastic bristles seemed like they were not nearly good enough for such a momentous occasion.

Some of the tension drifted away as Gabriel pulled the brush through my hair with long, sure strokes. Music drifted in through the window, an upbeat dance song about falling in love like a teenager.

"I was never a teenager like that," I said.

"Like what?" Gabriel asked.

"Like in the song. My mother died when I was so young. You'd think my life would have been one endless party with no parents leaning over my shoulder, but it wasn't."

"What was it like?"

"Scary, mostly. I became an Agent when my mom died. I was trying to feed myself and not lose the house. That's not the kind of information you can share with a potential boyfriend, or even a friend. I had to keep so much of my life a secret that I was never able to do normal teenage things, like go to the mall or sneak into R-rated movies or get trashed at parties. I never went on a date, never went to the prom. I never made out in the front seat of a car or got in a fight with my mom over a too-short skirt. One day I was a relatively normal kid and the next day I was responsible for the souls of the dead."

"We are not so different. I did not have a 'normal' childhood, either," Gabriel said.

I twisted to look at him and he stopped brushing. "What was it like, growing up with Azazel?"

Gabriel's eyes grew distant. "Difficult. There was never a time when I was not reminded of my status. Many of the Grigori disagreed with Lord Azazel's decision to raise me. I was often forced to battle creatures from other courts to prove my worth."

"What, like gladiatorial combat?"

Gabriel nodded.

"How old were you?"

Gabriel shrugged. "Eight, I believe, on the first occasion. It has been many years. I cannot remember exactly."

Eight. He'd been made to fight for his life when I was riding my bike up and down the street and reading Judy Blume books. I guess my childhood wasn't so bad after all.

"How old are you, Gabriel?" I asked. I couldn't believe I'd never thought to ask this question before.

He smiled briefly. "I am not certain it is wise to answer that question."

"Why not?"

"I believe you are already feeling self-conscious and the answer will make you more so."

"Don't you think your wife ought to know the answer?"

He sighed. "One thousand and twenty."

The light in the room flickered, or it just might have been black spots flickering before my eyes.

"One . . . *thousand.* With three zeros."

"Yes," he said. "But I do not wish for you to, as you say, make a big deal out of this."

I laughed. "Right, why would it be a big deal that you're nine hundred and eighty-eight years older than me?"

"Age does not matter," Gabriel said, his fingers under my chin. "Like you, I am not . . . experienced."

I hadn't thought about that. I'd been so wrapped up in my own worries that I'd forgotten that Gabriel had been forbidden from birth to have sex with anyone. The Grigori would not risk another child of the nephilim's line being born. And I'd thought I was the last virgin over the age of thirty in the U.S.

"So, I guess neither of us really knows what we're doing, huh?"

"Madeline," Gabriel said, and this time there was an undercurrent of implication when he said my name. "I believe we can figure out what to do."

"Gabriel," I said, with one last vestige of panic clinging to my voice. "The last time I was on a bed with a guy he tried to rape me."

He stroked his fingers over my cheek, and I closed my eyes. There was so much gentleness in him. I was amazed that Azazel had never been able to beat it out of him.

"I will never harm you," he said, and he kissed me again.

He leaned forward, wrapped his arm around my waist and pulled me backward on top of him. He was deliciously hot, and in this position all of our relevant parts were rubbing in all the right places.

But he didn't pull my robe off my shoulders, or attempt

to remove his own pants. He just kept kissing me, until I grew soft and warm and pliant, until my breath was short and my hands were roaming.

Only then did he untie the already loosened belt of my bathrobe and toss it away. Only then did his hands go everywhere that ached for his touch, and his mouth followed.

I unbuttoned his pants, slid my fingers inside, heard him gasp. I was suddenly aware of a power I had never really comprehended before—my power as a woman, the power I had to make a strong man weak—and I smiled.

He smiled back, and I felt my whole being suffused with joy. This was where I was supposed to be—with this man, with this love—and I saw that love reflected back in his face.

When, finally, we came together as one, the room was lit up like a solar flare. Magic exploded in my blood and in my eyes, and in Gabriel's. That magic mingled until the air was drenched with it, until it soaked our skin, until there was one tremendous explosion, a blazing burst of fireworks in the night sky.

The next morning I woke up with sunshine blazing through the windows. There was the smell of something good wafting from the kitchen. I groggily picked my head up and glanced at the clock. It was already midday.

I rolled over to my back. The sheets smelled like Gabriel, and I closed my eyes, remembering the night before.

Then I got up and pulled on my discarded robe, and went to look for my husband.

He was making pancakes, and whistling. I'd never heard him whistle before.

I leaned in the doorway, content to just watch him for a while. But he must have sensed me standing there, because he turned and smiled.

"Good morning," he said. I hadn't realized before how fraught with implication a "good morning" could be.

I crossed the kitchen to him and kissed him, because I could. Because I loved him, and there was no one to tell us not to.

Gabriel dropped the spatula on the counter so he could put his hands to better use. Things were just starting to get interesting again when someone cleared his throat behind me.

"The pancakes are burning," Beezle said.

I leaned my forehead against Gabriel's and rolled my eyes. "Why did I think you would give us a little privacy?"

"You had privacy. Yesterday. Now there are pancakes," Beezle said, flying to the cabinet and pulling out his favorite plate. It was a plastic child's plate with a cartoon of an owl and the word "night" above it.

He handed the plate to Gabriel, who shook his head at Beezle.

"I don't want any of those burned ones."

Gabriel obligingly loaded Beezle's plate with unburned pancakes. The gargoyle flew to the table and sat down next to his plate.

"Where's the syrup?" he asked, looking up at me expectantly.

I gave him an evil look, and he made a "pfft" noise at me. "What, did you think you were going to get some kind of honeymoon? You've got loads of stuff to do today. Does it really matter if I'm here right now?"

There was a tentative knock at the back door and Samiel stuck his head in hopefully.

I gave him a resigned wave. "Come on in. If you want pancakes, you'd better get them before Beezle eats them all."

An hour later Gabriel and I landed on the roof of the Agency. Since Beezle and Samiel had seen fit to break up our morning after, I decided it was best to just get on with my regularly scheduled business day. And that meant finding out what J.B. had wanted to show me the day before.

We entered through the rooftop door after a biometric scan of my face and fingerprints. Security at the Agency had been considerably increased since Ramuell's break-in a couple of months before.

As soon as we exited the stairwell we were all sent through a scanner. This scanner looked and acted a lot like a metal detector, except that it detected magical weapons and methods of concealment. A lot of Agents had worked overtime developing it, and it was now being duplicated at Agencies across the country. No one wanted to risk another massacre.

I had to turn in Lucifer's sword at the checkpoint—no weapons were permitted past the entry, Agent or not—and I felt terribly vulnerable without it. The sword had saved me more times than I could count since Nathaniel had presented it to me.

J.B.'s office had been moved to an upper floor to correspond with his rise in position to regional manager. His frizzy-haired secretary, Lizzie, typed away in the reception area with her usual look of long-suffering patience. She gave me a tight smile when she saw me.

"He wanted to see you as soon as you arrived. Go on in."

Usually Lizzie fussed over me like a substitute mother, so I was a little curious as to why she was so short with me, but I went to J.B.'s door and knocked. Gabriel followed closely behind.

"Come in," he called.

As usual, his desk looked like someone had blown up a bomb made of forms filled out in triplicate. J.B.'s eyes had bags underneath them and his hair stood up in every direction. He looked like he had gotten no sleep at all.

"You look like shit," I said baldly.

"Yeah, well, staying up all night trying to figure out how to calm dozens of screaming people will do that to you. Not to mention attempting to identify all of them so that they can be returned to their families—eventually," J.B. said with a touch of asperity.

I felt a little jolt of guilt. I'd been having the night of my life with Gabriel while J.B. had gotten stuck cleaning up the mess with the warehouse. But it did not seem prudent to apologize for my wedding night—particularly to a man who had wanted to date me—so I covered the awkward moment by changing the subject.

"So, what was it that you wanted to show me?"

J.B. pushed to his feet. "You'll have to come down to the basement. That's where we've been working on it."

"On what?" I asked as Gabriel and I followed J.B. out of the office and into the hallway.

"Not here," J.B. said shortly, and pressed the button for the elevator.

Agents bustled back and forth in the hall as we waited, most of them carrying piles of paper. The Agency was definitely stuck in the twentieth century, data-wise. A project had been undertaken to move all of our records to digital media but its importance had diminished after the attack.

Improving security had been the priority, and anyway, most of the upper brass wasn't completely sold on the necessity of moving to computers. I was sure that they'd felt this way when the Agency moved from papyrus to paper. There was definitely a culture of it's-always-been-this-way-and-it's-fine in my business.

We loaded onto the elevator with J.B. and stood in silence as the doors opened and closed, loaded and unloaded. I had a sudden memory of one of the elevators propped open by a severed human leg, and wondered if it had been this one. It was really a wonder that any Agents had returned to work after the place had been overrun by demons.

The elevator descended into the basement. The Hall of Records was down there, the place where every death in the Chicagoland area in history was recorded—even before there was a Chicagoland. The room was almost incomprehensibly big and filled with millions of index cards.

J.B. led us past the Hall, past the offices where Agents labored over the much-maligned data conversion, and to a door at the very end of the hallway. It looked to be solid steel and it was armed with another biometric scanner. J.B. swiped his I.D. card and then had his eyeball and both hands scanned.

The door clicked open, and we went inside.

The room was so secure that I expected there to be some fabulous treasure inside, or at the very least dozens of Agents working on some top-secret weapon. But all there was was one female Agent with short purple hair and both arms covered in tattoos, and a large pile of the cameras that I'd found with the wolf cubs and in the warehouse.

The Agent sat at a worktable with a lamp clipped to the edge. She hunched over one of the cameras, which had been disassembled into what looked like about eight million tiny pieces.

"This is Chloe," J.B. said. "Chloe, Madeline Black. And Gabriel."

Chloe gave us a little finger wave without looking up from her work.

"Chloe," J.B. said. "Can you show Agent Black what you showed me yesterday?"

She held up a finger to indicate that we needed to wait. I wondered if she knew how to talk.

J.B. tapped his foot impatiently while we waited for Chloe to finish whatever it was that she needed to finish. She seemed to be teasing apart the pieces of what looked like a circuit board. I am not technically minded in the least—I can barely operate my cell phone—but whatever she was doing was fascinating to me. I crept closer to get a better look.

"You're standing in my light," Chloe said.

Okay, I guess she could talk. I shuffled backward, cheeks reddening.

After a few moments she looked up and pushed away from the table. She seemed to notice Gabriel for the first time.

"Well, hello, gorgeous," Chloe said.

I felt strongly that it would not be good for me to act like an insanely jealous wife and rip her purple hair out at the roots, so I just said, "His name is Gabriel. And he's married."

She looked from my right hand to his left, saw the matching rings, and shrugged. "Worth a try. So, you want to see what we found?"

Chloe shot across the room on the casters of her chair and picked up one of the cameras from the pile. Then she used her feet to scoot back to the table.

She arranged the camera so that the lens pointed at the wall to our right. Then she lowered her hand over the camera and muttered something I couldn't catch.

"There's no on or off switch that we could find," J.B. murmured. "Chloe figured out by trial and error that you need magic to turn the machine on."

A second later the camera sprang to life and pictures were projected on the wall. Some of the pictures moved like video, and some were like camera images. All seemed random. There was a clip of a little boy catching soap bubbles, a gumball whirling down a ramp in one of those big gumball machines with the red top, a girl swinging on a piece of rope that dangled from a tree over a ravine, a half-eaten pepperoni pizza, a fragment of text that came and went too fast for me to read.

"What is this?" I asked. "It all seems random."

"Memories," Chloe said.

"Memories?" I asked. "Are you sure?"

"It's our best guess," J.B. said. "And it makes sense. The machine scans people's brains and extracts their memories, and then when they die the ghost is damaged because most of what made up its identity is gone."

I watched a white cloud shaped like a turtle drift by, a large buck leaping in front of a car's headlights, an older boy picking apples and laughing.

"Okay, I guess it makes sense. But why take the memories in the first place?"

"Don't know. We're trying to look into that now. Listen, Chloe, can you take a break?" J.B. asked.

Her eyes slid from me to J.B. to Gabriel. "Top-secret information about to be discussed. Got it. I'm sure I can use a milk shake."

She left the room with one last covert glance at Gabriel. I couldn't blame her for that. He was just about the prettiest thing you've ever seen.

As soon as the door closed behind Chloe, J.B. spoke.

"You were right—my mother is involved," he said heavily.

"How do you know?" I asked.

"The spiders," J.B. said. "My mother breeds them. No one else in the world has spiders like that. So either she's directly involved in this or she sold the spiders to whoever is. Either way, this goes back to Amarantha's court."

"And Beezle said that the charcarion demons are only present in two courts of the fallen. One of them sounded like a sneeze, and the other one was Focalor."

J.B.'s eyes glinted. "And we know that Amarantha and Focalor have worked together in the past."

"Yes, but how are they doing it?" Gabriel asked. "Lord Lucifer will surely be watching the two of them most closely to ensure that they do not continue their plans for sedition. They can hardly meet and plan, or even pass messages to one another without arousing suspicion."

"So, are we going to Amarantha's court to confront her or what?" I asked J.B.

"Well, you have a price on your head in the faerie kingdom . . ."

"And that's different from the regular world how? Lucifer's enemies try to kill me every other day."

"And I'm forbidden from coming to court at this time, as my mother is displeased with me for openly allying myself with you. I haven't been to court since I was there with you, and I have heard no communications since the edict to stay away."

"Come on, J.B., break the rules. Live a little. I'm forbidden from doing stuff that I do all the time," I said.

J.B. looked uncertain. It went deeply against the grain of his personality to even consider bending the law. J.B. is very devoted to order.

"It is the best lead that we have," Gabriel said.

"Yeah." I nodded. "This isn't just about the ghosts. I still need to find Wade. We know that the kidnapping is tied to whoever is responsible for these machines. If Amarantha provided security in the form of spiders while the machines did their work, then she might know where Wade is being held."

J.B. still hesitated.

"Look, I'm going whether you do or not. So you might as well come with me and try to mitigate the diplomatic damage that you know I'll do."

J.B. and Gabriel shared a look of acknowledgment of the truth of this statement.

"All right," J.B. said. "But we can't go now. I have things to finish here."

"Meetings to attend, paperwork to photocopy?" I said sweetly.

"I know you don't think much of bureaucracy, Black, but every cog needs to do their part for the machine to work," J.B. said, annoyed.

"People are being kidnapped and having their memories stolen. Many of them are dying. You really think the upper brass wouldn't cut you a break on your cog work?"

"No," J.B. said grimly. "You think I'm obsessed with paperwork? You should meet the board members sometime. I'll come by your house later with a car, around seven."

"Won't it take us a few hours to get to court by car?" I asked.

"More than a few," J.B. said. "We'll arrive in the early morning."

"That'll take too long," I said. "Let's portal it."

"You can't portal in and out of Amarantha's kingdom."

"It breaks the rules, right?" I asked. "Who cares?"

"No, I mean you literally can't. It used to be possible, but since you and Nathaniel burned down half her forest she's closed the magical loopholes that allow the creation of portals in her kingdom."

"Oh," I said, and rocked back on my heels, thinking. "Wait. What about portals that already existed, like the one that we found in the alley? The one that led to the swamp?"

The portal had been in the same alley where we'd found the body of a werewolf and later Gabriel had gone missing. It had been invisible, and I'd discovered it by throwing a magical net over the area.

"What about it?" J.B. asked. "Surely it's been closed by now."

"We might as well see," I said. "It will be faster than a car. Once we portal through we can fly to the castle."

"Fine, look into it," J.B. said impatiently. "And let me know what you find. I'll be at your house later regardless."

"Okay," I said.

We exited through the door and found Chloe sitting halfway down the hallway eating a gigantic burrito wrapped in foil. She gave the three of us a little finger salute and hopped to her feet, heading back to the room and her work.

J.B. parted ways with us on the floor of his office. I retrieved the sword from security and Gabriel and I exited through the rooftop door.

"Do you want to go to the alley now?" he asked.

"Nah, we'll wait and go with J.B. later," I said.

"Very well," Gabriel said.

He took my hand as we flew home. It was lovely just to be with him, not to hide my emotions, to know that I could touch him if I wanted and no one could take him away from me.

We landed in the backyard, smiling at each other.

"So I see that it is true," said a strained voice from the porch, and we looked up.

It was Nathaniel.

12

IF I'D THOUGHT NATHANIEL LOOKED MUSSED YESTERday at Samiel's trial, it was nothing compared to the way he looked now. He was positively ragged. He looked like he hadn't showered or combed his hair, there were huge bags under his eyes, his shirt had been buttoned incorrectly and the tails were left hanging out of his pants.

Nathaniel stalked toward us, and I backed up half a step. He had a slightly crazed look in his eye, and I wasn't sure what he would do.

"I did not believe when I heard," he said. "I did not believe that such a thing would be possible, would be *allowed*. I did not think you would defy your father and the laws of the kingdom so utterly by permitting this *thrall* to defile you."

Nathaniel raised his hand toward me but Gabriel stopped him with a hold on his wrist. Nathaniel wrenched his arm away.

"Do not touch me, slave," he spat. "You have already given me insult by touching my betrothed."

"She is not your betrothed," Gabriel said softly, but there was an undercurrent of steel. "She is my wife."

I stepped between them before Gabriel lost his temper with Nathaniel and went all nephilim-power on his ass. I didn't need another mess to clean up.

"Leave Gabriel out of this," I said. "And while you're at it, leave Azazel out of this, too. This is about you and me. I told you I wouldn't marry you. Repeatedly. I don't love you. I never felt anything remotely resembling affection for you. You convinced yourself that I would have to follow Azazel's word and marry you anyway, but I wasn't going to do it."

"You *must* follow the accords of Lucifer's kingdom!" Nathaniel shouted, and he looked totally unhinged now. "Even Lord Lucifer himself must cleave unto them!"

"Yeah, about that . . ." I said. "I think he just plays along with the Grigori because it amuses him to do so. Don't kid yourself that Lucifer has to follow anyone's whim but his own."

"You are speaking blasphemy," Nathaniel said, and his hand went around my wrist.

I felt Gabriel move behind me but I put my other hand on his chest, holding him back.

"Get your hand off me before I blow it off," I said to Nathaniel. "You'd better remember what I did to you the last time you touched me without permission."

The memory hung in the air between us—Nathaniel holding me down, me blasting him with so much power that it left his muscles and bone exposed, unable to heal for weeks.

He let go of me, his eyes narrowed. "You have done me an insult by treating me thus."

I resisted the impulse to rub the place where he had touched me, to wipe my skin clean.

"You're the one who's always going on about Lucifer," I said. "Fine. My marriage to Gabriel was Lucifer's will. I'd like to see you try to cross him."

Nathaniel backed away from me, his wings spread wide. "You have laid me low publicly, to be humiliated before all the courts. Everyone knows that Lucifer indulges you, that you are permitted to run wild. I do not blame Lord Lucifer for his affection for you, for I, too, was guilty of this."

I gave him a look. "The only thing you cared about was the status you would get when I married you. Now you've lost that. Don't act like it was love for me that's breaking your heart now."

"It is all falling apart," Nathaniel muttered. "I will not forget this."

He took flight in a whirl of anger, and we watched him go.

"Well, I didn't expect that," I said.

"I did," Gabriel said.

"Why?" I asked. "Nathaniel's like J.B. He's a rule-follower. I figured that whatever Lucifer said, he would go along."

Gabriel looked troubled. "You have insulted him on many levels. You have defied your father, who is the head of Nathaniel's court. You have publicly broken your betrothal. You have shown no regard for his feelings. And, worst of all, you have wed a thrall, the lowest caste of the courts."

"You're not a thrall anymore," I said fiercely, my hands on his cheeks.

"Not to you. Not to Lord Lucifer, perhaps. But although the members of the court must now treat me as a free man, they will always consider me a thrall. And it is that insult that Nathaniel will find hardest to swallow."

"I don't care," I said, and I kissed him. "You're mine

now, and none of them will take you from me. Not Nathaniel, not Azazel, not even Lucifer."

He smiled briefly. "My very small champion."

"I keep telling people not to underestimate me," I said.

"I don't," Gabriel replied. "Now let us go inside. Beezle is sure to be faint from hunger pangs by now."

I laughed, and we went into the house, a house that felt a lot more like home when he was by my side.

A little after seven the five of us—J.B., Gabriel, Samiel, Beezle and me—stood in the alley where I'd found the permanent portal. I cast the magical net again to pinpoint its location.

"It's still there," I said triumphantly.

J.B. shook his head. "I can't believe my mother wouldn't have closed the portal. You told her of its presence."

"Maybe she wasn't able to close it. I told Gabriel there was something about this portal that seemed very permanent," I said. "Regardless, we can get in from here a lot faster than if we drove."

Samiel tapped my shoulder. *I don't know if this is such a good idea. Beezle said the last time you came through here there was a big, tentacled monster.*

"Yeah," I said, remembering the horrible squishy thing in the swamp. "But I killed it, so there's nothing to worry about."

Gabriel raised an eyebrow at me. "You do not think that Amarantha will have replaced that monster with another? The portal leaves the border of her land open to attack."

"And I suppose you all think that Amarantha will just let us drive up to the front gates like we did last time," I retorted. "What with the price on my head and all."

"I suppose this is the best way," J.B. said reluctantly. "There is likely to be heightened security everywhere. My mother was paranoid even before you managed to kill two of her favorite pets."

"Five now," I said, remembering the spiders in the warehouse.

"I wouldn't mention that if I were you," J.B. said. "We want to gather information, not provoke her into trying to kill you on the spot."

"For Maddy those two things are often intertwined," Beezle said.

"Remind me again why you never stay home anymore?" I asked.

"Your life would be a lot more boring without me," my gargoyle said.

We all lined up in front of the portal, Gabriel staring at me blandly when I tried to step in front of him.

"You're not my bodyguard anymore," I said.

"Call it the right of a husband," he said, and disappeared inside.

And the right of a brother-in-law, Samiel added, nudging me out of the way and hopping into the portal behind Gabriel.

I looked at J.B., who appeared ready to knock me out if I tried to go before him, and sighed. "Fine, fine. Go on, be a man."

When they had all gone through I glanced over at Beezle, who was hovering near my right shoulder.

"Do you have some deep-seated need to prove your masculinity by going into the portal ahead of me?"

"Hell, no. I might get hurt," he said. "Put me in your pocket. I almost fell off last time we went through one of these."

I tucked Beezle into my inside pocket. Just his horns and his eyes were visible above the lapel of my coat.

"Heigh-ho, silver!" Beezle said.

I stepped into the portal, eyes squeezed tight, and felt the familiar sensation of being squashed into a pancake while traveling at approximately eight million miles an hour. A second later I flew out at the other end, determined not to land in the swamp on my face this time.

I needn't have worried. We weren't in the swamp. We were in front of Amarantha's castle.

"Well, I was right. It did take less time to get here than by car," I said.

I touched down lightly on the ground and joined the boys, who all stared at the castle. We were not in front of the structure but rather on the opposite side of the moat that surrounded it. The drawbridge was up and everything was weirdly silent. A half-moon shone, leaving way too many shadows.

"This isn't right," J.B. finally said, and his voice was barely above a whisper. "This is the time of night when the court is in full swing. It's usually like a never-ending party."

I looked up at the catwalk on the outer wall. There were no soldiers patrolling there and no torches lit anywhere that we could see. All was dark and quiet, almost as if the castle had been abandoned.

I expelled a breath. "We're not going to find out anything just standing here. We've got to go in."

Gabriel and Samiel nodded, but J.B. just stood there, fists clenched.

"J.B.?" I said, putting my hand on his shoulder.

He spoke through gritted teeth. "She is my mother. I hate her more than you can imagine, but she is still my mother."

And you don't want to go in there and find her dead, I thought, filling in the blanks. I squeezed his shoulder and made him look at me.

"Whatever is in there, you won't be alone," I said.

He nodded tightly, and we all took flight. As we soared over the outer wall and the courtyard I looked down. There were several cars in the courtyard, but they appeared abandoned. Doors were opened, and I thought I might have seen a skeletal hand hanging out of one of the windows, but I didn't stop to investigate.

We landed a few feet before the large front door. It was ajar, and there was a dark smear on the heavy wood that could have been blood.

The whole place had the unnatural calm that followed postapocalyptic calamity. I half expected rotting zombies to come shambling out of the castle at any minute.

"Does anyone else think it's a good idea to go home now and pretend that we never saw this?" Beezle said, his head sticking out of my jacket, and his voice seemed unnaturally loud in the extreme quiet.

I patted his horns. "Just make sure you stay in there when the inevitable freaky thing shows up."

"Don't need to tell me twice," Beezle murmured.

Gabriel conjured up a ball of nightfire. It floated above us and ahead, slipping into the crack of the open door.

He followed it silently, pushing the door open farther. The creak of the hinges sounded like an explosion, and we all paused, holding our breath, but nothing roared out of the darkness.

I fell in behind Gabriel, followed by J.B. and Samiel. We were in the receiving foyer, facing the long central hallway of the castle. The frozen knights that lined the walls stood like accusing sentries.

The ball of nightfire floated ahead of us, illuminating dust and cobwebs and the once-gleaming armor of the dead knights. There were more dark streaks on the floor, and rusty-looking splatters on the wall.

None of us spoke. I didn't know about the others but I was too tense to talk. The air seemed full of menace, and the sensation was not unlike the feeling I had when I entered the Maze. I wondered briefly if Amarantha was dead, and if so, could the horror that lived in the Maze break free?

We passed through the hallway and all of us turned instinctively toward the throne room. No faeries bustled to and fro; no one stood at the door to announce our presence. There was only a set of carved double doors, lit by nightfire and covered in blood.

J.B. pushed open the doors. I felt a little tremor of anticipation. We entered the throne room like four gunslingers looking for a fight. But again, there was no one to greet us.

Gabriel sent the nightfire dancing left and right, revealing smashed furniture and more splatters of dark red.

"Where are the bodies? What happened to everyone?" Beezle asked. He was still tucked inside my coat, his clawed hands gripping the lapel.

"A fair question, gargoyle," rasped a harsh voice. "What has become of the court of Amarantha the Fair, she who has ruled over this place for hundreds of years?"

We all spun in the direction of the voice, and Gabriel sent the nightfire higher, made it brighter so that it illuminated the room. The ceilings were so high that even Gabriel's light could not reach them, so we remained under an oppressive cloud of shadow.

A figure sat upon Amarantha's throne, face covered by the hood of a dark cloak. Behind the throne, a shadow shifted, as if hiding from the light. There was a whiff of sulfur in the air.

"How dare you show your face here so boldly, spawn of Lucifer?" asked the figure.

"Why do I have to keep telling everyone I'm not the spawn of Lucifer? It's becoming a bad running joke," I muttered. Then, to the figure on the throne: "Who are you? Do you know what's happened here?"

"Lucifer's justice," the person spat.

I looked around the room in horror. Had Lucifer punished Amarantha by slaughtering the whole court?

"He descended on this court like the god that he wishes to be, promising benevolence to those who would willingly give up the Queen."

I glanced at Gabriel and knew that we were thinking the same thing. There had probably been a stampede for the doors when Lucifer had shown up offering mercy.

"Did . . . a lot of people stay?" I asked tentatively.

"They fled like rats," the person said angrily. The voice was so strange, so harsh and low, it was difficult to tell if it was a man or a woman.

"Did anyone support the Queen?" J.B. asked.

"Prince Jonquil," the person said. "Why were you not in court to defend the integrity of your house, to demand that Lucifer respect the sanctity of Amarantha's kingdom?"

"The Queen sent me from her sight and bade me not return," J.B. said tightly.

"And if she had not, would you have stood before Lucifer and defied him? You, who have allied yourself with Lucifer's most beloved child? You, who have displayed contempt for your house and your family name?"

"What *happened*?" J.B. demanded.

The figure was still for a moment, and in the darkness and the quiet, I heard something shift. Something large.

"Gabriel," I whispered, sidling closer to him. "There's something . . ."

The figure stood abruptly, and again I smelled sulfur. "What happened? All those who swore loyalty to the Queen were marked for their fealty to Amarantha. They did only as they should have by staying loyal to their Queen. They should not have been punished for this. Lucifer has no dominion over these lands, whatever he may believe. He violated long-standing accords by treating another head of state as a subject of his will. The world is not his to carve up as he pleases."

"But there were no accords between the house of Lucifer and the house of Amarantha," I said. "The agreements between them had been broken. Amarantha invited his retribution by plotting treason against him with Focalor, and by trying to use his grandchild as a stud. And she tried to have me killed by proxy."

"And for that, Lucifer has claimed this court of faerie, has made it an outpost of his kingdom and rendered its inhabitants . . ."

The person under the cloak stopped speaking. The shadow behind the throne moved a little closer to the light, and I thought I saw a glint of green and scaly skin.

"What did he do?" I asked.

There was a sudden movement, a flurry of cloth, and the figure was revealed to us.

The creature was unspeakably ugly. It was humanoid, but it was impossible to tell if it was male or female. Its skin was green and armored like an alligator's. One large black horn protruded from the left side of its head. The right side of its face was covered in gigantic pustules that oozed slimy-looking fluid. A long, heavy, lizardlike tail dragged behind it.

And shining from that hideous face were the blazing blue eyes of Queen Amarantha the Fair.

"This is what Lucifer did to me, to those who swore loyalty to me. He stole our beauty and our magic, and made us hideous to look upon, so that anyone who dared contemplate defying *Lord* Lucifer would see my court as a cautionary tale, and reconsider."

"Mother?" J.B. said. He seemed to be in a trance, approaching the thing that no longer looked like Amarantha.

"Mother," she said, and there was a wealth of contempt in her voice. "You have never been a child of mine. You belonged to your father, always. Always duty, always Death."

"I could not abandon the souls that needed me because you would have preferred that I played the role of a courtier," J.B. said angrily.

"Souls!" Amarantha said with a sweep of her hand. The beautifully manicured nails had been replaced by long and ragged claws. "What are humans to faeries? Lesser beings, beings to be used when needed and then discarded."

"Like my father," J.B. said.

"Yes," Amarantha replied.

"You know," I said thoughtfully. "I think this new look suits you. It reflects what's on the inside a whole lot better."

"And you, Madeline Black," Amarantha said. "Do not think that I have forgotten that this occurred because of you, Lucifer's best beloved."

"Why should I get blamed for this mess you're in? Because I'm the one that caught you at it? I called you a child once, and that's exactly what you're acting like—a child. When are you going to grow up and take responsibility for your own actions?"

"You dare—" Amarantha began.

I moved my hand to look like lips flapping. "To defy me,

to disrespect me, blah-de-blah blah. I swear, you immortals need to get a new script. You haven't learned a thing, have you? Lucifer took your power and your court from you, and you're still plotting against him. You're asking to get squashed like a bug."

Amarantha drew herself back, gave me a crafty look. "I do not know of what you speak."

"The spiders," J.B. said. "We found the warehouse protected by spiders."

"What warehouse?" Amarantha asked.

"Gods above and below," I said, losing my temper. I pulled the sword from its sheath and stalked toward Amarantha. "Do you think I'm going to stand here all day and let you play dumb with us? You're the only one who breeds spiders like that."

I swung the sword toward her neck, intending to threaten her. I wouldn't actually cut her head off, no matter how much I would like to.

Someone cried, "No!" and a creature leapt from behind the throne. It looked like a mad scientist had welded the head of a snake on the body of a human and then covered it in snakeskin. I stepped back, swung the sword up to meet the new threat, but Samiel had already flown to the rescue. He crashed into the creature and they fell to the ground behind Amarantha, rolling over as Samiel punched and the creature slashed out with its claws.

A moment later Samiel had the snake-thing pinned under him. I'd yet to meet any creature that was stronger than Samiel except for Metatrion. It occurred to me that I had accidentally gathered quite a powerful collection of beings around me, and I wondered if that had added to the general perception that I was a threat.

Samiel looked up at me, questioning. I swung the sword

back so that the tip was at Amarantha's neck. She looked terrified, but it wasn't for herself. Her eyes were pinned on Samiel and the snake-thing.

"Do not let him hurt her," she said, and there was a pleading in her voice that I had never heard before.

The snake-thing snapped its fangs at Samiel and he punched it in the jaw. I heard something break, and the snake let out a hideous cry.

"Don't let him hurt her!" Amarantha screamed. "She's all I have left."

"Who is it?" I asked, although I had a strong suspicion already.

"Violet," the Queen said, and a tear burned down her misshapen cheek. "She would not leave me."

I dropped my sword to the ground. She seemed so broken, so pathetic, but we still needed information.

"I want to know where Wade is," I said. "And what you're doing with the souls."

"Why should I tell you?" Amarantha said.

"If you don't, you can stand there and watch Samiel beat Violet to death," I said, and held the tip of the sword near her face. "And then I'll see if I can improve upon Lucifer's handiwork."

J.B. and Gabriel didn't speak behind me. I hoped that they knew I'd never follow through on the threat. It made me feel a little sick just to say it aloud. I did not have the stomach or the will for torture, but it's the kind of thing that Amarantha would have done. Monsters are always willing to believe in the monstrosity of others.

Amarantha narrowed her eyes at me, like she was taking my measure. I raised my eyebrow at her, and nodded at Samiel, hoping it wouldn't be necessary to do too much to convince her.

He seemed to understand what I wanted. He grabbed one of Violet's hands and broke two of her fingers. I winced, but Amarantha didn't see it. She had taken a step toward Samiel and Violet, eyes wide. The snake screamed and thrashed, and Amarantha fell to her knees, held her hands up in front of her.

"Stop," she pleaded. "Please, stop."

It gave me no pleasure to see such a once-proud creature submit in humiliation. It didn't matter that Amarantha had tried to destroy Lucifer's kingdom, that she had cast a spell to have me raped by Nathaniel, that she'd sent me into the Maze with every intention of me coming out in a body bag. I was sorry to be the one who had to lay her lower than she already was, and that I'd had to act like a monster to do it.

"Where is Wade?" I asked.

"The wolf is hidden in the castle," she said in a whisper.

"Where?" I nudged her with my boot.

"In the south tower," she said, looking at J.B.

"J.B., you and Samiel go," I said. "You'll be able to get there fastest."

"Umm, I don't think splitting up is a good idea," Beezle said. "That usually leads to certain death."

"You watch too many horror movies," I said. "Besides, someone needs to watch these two, and I'm not leading a parade to the tower."

"What's guarding it?" J.B. asked.

Amarantha looked annoyed that we'd asked. "Charcarion demons."

"How many?" I said.

"Why should I tell you?" Amarantha snapped.

I looked at Samiel and he broke another one of Violet's fingers. She screamed in pain and Amarantha cried out, stepping toward them. I held the sword to her throat to stop her, and tried to remember that there was a greater good here, and I was supposed to be a part of it.

"Fifty," Amarantha said through gritted teeth.

"Fine. The two of you can easily handle fifty demons," I said to Samiel. "Gabriel, you take over the watch on Lady Violet."

Gabriel walked forward and put his hand on Samiel's shoulder, and his half brother rose. Gabriel offered a hand to Violet and she accepted, her face confused. When she stood Gabriel nodded to her respectfully and then conjured another ball of nightfire. It hovered over his palm, the threat clear. Violet looked at the nightfire, then at Gabriel's face, her expression resigned.

I backed up a little from Amarantha, confident that she wouldn't risk Violet's life by doing anything stupid. I pulled J.B. close to me so I could whisper to him.

"Do you think she's lying?" I asked.

"There are probably twice that number of demons up there, but I think we can manage them," he replied.

"Don't worry about killing all of them," I said. "The priority is to get Wade and get out of here. Do it as quickly and as safely as you can, and don't bring him back into the throne room. Go right out to the portal."

"Yeah, before something else horrible happens," Beezle muttered. "I still think this is a bad idea."

"Duly noted," I said.

"How will we let you know we have Wade?" J.B. said.

"I'm going to move Amarantha and Violet into the courtyard," I said. "We'll see you when you come out."

"And then we'll all run like hell," Beezle said.

"Some of us will. Others will allow themselves to be carried," I replied.

"Hey, you're the one who wants to lose thirty pounds. I'm helping you out by adding extra resistance," he said.

"Okay, going to get Wade now," J.B. said loudly.

"Be careful," I said.

"I'm well aware of my mother's ability to set traps and spring them," he said. "I will be."

I waved Samiel over and signed to him. *Watch out for a sneak attack. We don't know if any other faeries loyal to Amarantha are still in the castle.*

He nodded. *Beezle told me about the secret passages.*

The two of them left the room. I hoped that there was nothing between here and the south tower except the char-carion demons. Samiel had managed to hold off hundreds of them in the cave where we'd found the cubs, so I was confident that he could take care of them. If that was all there was.

"All right," I said to Amarantha. "We're taking this outside."

She smiled, and I did not like the look of that smile.

"And why should I obey you, Lucifer's child?"

I dropped my shoulders in annoyance. "Do I really have to repeat this again? I am not Lucifer's . . ."

That was when the spider landed on top of me.

13

I FELL TO THE GROUND, LANDED ON MY FACE, FELT THE horrible weight of its furred body above me. Beezle cried out as he was squashed by both the spider's weight and mine. I rolled to my side, saw its fangs descending toward me, and plunged my sword into its abdomen.

A gush of dark fluid poured from the wound, and I scrambled out from beneath the giant arachnid as it collapsed to the ground.

I pushed to my feet, wiping goo from my eyes, and saw Gabriel holding off two larger spiders with nightfire. There was no sign of Amarantha or Violet.

"That was *disgusting*," Beezle said from inside my jacket. "We are not doing that again."

I knew from experience that nightfire was useless against spiders, so I shot the one on the left with electricity. It screeched and reared up as little arcs danced over its body. Gabriel got the message pretty quickly and conjured up the white nephilim fire to take out the other one. The air was filled with the smell of cinnamon and sulfur and rotting blood.

Gabriel flew over the twitching, burning corpses of the other two spiders to my side.

"You are unhurt?" he asked, taking my hand.

"Yeah," I said. "I'd kiss you, but I have spider goo in my hair."

"Again," Beezle said.

"Did you see where Amarantha and Violet went?" I asked.

He shook his head. "They disappeared into the wall passages. They are likely far from here by now."

"I told you we shouldn't split up," Beezle said. "They were just waiting for us to divide our forces before they let the spiders attack."

"Yeah, yeah," I said. "You can have a doughnut if we get out of this alive."

"We must locate Samiel and J.B. Have you any notion of where the south tower is?"

I thought of how often I'd gotten lost in the couple of days I'd stayed in Amarantha's castle the month before. I shook my head.

Beezle sighed. "Can't either of you tell which way is north?"

"I know Lake Michigan is to the east," I said.

"That doesn't help you if you're nowhere near Chicago," Beezle said. "You're not on the grid system here."

"Well, do you know which way is north, smarty-pants?"

"Yes, as a matter of fact," he said. "It's that way."

He pointed toward the doors we'd entered.

"Are you sure about that?"

"I'm sure about everything," Beezle said.

"Confidence does not necessarily equal accuracy."

"It does for me."

Gabriel shared a look with me. "Do we have a better option?"

"No," I said. "If you're wrong, you're out that doughnut."

"I'm not wrong," Beezle said.

We crept quietly into the hall. I was in front and Gabriel walked behind me with his back pressed against mine. We weren't sure if more spiders were lurking on the ceiling or if Amarantha and Violet might leap from the walls and try to take us out from behind.

The hallway was still eerily silent. We walked slowly, listening for threats, all three of us strung tight with tension.

I hoped that I hadn't sent J.B. and Samiel to their doom because I'd foolishly trusted Amarantha's word. Over and over again Gabriel and Beezle had warned me against taking immortals at face value. It seemed that I had trouble learning that lesson.

We turned south according to Beezle's directions and entered a hallway that was filled with spun silk. The bodies of dead faeries hung in the webbing.

"There had better not be any more spiders down here," I said. "Because I just can't take another one."

It was difficult to get through the hall without disturbing the webs. We had to stop and untangle from the sticky stuff more than once. I was hyperventilating by the time we got to the end—without encountering any more spiders, thank goodness.

There was a wide set of stone steps at the end of the hall and we followed them up. At the top of the stairs was another long hallway. Both sides had large arched window openings cut out. The left side windows were covered in multicolored glass and looked out over the forest that bordered Amarantha's castle. The right side windows were free of glass. I stepped forward to peek around the arch, and my heart stopped.

The windows looked over a large, long room that might have been a dining hall once. It was still a dining hall—of a different sort.

The room seethed with spiders of all sizes. They fed on faeries and charcarion demons—obviously Amarantha was willing to use whomever she had on hand to keep her pets satisfied. Everywhere I looked there were clutches of eggs hanging in the webs.

"An average-sized spider will lay about a hundred eggs in one of those sacs," Beezle said quietly.

"Those aren't average-sized spiders," I replied. "There are probably thousands of them in there."

"What shall we do?" Gabriel asked. "We cannot leave them here to breed further. If Amarantha releases these upon a large population of humans . . ."

"They could wipe out half a city in a day," I said. "Normal people aren't prepared to deal with monsters like this."

"Are you going to set everything on fire again?" Beezle asked.

I looked at Gabriel. "Probably. It's the most effective way to take out a bunch of them at once. But if I do that, we have to make sure that Wade and J.B. and Samiel are clear of the building first. And then we have to make sure that the spiders can't escape from this room."

"Well, I don't think they can open doors," Beezle said.

"But they can break them down if they're in a room filled with smoke and flame," I replied. "And the smaller spiders can easily escape up the walls and out these windows. Every creature has a self-preservation instinct."

"I know. Mine is kicking in right now," Beezle said.

"Let us find the others, then return for this," Gabriel said. "We do not want to attract the creatures' attention."

I crouched to the ground and duckwalked below the bottom sill of the arches until we reached the end. I was terrified the whole time that I'd see the hairy leg of a spider creeping through a window, but we managed to make it through safely without being attacked.

We climbed another set of steps, came to another hallway.

"They all look the same," I said desperately.

"We're heading in the right direction," Beezle insisted.

"But are we choosing the correct passages?" Gabriel asked. "One wrong turning and we will miss them."

Then we heard it—the clatter of footsteps, angry cries, and the howl of a wolf.

"This way," I said, turning to the right and running down the hall to another junction.

I was knocked from my feet by a large furred body, and when I stopped seeing stars I looked up to see a panting black-and-gray wolf standing on my chest. He licked my face.

"Wade," I said, putting my arms around his neck. "Wade, thank goodness."

J.B. and Samiel pounded up behind him.

"No time for happy reunions," J.B. panted. "There are about a hundred demons behind us."

"And we're running for our lives again," Beezle said grumpily.

Wade leapt off me, and Gabriel helped me to my feet.

"We don't have time to fight off all those demons," I said. "We still have to destroy all those spiders."

Wade whined, nudging my leg.

"I know—walk and talk," I said, and we ran into the hallway. "J.B., do you think we could collapse the passageway behind us?"

"This castle is bound by more than brick and mortar. There's magic in every crevice. You'd never be able to knock even a part of it down," J.B. said. "Besides, it wouldn't really help. There are multiple ways in and out of every part of the castle. If you collapse the passage, they'll just go through the walls."

"Right, too easy," I grumbled. I could hear the demons shrieking behind us now, getting closer.

We pounded down the steps, Wade leaping ahead of us, and stopped at the bottom.

"Why are we stopping?" Beezle asked, alarmed.

"If we run across that passageway, we'll attract the spiders," I said.

"If we stand here, a whole bunch of demons are going to fall on our heads," Beezle said.

Everyone looked at me.

"Why do I have to be the one who decides?" I muttered.

"Because you're our leader, Morningstar help us," Beezle said. "So lead."

"Okay, everyone get low and get through the hall as quietly as you can. I'll hold the demons off here until you're through."

"No," Gabriel said.

"Look," I pleaded. "Just trust me. I need the rest of you to be safely out of the castle. I'll come back another time for the spiders."

"No," he repeated.

"We don't have time to argue about it," I said. "All of you, go."

Wade, Samiel and J.B. carefully made their way through the hall. I turned to face the stairs and readied my magic. Gabriel stepped up beside me.

"I will not leave you," he said. "And you cannot make me go."

"I've never been able to make you do anything," I said.

"Nor I you," he replied. "So we are even."

"Oh, my gosh, the two of you are just the cutest," Beezle said. "Is there some reason why I couldn't go with Samiel and get away from the lovefest?"

I shoved Beezle back inside my jacket. "Why can we not do anything without a running commentary?"

Beezle popped his head out again, looking disgruntled, but he didn't say anything for a change.

The demons were getting closer. I could hear them thundering in the hall above us. My heart beat faster.

"You know, all this noise is bound to attract the spiders anyway," Beezle said.

"I *know*," I replied. "I want the others to get out of the castle."

Beezle snorted. "And you think they're going to leave without you?"

"Well, I told them to . . ." I said, turning to check, my voice fading.

J.B. and Samiel and Wade had gotten through the hallway without the spiders noticing them, but they all stood expectantly at the other end, beckoning to us.

"What is the point of being the leader if no one will listen to you?" I asked.

I didn't know if Gabriel or Beezle answered, because that was when the demons poured down the steps.

There were a hell of a lot more than fifty, and I was sure that Samiel and J.B. had taken plenty out already while freeing Wade. Gabriel and I fired at them with everything we had. Demons fell screaming, acidic blood splattering on the steps and on us, burning our faces and hands. I was already covered in spider goop so I was sure I looked just delightful.

J.B. cried out behind us, and when I glanced back I saw that several of the smaller spiders were crawling through the arches behind us. J.B. and Samiel shot spells at the spiders while Wade tore several of them apart with his teeth and claws. I did not want to think about how completely gross it was to have a spider in your mouth.

"Of course," I muttered, throwing magic at the demons. I could feel my temper rising, and the hall was lighting up. Several of the demons stopped where they stood and covered their eyes, which made it a lot easier to kill them. "Of course. Nothing can ever be easy. I can't just rescue Wade and get out of here, no. There have to be giant . . . freaking . . . spiders . . . again!"

There was a sudden buildup of magical pressure, something I hadn't felt for a long time—not since I'd fought Ramuell in the cave in the Forbidden Lands.

"Get clear," I said, gasping for air.

"I will not . . ." Gabriel began.

"GET CLEAR!" I shouted, thrusting Beezle at him.

Something in my face or my voice convinced him, because he took Beezle and ran down the hallway. I didn't stop to check if he gathered everyone else—I knew that he would.

The demons stood frozen on the stairs as light and magic burst from me like a star exploding. I let the power flow through me without fighting it, but it still hurt. It hurt to breathe; it hurt to be a conduit for something not meant to be contained inside a mortal body.

All of the demons disappeared as the light touched them, just fell to ash like a nuclear blast had hit them. Any spiders that were within the reach of the light were destroyed, too. The power inside me cut off abruptly, and I felt drained. I knew I would not be able to use my magic for a while, but hopefully I wouldn't need to. Maybe Amarantha's castle was out of tricks.

There was a sudden rumbling, and chunks of stone fell out of the ceiling.

"Oh, damn," I said, turning to run to the others, but it was already too late.

The passageway collapsed in front of me, rock raining down. I backed up, coughing, covering my mouth with my sleeve.

Now everyone was on the other side, and I had no idea how to get out. And there was far too much stone between us to communicate.

All I could hope for was that they would try to exit the castle and meet me by the portal.

"Which is what I wanted in the first place," I muttered.

The only passage left to me was going up, so I climbed the steps, kicking piles of demon ash aside as I went. The building rumbled ominously and the stairs shifted beneath my feet. I scrabbled at the wall so that I wouldn't fall down the stairs and get a concussion on top of everything else.

"Are you kidding? I thought J.B. said that you were bound by magic and all that," I said to the wall. Then I rolled my eyes. "I am losing my mind. It's all those spiders. That would put anybody over the edge. Nobody should ever have to see one giant spider, much less dozens of them over and over."

It didn't seem smart to continue going up when the castle might fall down at any moment, but I needed to find a window to the outside. I could fly out and get around to the front of the castle and find the others.

I sped up the steps and entered yet another hallway filled with the bodies of demons. The passage was lined with more multicolored windows.

I covered my hand as best I could with the sleeve of my coat and used the pommel of the sword to break the glass. Despite my precautions I ended up getting little cuts all over my face and hands from glass shards. I squeezed though the hole I'd broken—*must lose thirty pounds*—and emerged into the dark night.

The moon hung low over the trees. I had no idea how much time might have passed while we were inside the castle. I flew around the castle to the front door, where I hoped I'd see the others waiting for me. There was nothing except the abandoned cars and bodies that had been there when we arrived, which meant that I had to go back inside the castle to find them.

"We need some kind of magical IM-ing," I said. I could probably text Gabriel, except that if he was fighting for his life, he doubtless would not be checking his cell phone.

The open door yawned before me, the empty foyer black and menacing. The last thing I wanted to do was go back inside, but I would never leave my husband and my friends behind. I pulled the sword from its sheath and held it before me like a talisman.

I crossed the threshold, my boots unnaturally loud in the silence. Far away inside the castle I heard the howl of a wolf.

I ran across the entryway, trying to figure out what direction the noise was coming from. And that was when I was hit from behind.

A heavy body crashed into me, sent me face-first to the ground. Fangs pierced the back of my neck and I screamed in pain. I elbowed Violet with all the strength I could muster—not much, considering how tired I was, but it was enough to make her weight shift.

I wriggled out from beneath her and rolled onto my back

as she dove at me again. I slashed out with the sword and felt the blade slice through bone. Violet screeched and fell away from me, clutching her left arm with a clawed hand. The arm hung by a few ragged strands of muscle. She glared at me in hatred.

I struggled to my feet, dizzy and bleary-eyed.

"Poison," I gasped.

Someone trilled a laugh to my left, and I swung the sword awkwardly in the direction of this new threat.

"Yes, of course there's poison in her fangs," Amarantha purred. "And there is no thrall here to heal you."

I wiped dripping sweat out of my eyes. Amarantha was just a blurry shadow in the hall. I could feel my heartstone throbbing in my chest as the poison careened through my bloodstream.

Violet lunged for me again and I swung the sword at her, both of my sweaty hands gripping the hilt so that I wouldn't lose it. She danced backward away from the blade. I kept my eyes on her. Violet seemed more inclined to do me physical harm than Amarantha. The Queen liked to keep her hands clean.

"What will you do now, Lucifer's child?" Amarantha taunted. "The poison will kill you long before your friends get here—if they get here. I've left a few obstacles in their way."

"You really are a gigantic bitch, aren't you?" I said. My tongue felt thick and heavy in my mouth. "That's your son up there. Don't you care if he lives or dies?"

Amarantha was silent for a moment. I didn't want to steal a glance at her since all of my attention needed to be on Violet.

"Once, I would have cared," Amarantha said finally. "But he chose his loyalty long ago."

"Because he fulfilled his duty?" I asked. This was an argument I'd had with Azazel several times. "Because he chose not to abandon the dead to dance at your heel?"

"Yes," she said. "He is no son of mine."

"Well, if that's the way you feel about it," I said, and I turned and threw the sword at her.

She didn't expect it, and neither did Violet. There was a moment when time seemed to slow down. The blade flew through the air and passed through her chest, throwing her backward to the floor. I saw blood pooling beneath her.

Violet howled and ran at me. I had no magic, no sword, and it was becoming increasingly difficult to stand. So I didn't. I threw myself to one side and cleverly dodged her attack by falling to the ground. Then I kicked out with both legs as hard as I could, aiming for her knee. I'm not as strong as Samiel, but I am significantly stronger than the average person. There was a satisfying crack and she tumbled forward.

I scrambled backward just enough so that she couldn't grab at me, but Violet was no longer interested in fighting. She was dragging herself on her one good arm and leg to her Queen's side.

The snake on my palm wriggled in warning. The sword was still embedded in Amarantha's body. Violet wasn't trying to hear the Queen's last words—she was trying to get the sword so she could chop my head off with it.

"Damn it all," I said, trying to stand and falling again as my head swam.

I army-crawled toward Amarantha's body as fast as I could, but I wasn't going to make it.

Violet used one of the columns to pull up to her feet and yanked the sword from Amarantha's body. She stood unsteadily on the dislocated knee, but her expression was full of triumph and malice. I heard the last rattle of breath from the Queen, and the misty ectoplasmic form of her soul emerged. The soul looked as Amarantha used to, a vision of otherworldly beauty, not like the twisted demonic body Lucifer had given her.

"Kill her," Amarantha said.

I pushed to my knees as Violet ran toward me with the sword raised. As she did, the castle began to tremble alarmingly, as if an earthquake had struck. Pieces of the ceiling rained to the ground. The magical spell that bound the castle together must have broken completely with Amarantha's death.

I heard voices coming closer, J.B. and Gabriel, and Wade's barking. Violet tumbled to the ground as the castle shook, the sword flying free of her hand. I crawled toward it, sickness rising in my throat, my body on fire. The poison was going to kill me before Violet had a chance.

My fingers closed around the sword. Stars filled my eyes and I rolled onto my back, coughing blood. The poison was in my lungs. It was burning me alive.

Violet closed her good hand around my wrist, tried to wrench the sword from me. We must have looked pathetic, two mauled and half-dead creatures wrestling over a sword as the building came down around our ears.

"Kill her!" Amarantha's soul screamed.

"Shut . . . up," I slurred. "I killed you so I wouldn't have to listen to you anymore."

Violet slashed at my face with her claws and my cheek split open. I punched her where Samiel had broken her jaw and she rolled away from me, thrashing in pain. A chunk of the ceiling landed on my stomach and all the breath whooshed out of my body.

I rolled over, knocking the rock to the floor, and tried to

fly since I couldn't walk. But I was too tired to hold myself up and I managed to flutter only a few feet before collapsing again. I didn't know where Violet was.

The floor cracked underneath me. I could barely see now, between the salt burning my eyes and the pain that turned them black. Even the rumbling of the castle seemed a distant thing.

"There, there, you idiot!"

Beezle. That was Beezle.

Hands underneath me, a cold wet nose pressed against my face, my body lifted and slung over a broad shoulder. I smelled apple pie baking, and heard Gabriel murmuring.

Then I felt cold air on my face, and went out.

14

I WOKE IN THE COURTYARD, SORE ALL OVER, GABRIEL'S lips on mine. I opened my eyes and felt everything whole again, although angelic healing doesn't do anything for dirt and encrusted blood and spider goop all over you.

"I can't believe you're kissing me in this state," I said.

"You have looked worse," Gabriel said, smiling.

"I find that difficult to believe," I said.

There was a crack of thunder behind me and I twisted to look at the castle. Or rather, what remained of the castle. It was nothing more than a jumble of stone and mortar now, the broken spell spewing arcs of light into the night sky.

Beezle landed on my chest and examined my face. "How did you manage to make the whole castle fall down, huh, Maddy?"

"She killed my mother," J.B. said from behind Gabriel.

I sat up more fully, nudged Gabriel aside so I could look at J.B. He had his hands in his pockets and was staring broodily at the remains of his family court.

"I did," I said steadily. I wouldn't offer any excuses.

"I knew that you would," he said. "She wouldn't stop trying to kill you."

"I'm sorry that I'm unreasonable about that," I said, a tad defensive. "But people keep trying to make it a question of them or me."

"I'm not blaming you," he said. There was no sorrow in his voice, and his eyes were dry. "I just knew that it would happen, sooner or later."

"Well, the upside of Destructo-Girl's actions is that the room full of spiders is destroyed, so we can cross that off our to-do list," Beezle said.

"And we got Wade back," I said.

"For which I am heartily grateful, Madeline Black," said Wade.

He stood next to Samiel, wrapped in Gabriel's overcoat. He looked a lot thinner than the last time I'd seen him. Exhaustion had etched his face in new lines, and his salt-and-pepper beard was ragged.

"What of the cubs?" Wade asked. "Did you find them as well?"

"Yes," I said, and explained what had happened. "But we still don't know how to . . . fix them."

I looked at J.B., who turned away from the castle to face Wade. "We're trying to find a way to heal them, but it's difficult. We've only just determined that it's their memories that have been taken from them."

"Yes," Wade said grimly. "That, I knew."

"Why didn't they take yours as well?" I asked.

"Amarantha and Focalor had some other intention for me. They would not reveal it. But they did force me to watch as they tore the first memories from our cubs."

"What are they doing with the memories?" I asked.

"They're selling them," Wade said. "To vampires."

"Selling them?" I said blankly. "Why?"

"Human sensation is like a drug to these creatures. They feed off it. When a vampire kills a human he experiences all the moments of that human's life before death. Many vampires become addicted to the thrill of memory. But it is impractical to kill humans all the time."

"It attracts too much attention," I said.

"And depletes your food supply," added Beezle.

"So Amarantha and Focalor decided to get together and sell memories to vampires? How did they come up with the technology for extracting the memories in the first place?" I asked.

Wade shook his head. "This I do not know. There is a third party in this game. Whoever that is presented the technology to Amarantha."

"Awesome," I said. "There's an unknown factor running around."

"Madeline," Gabriel murmured. "I know that it is important to find the source of these problems, but do you not think we should return Wade to his pack? They have been grieving for their alpha."

I rubbed my face, tired beyond comprehension. "Right. Return Wade to pack."

"Jude is going to grind his teeth to dust when you bring Wade back," Beezle predicted. "He didn't believe you."

"Believe what?" Wade asked.

"Maddy promised to bring you back," Beezle said, landing on my shoulder as I got to my feet.

Wade grinned. "That is why I told Jude to go to her if I went missing. Madeline's loyalty is her finest quality."

My cheeks reddened as everyone looked at me. "Don't we have somewhere to be?"

Gabriel touched my cheek. "You should not be embarrassed. Everyone here knows that you would fight to the death for them. It is why we put our own lives in peril when you ask. It is why the Grigori fear you, why Lucifer wants so badly to collect you."

"Because she's stubborn?" Beezle said. "I never really considered that a positive quality."

That's because when you want a doughnut and she says no, you know you'll never get it, Samiel signed.

"I'm more stubborn that she is," Beezle said. "If it's one thing gargoyles know how to do, it's outlast."

"Ooookay," I said, very uncomfortable with the direction of the conversation. I didn't want any more discussions of my qualities while I could hear them. "Let's get this show on the road."

I turned away in the direction of the portal, but not before I saw them all smile at one another, like they knew something I did not.

I crashed into bed when we finally got home. It was midday, but the sky looked like it was threatening snow so my bedroom was pleasantly dark. Gabriel kissed my cheek and then I conked out.

When I woke up I was painfully aware of the fact that I had slept unwashed and in my clothes. I rolled to my feet and wandered over to the window. Snow had fallen while I slept—a great deal of it. The rain barrel in my backyard was covered to about half its height, and the snow was still coming down. It looked like we were having a genuine Chicago blizzard.

I stripped out of my clothes and went for the bathroom, wondering vaguely where everyone was. The bathroom door opened just as I finished shampooing all the gunk out of my hair.

"Gabriel?" I called.

"Yes," he said, and pulled aside the shower curtain.

He stepped inside, and I looked up at him. His eyes were burning.

"I've never taken a shower with anyone before," I said, smoothing my hands over his shoulders.

"Neither have I," he replied, and he kissed me. "But I think we can figure out what to do."

"I think we need to burn those sheets," I said as we got dressed in the bedroom a little while later. "We'll never be able to get the spider goop out of them."

Gabriel gave the sheets a critical look. "You may be correct. The spider ichor seems to be very . . . persistent."

"And very smelly," Beezle said as he flew into the bedroom and landed on the dresser.

I pulled my sweater over my head and glared at him. "Haven't you ever heard of privacy?"

"That is a concept with which I am unfamiliar," Beezle said.

"Newlyweds usually enjoy being alone," I said pointedly.

"Gargoyles usually enjoy being fed in a timely manner," he replied.

"Go bother Samiel," I said.

"I've been bothering him all morning. It's your turn," Beezle said.

"Your cell phone is ringing," Gabriel said, cutting in.

I kicked around in the pile of filthy clothes on the floor

until I found my peacoat. The phone was in the inside pocket, and I had to very carefully unfold the jacket to get at it without getting dirty again.

I glanced at the caller ID. "What's up, J.B.?"

"You need to get downtown as soon as you can," he said, and there was suppressed excitement in his voice. "I think Chloe's figured out a way to cure the victims, but I need your help first."

"We'll be there soon," I promised, and clicked off.

I told the other two what J.B. said.

"We can go as soon as I get fed," Beezle said.

"Why are you coming?"

"Because I was there when you found the cubs, and I want to see them fixed," Beezle said.

Sometimes I don't think I give Beezle enough credit.

A couple of hours later the four of us—me, Samiel, Gabriel and Beezle—had passed through security and were on our way to the basement room where Chloe worked on the machines. When we arrived we found Wade and Jude were already there with J.B.

"*En Taro Adun*, Madeline Black!" Wade said.

Jude grunted at me. He had been thrilled to see that Wade was alive, but he had been less pleased that I had been the author of Wade's escape from Amarantha. Jude still had trouble comprehending that I was not Lucifer.

We all crowded into the small room. Chloe looked less than pleased to have so many people in her space—that was, until she saw Samiel.

"Well, helllllo," she said, giving him the up-and-down.

Samiel looked slightly panicked.

"Quit messing around, Chloe," J.B. said. "Show them."

Chloe lifted one of the machines from the pile on the table. "So, it's been pretty well established that what's being stored in these machines are memories. What I couldn't figure out was how the memories were being extracted and then manipulated. It was clear after a while that the solution was part mechanical and part magical."

"There is a spell embedded in the machine?" Gabriel asked.

"Exactly," Chloe said, and winked at him. I got the feeling that she enjoyed flirting and that she wasn't particularly discriminatory.

"The spell uses the eye scanner on each machine to extract the memories. Once they are removed the memories are embedded in this chip," she said, pointing to a tiny computer chip. "It seems, from what Wade told us, that the chips are then taken out of the machines and put in some kind of virtual reality headset that is probably also enspelled. It would actually help us to have one of those headsets so I can see how the spell operates, which is why you're here."

I looked at J.B. "How are we supposed to track down one of the headsets?"

"We've got a line on the location of a vampire nest," J.B. said.

"Didn't we do something incredibly stupid yesterday?" Beezle complained.

"I think I may have broken down the components of the spell enough that we can rebuild it to work in reverse if I can get this final piece. But it's going to take time—a lot of it. First we have to match the correct camera to the correct person. We'll have to remove the magic embedded in each machine, carefully rebuild the spell, and then . . ."

"The only way to test if it will work is to try a machine on a person," J.B. said, and looked at me. "At least you had the unbelievable foresight to collect all the cameras. With those we can actually restore the right memories to the right person."

I did not like the sound of trying out this sketchy process on a person without some other kind of testing first.

"What if we kill the victims when we're trying to restore their memories?" I asked.

"Could it really be worse than they are now?" J.B. asked. "They don't know where they are. They don't know anything except that they've been taken from the machine. Most of them have screamed themselves hoarse. We had to pad the walls so that they don't kill themselves walking into solid objects."

"Madeline was able to make the cubs obey her commands," Gabriel said. "Why not have her attempt the same with the other victims? At the very least we could prevent them from harming themselves further."

Wade cleared his throat. "I am not certain that will work. When we were taken, I instructed the cubs to follow Madeline Black if she arrived to rescue them. I told them to listen to her and do exactly as she says."

"So . . . even though the cubs were completely damaged, they still followed Maddy and listened to her because you said so?" Beezle asked.

"The power of an alpha over his pack is absolute," Wade said.

I'd never realized before how strong the magic bond was in a wolf pack. There was something so earthy about the wolves that it was easy to forget they were supernatural at all. Even their shift from human to wolf form seemed natural.

"So that's out," I said. "I can't help the victims here because they weren't instructed by Wade to do what I said."

"We have to try the machines on them, Maddy," J.B. said. "The life they have now is worse than death."

"Tell that to the cubs' mothers," I said fiercely. "I don't think one of them would risk their child's life, even if it is a half life."

"We won't try it on the kids first," J.B. said.

"So you'll risk some other mother's son?" I said. "It's okay if they're past puberty? I found them. I'm responsible for them. I won't let you risk their lives needlessly."

"What do you want me to do?" J.B. said angrily. "We have no way to test the efficacy of the method. We can either try to return the memories or leave these people as they are. That's not an acceptable option to me."

Wade put his hand on my shoulder when I would have retorted further. "Madeline Black, you have an admirable respect for life."

"I see enough death," I said dully.

"But J.B. is correct. These people have had their lives and minds torn from them. We must at least try to restore them."

"Will you risk the cubs?" I said, looking up at him.

His eyes were full of sorrow. "Yes. If it will lift the darkness that has fallen over my pack, if it will restore even one child to her mother. Madeline Black, my daughter is one of the cubs that you found."

Saying "I'm sorry" didn't seem to be enough. If Wade was really willing to take the chance with his own child's life, then I couldn't stand in the way.

"Okay," I said to Chloe. "Do what you need to do. I'll find the missing piece that you need."

I was the last one to leave as we filed out. I passed Beezle to Gabriel and let the door swing shut so that it was only the two of us in the room. Chloe had already returned to her worktable, a headlamp with a magnifying glass attached to it over her eye.

"Don't try anything unless you are ninety-five percent sure that it's going to work," I said to her, and she looked up. "I can't ask for a hundred percent. I know that's not possible. But wait until you're almost sure."

"Don't worry. I won't mess this up. Besides, everyone here knows about you. I'm not going to want Madeline Black pissed off at me."

She smiled and winked at me. Maybe she just liked winking. I left the room before she said or did anything else unsettling.

J.B. and Gabriel were waiting for me in the hall.

"Where's Beezle?" I asked.

"He went with Samiel," Gabriel said. "He prefers the company of my brother."

"Because Beezle likes to hear himself talk and Samiel can't talk back," I said.

"It'll be easier to get into the nest with just the three of us, anyway," J.B. said.

I looked at J.B. "Chloe said something weird. She said that I have some kind of . . . reputation here."

J.B. looked amused. "You haven't been spending very much time in the office. You've become something of a legend around here. They talk about you like they do the Retrievers—'If you do something bad, Madeline Black will come and get you.'"

"Great," I said. "Awesome. I am now a bogeyman for bad Agents."

Gabriel laughed. "If they had seen you yesterday, they certainly would have believed you a bogeyman."

"You've been spending too much time around Beezle," I said crossly. "It's giving you a smart mouth."

"I do not want to be the only unarmed member of the family," Gabriel replied.

"You still have a long way to go," I said as we walked toward the elevator. "Beezle and I have years of practice on you."

"And I have years to catch up," Gabriel said, and took my hand.

J.B., Gabriel and I left the Agency and headed west.

"How did you find out about this nest?" I asked J.B.

His eyes slid away from me. "I asked around."

"Asked who?" I said suspiciously. Then it dawned on me. "You asked one of the seers to tell you about the death of a human at the hands of vampires, didn't you? J.B., you actually broke the rules?"

Agents are allowed to know the time and place of a death, but that's about it. We're not allowed to know what is going to happen or why or how. I'm pretty sure it's a measure that's been put in place to prevent us from trying to stop deaths. Like I've said before, it can be difficult to stand back sometimes, to let death happen even when you know that it should.

"I had to break the rules," J.B. said. "We've got to find some way to cure these people. So I hid under a veil and followed a vampire after it killed a person."

I shook my head. "You're getting wild in your old age, J.B. One of these days you might forget to fill out a form."

"That will never happen," he assured me.

"What do we do if this nest doesn't have any vampires that are using memories?" I asked.

"It had better," J.B. said. "I'm not asking another seer for information. I could lose my position if anyone found out."

"How do you know this particular seer will not betray you?" Gabriel asked.

J.B. was silent, and when I looked at him I saw a faint pink tinge on his cheeks. "She, um, likes me."

I could think of a million things to say in response to that, but I didn't. Gabriel turned his head away so J.B. wouldn't see him smile.

We continued west and south until we hit the Ukrainian Village area. J.B. indicated that we should land, and we touched down on the sidewalk in front of a three-flat apartment building.

The snow was piled high in drifts and the sidewalk had been imperfectly shoveled, leaving lots of icy patches. And of course I promptly slipped on one and landed on my butt in a pile of snow. Since I was still wearing the peacoat, my jeans got soaked almost immediately. Luckily no one could see me except J.B. and Gabriel. As long as my wings were out I was still invisible. J.B. was snorting with laughter. Gabriel knew better.

I stood up, dusted snow off my bottom and gave J.B. an evil glare. "I thought that all the Agents were afraid of my wrath."

"The Agents are. I'm not," J.B. said. "I've seen you come to work in your slippers."

"Anyway," I said, not wanting to rehash one of my least favorite moments, "is this the place?"

"Yes," J.B. said, sobering. "I didn't have time to do a lot of reconnaissance, so I'm not certain exactly how many of them are in there."

"But they are all, presumably, asleep," Gabriel said. "The sun will not go down for at least two more hours."

"Yeah, but they could have magical defenses in place in case their home is breached," I said. "Any smart vampire has them; otherwise their enemies could just waltz in the front door while they were sleeping."

Vampires and goblins don't have a protective threshold like other creatures. I'm not sure why. It probably had something to do with the concept of "home." Humans, faeries, and a lot of other supernatural creatures made permanent homes, and a home is a lot more than a space to rest your head. It takes on the essence of the people who live there, who love and laugh and fight and make memories in that space.

Vampires don't do that. They just . . . exist. As far as I can tell they pretty much eat and sleep and have sex. So in order for them to be protected during the day, they either needed magical defenses or hired humans to watch over them. The slightly run-down air of the three-flat told me that these vampires could probably not afford to hire help.

The windows were all blocked by blackout shades, so we weren't going to get any information that way. There was nothing for it except to try to ease through the defenses and hope we didn't set off any alarms, and I told the other two as much.

"Well, let's try to find the defenses before we go rushing in," J.B. said.

We all went silent, each of us drawing on our power. I'd done something like this before when I detected the presence of the portal in the alley that led to Amarantha's kingdom. I pushed out my magic, spreading it away from me like a cloak of fine mesh, and watched it settle. There were several places where the cloak bulged, and I could see the little flares of magic set at regular intervals around the perimeter of the house.

"Do you see them?" I asked the other two.

They both nodded, frowning.

"But there's nothing on the second floor," I said. "Stupid."

"We'd have to break a window to get in that way," J.B. said.

I shrugged. "So?"

He sighed. "You're right."

"Wow, I never thought I'd hear those two words pass your lips," I said.

"Let us enter from the back of the building," Gabriel said. "A passerby may notice if one of the windows seems to be breaking open with no cause."

We flew around to the back. I took one look at the wooden fire escapes and shook my head. "No way. They're going to have this area covered."

I performed the same spell again and noted that the defenses were significantly stronger back here.

"It's the front or nothing," I said.

We all looked at one another. Breaking a window in the front definitely increased the risk that attention might be drawn to the house. But it wasn't as though we had a lot of choice.

Gabriel wouldn't let me break the window. I let him do it because he was stronger than me and J.B. put together. He swung his arm back and blasted his gloved fist through the glass as if it were water.

The glass made an awful noise, and we all froze except for the slightest flapping of our wings. No one was walking down the street at the moment, so it was unlikely there were any witnesses.

Gabriel cleared the frame of the remaining shards so that we could climb in safely. He swung his leg over the sill and pushed the blackout shade to one side.

There was an inhuman hiss from inside the room and the blackout shade dropped back into place as Gabriel let go.

"Gabriel!" I whispered fiercely.

"It is all right," he said calmly through the shade. "The

vampire that occupies this room is still asleep. His unconscious was simply responding to the touch of sunlight."

He lifted the shade on the opposite side so that we could climb in without disturbing the vampire further. Although the daylight was not their natural time, a vampire could certainly rouse itself if it felt threatened in sleep. We didn't want to antagonize the vampires any more than necessary.

J.B. climbed in and I followed, wrinkling my nose. The room smelled like decaying corpses. A single male vampire lay stretched out on a filthy bed splashed with blood. In the corner was a pile of rotting limbs and human skulls. My blood ran cold. Some of those bones were very small.

I covered my mouth and nose with my sleeve. "I thought most vampires don't kill their food."

"They don't," J.B. said thoughtfully. "But this is the vampire I followed home from the kill, so obviously he's gotten a taste for it."

"We should stake him," I said fiercely. "He's a serial killer."

"That's not what we're here for," J.B. said. "Look around for a headset."

"It's not going to be in this room," I muttered angrily. "This asshole gets his memory high the natural way."

As I predicted, there was no equipment in this particular vamp's room.

We entered the hallway stealthily, still on the lookout for any humans that might be living in the building. We didn't find any. We did find more sleeping vampires, although none of their rooms looked like the charnel house of the first one. Most of the vamps' rooms looked like ordinary twentysomething bedrooms, with posters on the walls and clothes all over the floor. We split up to make the search go faster. There were a lot of vampires living here.

Finally, in the seventh room, I found it. It did look like a VR headset from that movie where Russell Crowe is a virtual killer and Denzel Washington hunts him down. The headset was casually tossed on a dressing table scattered with drugstore makeup.

I snatched it up, contemplating the sleeping female vampire on the bed. Was she any better than the killer upstairs? Her addiction had cost someone their life even if her own hands hadn't been bloodied.

I walked toward the window.

"Madeline." Gabriel's voice in the doorway.

I turned around, and he could see the intent on my face. His eyes widened when he saw the headset in my hand.

"Do not do it," he said. "We need to get that device to Chloe."

I looked back at the window.

"What if she wakes while she is burning?" Gabriel said softly. "What if the others hear her distress and awaken as well? Would you risk our lives needlessly, possibly putting our mission in jeopardy?"

I tightened my grip on the headset. Should I help the living, or take revenge for the victims who had already fallen?

In the end, it wasn't a difficult choice. But as we exited the window that we had entered I yanked on the blackout shade in the killer vamp's room. And smiled in satisfaction as we flew away to the sound of a monster screaming as it burned to death.

After we delivered the headset to an ecstatic Chloe, there was nothing to do but wait. A couple of days passed in a relatively normal fashion. I picked up souls; Beezle ate;

Gabriel and I thoroughly explored all the benefits of marriage.

One thing I was not enjoying were the constant phone calls from Azazel. He would not accept my marriage to Gabriel, and he didn't care in the least that Lucifer had willed it.

"Lord Lucifer would not override my wishes in this matter," Azazel said angrily. "I have betrothed you to Nathaniel before the court. No daughter of mine will marry a thrall."

"He's not a thrall," I said. "Lucifer freed him."

"A thing which he is not permitted to do," Azazel replied.

"Just because he hasn't done it before doesn't mean he's not permitted to do it. Is he your lord or is he not?" I asked.

There was a long silence at the other end of the line.

"Well?" For Azazel to say otherwise was treason. I knew it and so did he.

"Of course," Azazel said. "But he has always respected the autonomy of each court."

"Why don't you just check with him if you don't believe me?" I said.

"Lord Lucifer is not returning my messages to him," Azazel said tightly.

"I wonder why," I replied.

After a few of these calls in which we repeated the exact same conversation over and over I finally stopped answering when I saw my father's name pop up on the caller ID. He filled my voice mail message box to the limit so often I couldn't delete them fast enough.

"Not that I'm not insanely happy with you," I said to Gabriel on the third morning after the meeting at the Agency. "But why do you think Lucifer freed you and let us marry? He'd been holding the risk to you over my head for the last two months. What made him change his mind all of a sudden?"

Gabriel sipped his coffee and looked thoughtful. "I

believe we can agree that Lord Lucifer's motivations are often deep and mysterious."

"You can say that again."

"I also believe that Lord Lucifer has some limited ability to see the future," Gabriel said. "If he perceived that it was a strategic advantage to him to have us married, then he would allow that to happen."

"I'd rather not find out that we're only married to assist Lucifer in his long-range plans for world domination."

"For all your strengths, Madeline, you do not comprehend Lord Lucifer. He is a creature so old and powerful that your mind cannot fathom it. He was born at the same time as the stars in the galaxy. He has seen millions of days pass since his creation."

"And in all that time the best he can do is think up ways to amuse himself by moving the rest of us around on the game board?"

"Lord Lucifer has never had an equal to him—in strength, in cunning, in magic. I believe, truly believe, that we are permitted to exist only at his sufferance, and because it does, as you say, amuse him to watch us."

I felt a chill in my blood that had nothing to do with the temperature. If Lucifer really was that powerful, then he could wipe out everyone on Earth with one swipe of his hand.

Gabriel watched me, and something of my thoughts must have been in my eyes because he took my hand. "It is why we all fear him so absolutely, even those courts of creatures that are not of the fallen. It is why after Amarantha and Focalor's rebellion so many of the smaller courts are banding together to protect themselves."

"Banding together won't help them if he's as powerful as you say he is," I said.

"He is," Gabriel said grimly.

We both sat in silence, contemplating a world where Lucifer ruled absolutely. The ringing of my cell phone broke into our thoughts.

"We're ready to test Chloe's solution," J.B. said.

"We'll be there in half an hour," I said and hung up, looking at Gabriel. "What are the chances that we can get out of the house without Beezle noticing?"

"Zero," Beezle said, coming in through the side window. "Let's go."

So I left for the Agency with my entourage escorting me (because of course Samiel wouldn't be left behind, either). When we landed on the roof, I got a terrible shock.

Amarantha stood there.

15

AFTER A MOMENT I REALIZED IT WAS NOT AMARANTHA, but her ghost. She looked more than a little unhinged, and her appearance reflected her state of mind, as it often does with ghosts. If they remember themselves as young and beautiful, that's how they will look in the afterlife, even if that person died in their dotage. If they pull at their hair and scratch things, then their ectoplasmic form will reflect the ghost's perception of what they should look like after they've tugged their hair and broken their nails.

Amarantha looked like she'd been doing both, and she looked a lot more like a wild bean sidhe than either her perfect faerie self or her freakish demonic form.

"Somebody here needs a salon," Beezle said. "You've looked better."

"You! YOU!" she screeched, and she pointed her finger

dramatically at me. "You stole my life from me. I demand justice!"

And then she flew at me with her arms outstretched, fingers bent into claws.

I stood still and waited for her to pass through me. She did, and I shivered. Ghosts draw energy from the air around them, and it means that they make cold spots. When a ghost passes through you it's a lot like having ice water poured down your spine.

I waved to Gabriel and Samiel to follow me and walked toward the door. Amarantha flew after me, cursing.

"This is not over, Lucifer's spawn," she hissed.

"It is for you," I said.

"I will haunt you to the end of your days!" Amarantha vowed. "You will never be free of me."

"We'll see about that," I muttered.

We went inside and down to Chloe's secret lab. J.B. was waiting for us in the hallway.

"Uh, why is your mom hanging around on the roof?" I asked.

"Because she refused the Door," J.B. said. "She's been following me around for the last couple of days. I had to have a spell put up around my condo to keep her out."

"Can I get one, too?" I asked.

"She threatened to haunt Madeline 'until the end of her days,'" Gabriel said.

J.B. rubbed his eyes. "I'll see what I can do. Come on—Chloe is anxious to run the tests."

We crowded into the small room. Chloe's worktable had been removed. In its place was a tripod with one of the machines on it, and a man tied to an office chair so that he faced the lens. He looked like he was in his mid-forties, paunchy and balding. He was dressed in a jumpsuit that looked a lot like the sort of thing that prisoners wore. He wasn't screaming, but he kept rocking back and forth in the chair. Chloe was making some adjustments to the machine when we walked in.

"We had to tie him; otherwise he kept trying to bang his head against the wall," Chloe said apologetically.

Her hair was pink today, and she wore a leather vest with a tiered black skirt. She gave Samiel a very suggestive smile.

"Okay," she said, clapping her hands together. "Let's get this party started."

Nobody spoke as Chloe pushed a button to turn on the camera. Gabriel took my hand and squeezed it. My whole body was taut. The man in the chair went rigid as the scanner met his eyes.

"We've attempted to speed up the reinsertion process," Chloe said as the machine did its work. "It seems, from what we could determine in analyzing the spell, that the memory extraction takes a number of hours."

"And you think it's safe to put the memories back in there faster than they were taken out?" I asked, skeptical. A human brain is a delicate and complicated organ. It didn't seem that quickness was wanted here, but rather care.

"We have no idea if this is safe at any speed," Chloe said frankly. "I erred on the side of rapidity only because we have so many victims to restore."

"Plus, we don't know how many more may be out there. Our resources are taxed as it is taking care of the ones that are already here," J.B. said. "I've got special teams all over the city looking for warehouses like the one you found."

"I can help with that," I said, surprised that he hadn't asked me.

"There's no point in putting you in charge of a team,"

J.B. said. "Chaos follows you everywhere you go, and I don't need to deal with any more property damage."

"I don't think you are taking the long view," I said, my cheeks reddening. "The people in the warehouse were saved."

"By J.B. and his team," Beezle pointed out.

"Who didn't have to deal with the monster arachnids," I said.

"Enough," Gabriel said.

Beezle and I both subsided, glaring at each other.

The man in the chair moaned. We all stared at him. I would have squashed Gabriel's knuckles into powder if he hadn't been supernatural. J.B.'s hands were balled into fists in his pockets. Chloe had her arms crossed, her mouth drawn in a straight line. On my other side Samiel slung a comforting arm around my shoulder. Beezle fluttered around the room nervously.

The man moaned again, louder this time, and then he shouted, "Janie!"

He began to thrash in his restraints. I released Gabriel's hand and stepped forward, only to have Chloe cut me off.

"Wait," she said.

The man tore back and forth, screaming now. It was a different kind of screaming than when we had removed the victims from the cameras. That screaming had a kind of dull, automaton quality to it. This screaming was a soul-deep cry of pain. Blood leaked from the corners of the man's eyes.

I started to move around Chloe, to go to the man who was screaming so hard and long it was breaking my heart.

"Wait," she repeated, her hand on my chest. "The process isn't complete yet."

"His *eyes* are bleeding," I said furiously. "You think that's a good thing? He could be having a stroke."

"Trust me," she said, her face desperate.

I think she knew I could blast her out of the way if I wanted.

"Wait, Maddy," J.B. said. "Just wait."

He sounded as deeply unhappy as I felt. Beezle landed on Samiel's shoulder and covered his little ears.

Gabriel touched my shoulder, pulled me back to him. "Wait."

We all watched in various states of distress as the man howled, rocked, tried to tear at his bindings. But his eyes never moved from the camera.

Suddenly the man went completely rigid and silent, and then he slumped forward, his eyes closed.

I pulled away from Gabriel and ran to the man. Chloe was right next to me, untying the restraints. Together we eased him down to the floor and I checked for a heartbeat.

"He's still alive," I said, lifting his eyelids. His pupils were normal, but there were streaks of blood on his cheeks.

"Good," Chloe said. "I think he'll sleep for a while now."

"And when he wakes up he'll be good as new?"

"Well, sleeping helps memory function in normal people," Chloe reasoned. "So we assumed that after the memories were restored, the victims would need to sleep for several hours. Their brains need to process the restored information."

"Don't try this on anyone else yet," I said.

She shook her head. "We'll wait and see if it takes."

Chloe stepped into the hall to find someone who could help her bring the man back to the rooms they had prepared for the victims.

I stood, feeling drained, and looked at J.B. "Call me if you want me to help the special teams."

He nodded. "I think we have it under control, but you

could help by trying to find out where Focalor is. We know from my mother that he's part of this."

"He may just be in his court," I said, thinking of Focalor's appearance at Samiel's trial.

"We're not going to try to beard the lion in his den again, are we?" Beezle asked. "Because that didn't go so well last time."

"No," I said. "I think I'll give Grandpa a call."

I dialed Lucifer's number—yes, that really is as weird as it sounds, giving Satan a phone call—and waited for him to pick up. I got his voice mail.

"Azazel said Lucifer hasn't been answering his calls," I said to Gabriel.

"You think Lord Lucifer is in some kind of danger?" Gabriel asked.

"More likely he's on vacation in Aruba and has his phone shut off," I said.

"Or he's decided to see if you can handle the pressure from your marriage yourself," Beezle said.

"What do you mean?" I asked.

"He gave you what you wanted; now he wants to see if you deserved it," he replied. "I could kill for a cupcake right about now."

"Forget it," I said, thinking over the implications of what Beezle had just said. "You think Lucifer is purposely waiting to see what kind of fallout there is because I married Gabriel?"

"It is an excellent way to see which of his courts would openly object, and which would fall in line," Gabriel said. "Remember what we discussed this morning."

I believe, truly believe, that we are permitted to exist only at his sufferance, and because it does, as you say, amuse him to watch us.

"If that's the case, then Beezle's probably right—"

"I usually am."

"—and Focalor probably will send someone to kill me."

J.B. looked troubled. "Should I assign a team to you for protection?"

I shook my head. "I can handle whatever Focalor's got."

And I don't want any more blood on my hands than I have already, I thought. Most Agents, even highly trained ones, were not even remotely prepared for the kinds of horrors that lurked in a demon court.

"Make sure she doesn't get hurt," J.B. said to Gabriel, and they shared a long look.

"Why is it that when you two decide to be manly men you act like I'm not in the room?" I said crossly. "Come on, I'm sure we need to feed Beezle something healthy."

"Carrot cake has carrots in it," Beezle said hopefully.

"Yeah, and cream cheese frosting has calcium, too, I suppose," I replied.

"I think the food pyramid is really about interpretation," Beezle said.

We retrieved our weapons from security and went out onto the roof. Amarantha was missing, thank goodness.

"I forgot to apologize to J.B. for setting his mother on him full-time. He can't be happy about that," I said as we took flight. It was starting to snow lightly—like we needed more snow. It had taken me, Gabriel and Samiel hours to shovel the walk and the gangway.

Samiel tapped my shoulder. *Do you think that Amarantha would try to stay in touch with her cohorts, even though she's a ghost? We still don't know who the third party is, the one who provided the technology to extract memories.*

"You think we should track her?" I asked, intrigued. "That's a good idea. She may try to get in touch with Focalor or with this other character. I'll ask J.B. about it. We can probably take turns keeping an eye on her."

"I wonder what happened to Violet?" Beezle said.

I shrugged. "She must have chosen the Door. Otherwise she'd be hanging around Amarantha, I'm sure."

Beezle climbed inside my (dry-cleaned) jacket for warmth. I wiped snow out of my eyes, thinking it would be a good idea to get some goggles for this time of year. We landed in the front yard, shaking snow out of our hair.

Samiel scooped up a snowball and threw it at Gabriel's face.

My exceedingly dour husband gave his half brother the evil eye. It was slightly less effective with snow and ice dripping off the end of his nose.

Samiel gave Gabriel a taunting look and scooped up another handful of snow. Gabriel raised his eyebrow at Samiel but made no move to defend himself. Samiel tossed the snowball toward him and Gabriel blasted it out of the air with nightfire so that it backfired all over Samiel.

"That's not conspicuous or anything," Beezle said, peeking out of my jacket.

"Yeah, guys," I said, laughing at the outraged expression on Samiel's face. "No magic . . ."

Samiel threw a bolt of nightfire at Gabriel's feet and made the snow fly up underneath Gabriel's overcoat. Gabriel narrowed his eyes.

"Uh-oh," I said. "Whatever you're thinking, I don't think it's a good . . ."

Gabriel sent out a bunch of tiny nightfire pulses, almost like an automatic weapon. They surrounded Samiel's feet and sent high shooting sprays of snow and ice onto his face and coat.

Samiel must have decided that it wasn't worth it to try to

beat Gabriel magically, so he dove for his brother and tackled him. Gabriel landed on his back in the snow and Samiel smashed a handful of it in Gabriel's face.

I was now laughing so hard I could barely breathe.

"You think this is funny, do you?" Gabriel said menacingly.

Samiel turned and gave me an appraising look.

"Don't even think about it," I said, holding my hands up and backing toward the porch.

Gabriel rolled lightly to his feet and stalked toward me.

Beezle flew out of my jacket. "I'm not playing this game."

Samiel snatched Beezle by the ankle out of the air and buried him in a pile of snow. Beezle came out spluttering and glaring.

"That's it, nephilim boy," Beezle snarled.

Bring it on, gargoyle.

I turned to run up the porch steps as Gabriel reached me. He grabbed me around the waist as I laughed and screamed. "No, don't, no, don't!"

He tossed me into the snow face-first and I got a mouthful. I rolled over as he landed on top of me.

"Well, this is nice," I said, and kissed him.

I vaguely heard the sounds of Beezle and Samiel's continued battle.

"We should go inside and leave them to it," Gabriel murmured.

"Good idea," I said.

Then a familiar voice broke into our reverie.

"Gabriel ap Ramuell, you are under arrest for defiling my daughter."

Gabriel lifted his head, a shocked expression on his face. I twisted around in the snow.

Azazel and two of his flunkies stood in the front walk. Samiel and Beezle were frozen in place, staring.

"Let me up," I said to Gabriel urgently.

He stood, pulling me to my feet.

"Get off my property," I said to Azazel.

"I am here to take this thrall into custody so that he can be tried before the court of the Grigori for his crimes," Azazel said coldly.

"Not this again," I said, rolling my eyes. "You're not taking him. He's not a thrall anymore and he's not defiling me—at least, not against my will."

Beezle snorted.

"I have had quite enough of your insolence, daughter," Azazel said. He waved to the two foot soldiers that stood behind him. "Take him."

I pulled Lucifer's sword from its sheath. "If you take one more step toward my husband, I will make sure you don't leave here with all your limbs."

They stopped, uncertain, and looked at Azazel.

"You cannot defy the will of the Grigori!" Azazel shouted.

"And you cannot defy the will of your lord," I replied steadily, keeping my eyes on the two flunkies. "Lucifer freed him, Lucifer married us, Lucifer is not going to be happy that you're still annoying me about this."

"You are my daughter. It is my will you obey. I have betrothed you to Nathaniel ap Zerachiel, and you will marry him. The thrall will be killed for his insolence," Azazel said. "I will take him myself if I have to."

"No . . . you . . . will . . . not," I said, and I felt the power of the Morningstar flowing through me.

I was putting on another light show for the benefit of my normal neighbors. One of these days video of me acting like a freak was going to wind up on the Internet, and then the government would be knocking at my door asking if they could use me as a weapon. I wondered if Lucifer would help me then, or if it would suit him to see me get carried away to some top-secret bunker.

"For the last time, I am your father."

"In name only," I spat.

"In the only way that matters. You will do as I say, or you will be punished."

"No," I said.

One of the foot soldiers made a sudden move toward me, but I was ready for him. I kept my right hand on the sword, and with my left I blasted him with regular fire. His designer trench was set ablaze immediately and he ran screaming for the nearest snowbank.

"Anyone else want to try?" I said innocently.

"Do you truly think your powers are superior to my own?" Azazel said softly. "I am the right hand of Lucifer, and have been for ages untold. Do you believe that you could defeat me in a fight?"

"Try me," I said, and then, in an undertone to Gabriel, "Take out the other one before he gets any stupid ideas."

Gabriel blasted the second soldier with nightfire. This one was a little more savvy than his friend and so managed to dodge out of the way. He threw his own spells—some kind of purple sparks—at Gabriel and the two of them dueled their way across the tiny front lawn and onto the sidewalk. I really hoped that no one decided to walk down our street at just this second.

Samiel and Beezle dodged out of the way of the other two.

"Sam, take Beezle inside," I said.

"Why should I miss all the fun?" Beezle complained.

"You can watch from the window," I said, keeping my eyes on Azazel.

My father looked cool and stone-faced and not at all scared of me. I, on the other hand, was terrified. Not of defying Azazel—that had been a long time coming—but of the consequences if I lost. Azazel might lose status among the Grigori. I would lose the love of my life. I had to win.

Maybe some of this was on my face. Maybe Azazel saw me waver for a moment. He struck before I had time to prepare.

A bolt of lightning shot across the space between us and hit me square in the chest. Electricity sizzled all over my body and my teeth rattled in my jaw. I kept a tight grip on the sword and slashed up with it as Azazel leapt to me, another lightning bolt ready at his fingertips. The bolt bounced off the sword and into a nearby tree, which gave an ominous crack.

We have some fairly large trees on the north side, and this was a three-story catalpa. I sincerely hoped it did not crash into the street and smash my neighbors' cars.

I jumped to my feet and swung the sword at Azazel, who looked surprised that I was actually doing it.

"You dare . . ." he said.

"I swear to the gods, I can live the rest of my life without hearing that phrase," I said.

Azazel blasted me again, this time with some spell made of small gold sparkles. Wherever they touched me, they burned like acid.

"Thanks for ruining another jacket," I said. "I'm not made of money, you know."

I slashed down with the sword. He danced out of the way but the blade managed to slice through the arm of his coat, which was much nicer and more expensive than mine.

"Now we're even," I said.

Azazel narrowed his eyes at me. "You have never truly given me the respect I deserve."

"You have never earned it," I replied.

We stared at each other for a moment, taking each other's measure.

"I will not yield to you," I said.

"I gathered as much," my father said.

I slashed forward with the sword. I wasn't about to engage in a magical tête-à-tête with a creature who had significantly more power than I did. Azazel blocked the blow with some kind of shield spell and began shooting various forms of fire, electricity and other things that hurt me.

I grimly settled in for the long haul. Some of his spells hit me. Some of them I managed to knock away with the sword. At every opportunity I pressed forward, looking for an opening.

Azazel's remaining flunky cried out, and Azazel's eyes slid to left, just for a moment. I had him.

I slashed him across the face with the blade, slicing open his cheek. He staggered backward, more in shock than in pain, I believe.

"I think that will leave a mark," I said. "Something tells me Lucifer's sword will defy any permanent healing."

My heart was cold. There would never be space there for Azazel. I'd wanted a father all of my life, and when he finally showed up he was interested only in obedience, not love.

Azazel stood alone. His foot soldiers were down for the count. I held the sword before me, his blood still fresh upon the blade. Gabriel moved beside me, prepared to strike.

"This is not over," Azazel said, taking in the situation and correctly interpreting that he would have his butt kicked if he stayed any longer.

"Yes, it is," I replied. There was no anger in my voice, only steady determination. "I renounce you as my kin. You may be a father in name, but that is all that you will ever be. I refuse the inheritance of your court and the appellation of your name. From this day forward you will have no platform from which to demand obedience from me, and I will not give it. I renounce you and everything to do with you."

The air between us shimmered with heat, and then there was a heavy crack, as if the cord that bound that two of us by blood had been severed.

Azazel appeared stunned. Blood dripped from his cheek, the slash that ran from the top of his ear to his chin.

"You . . . you . . . cannot . . ." he said, spluttering.

"I just did," I replied.

Gabriel was by my side, taking my hand. "Let's go inside."

We walked away from Azazel, and my heart was a fist of ice.

16

THE DAY AFTER THE INCIDENT WITH AZAZEL I CALLED J.B. to check on the progress of the victims. The first man that they'd tested had woken up disoriented but cognizant of his surroundings. They were proceeding with cautious optimism through some more people before going full-scale. J.B. was convinced the prognosis was good, but he didn't want to call Wade to bring in the cubs until they were sure. During the same conversation I convinced him that keeping track of Amarantha's ghost was a good idea.

"But I don't want you to do it," J.B. said over the phone.

He sounded distracted. I imagined he had a lot on his plate. Upper management at the Agency wouldn't give him a break on his regular duties just because he had to deal with this other massive issue of memory stealing.

"Why not?" I said. I was a little offended that my services

were being refused for a second time. "You don't think I'm competent enough?"

"You're too competent—that's the problem," J.B. said. "Do you know how many phone calls we intercepted yesterday about an altercation on your front lawn between three angels and a crazy woman with a sword?"

"Umm, my father was being an . . ." I began.

"Sixty-two," J.B. said. "Sixty-two phone calls. Do you know how hard it is to keep these calls from actually reaching the authorities? Do you know how much trouble I get into every time you do something like this?"

"I don't know why I get the blame," I said angrily. "Azazel was the one who showed up on my lawn threatening to take Gabriel away to his death. What was I supposed to do, let him?"

"No," J.B. sighed. I could almost hear him pulling on his hair. "I'm just grateful no one has caught you on their phone's video camera—yet."

"J.B.," I said. "I'm sorry I'm nothing but a headache for you."

"You're worth it," J.B. said.

He hung up before I could apologize again.

So another day passed, with our little family behaving as normally as we knew how to be, given that we were composed of an Agent, two angel/nephilim crossbreeds and a gargoyle. Lucifer still wasn't returning my calls, which gave credence to the notion that he wanted to see how I handled the fallout from the marriage.

"The least he could do is make some sort of proclamation from afar," I said to Gabriel the next evening as we walked home from the grocery store.

The trudge through the snow was not pleasant. We lived about eight blocks from the nearest grocery. Many people had done a half-assed job of shoveling the walks in front of their buildings. The snow was tamped down into an icy, slippery crust in many places, and it made for treacherous walking even when you weren't laden with bags of food.

Something gray and misty darted across the road when we were about a block away from home.

"Hey," I said, staring. "That's Amarantha."

Gabriel frowned. "Do not get any ideas, Madeline. J.B. asked you not to follow her."

I looked around, but I didn't see any Agent in the vicinity. "No one else is doing it."

I was already pushing my wings out, disappearing into the night. The grocery bags fell to the ground.

"Madeline," Gabriel said, scooping up the bags.

"I want to know what she's up to," I said.

"She is near our home. Doubtless she was attempting to haunt you and found that she was unable because of the spell the Agency provided."

"She's not hanging around as a ghost to haunt me or J.B. That's a side benefit. She's still out to get revenge against Lucifer. I'm sure of it."

Gabriel sighed as we chased after her as inconspicuously as we could. She glanced around a lot, obviously expecting a tail.

"She must have shaken off whoever was following her before," I whispered.

"I am not going to carry this food all over creation while you do the exact opposite of what was asked of you," Gabriel said.

"Why do I hear J.B. in your voice?" I said. "Just stow the groceries somewhere and we'll come back for them. Come on, she's getting farther away. I don't want to lose her."

Amarantha was drifting along the sidewalk, her head

moving around constantly. I got the impression that while she was concerned about being followed, she was also unsure exactly where she was going. She seemed to be checking landmarks.

Gabriel quickly flew to the top of a multi-unit apartment building and put our groceries on the roof. The building was only a couple of blocks from our house so the stuff would be easy to find later. I can't afford to throw away groceries, and I was glad that Gabriel was conscientious enough to remember that even when I couldn't.

Amarantha turned on Lincoln just past the Metra tracks and went north. She went past the underpass where Ramuell had killed Patrick. I always have to swallow the lump in my throat when I pass by that place.

Gabriel murmured something and I felt a weight like a heavy cloak settle over me.

"What did you do?" I asked.

"Redoubled our spell of invisibility," he replied. "It will better protect us from the eyes of supernatural creatures—or ghosts."

"Cool," I said. "When are you going to show me how to do all this neat stuff?"

Gabriel gave me a half smile. "We have plenty of time."

We followed Amarantha for more than a half hour. She seemed to be wandering aimlessly at times, stopping to stare at sculptures or the glowing signs of chain stores.

"This is really boring," I muttered.

"As I understand it, this is what surveillance work is usually like," Gabriel said.

"Who told you that?"

"Beezle. It seems he spends a great deal of time watching police procedurals on television. We can always contact J.B., let him know her location and return home."

It pained me to admit that he might be right. Amarantha seemed to have no clear purpose in mind, and my stomach had been rumbling for a while. I pulled my phone out to make the call to J.B. It was a given that he would scold me for ignoring his wishes, and I braced myself for the argument that would follow.

We followed her into Welles Park, which is across the street from Sulzer, the large regional library branch on the north side. Amarantha floated over the baseball fields, which would be crowded with leagues for the young and old in the summer. Now they were covered in drifts of snow.

There was a large gazebo in the center of the park, just south of the complex that housed a fitness center and pool. Several feet to the right and left of the gazebo were play lots filled with swings and slides and things from which children could jump. Between the two play lots was a wide, empty field.

A shadowy figure stood inside the gazebo.

Amarantha moved with purpose now, shooting across the snow directly toward the gazebo. I dropped my phone back into my pocket. This was what she had been up to all along.

She entered the gazebo, and the figure turned to speak to her. There was very little light in the center of the park this time of year. I couldn't see the other person clearly. I had an impression of height, but the deep shadow may have been distorting my perception.

"We have to get closer," I whispered.

"This is exceedingly foolish," Gabriel said. "I am calling J.B. so he can deal with his mother's ghost."

"Call him after we find out who she's talking to," I hissed. "It's not helpful if we call him with no new information."

I again had the impression of a heavy weight thrown over me.

"Are you adding to the invisibility spell again?" I asked.

"Yes," Gabriel said grimly. "Since you insist on staying, the least we can do is ensure that we are not detected."

"Are we having our first argument as a married couple?" I asked innocently.

We flew closer to the gazebo. Amarantha and the other person talked in low whispers, and I couldn't make out what they said.

"I never thought I would say this, but I wish Jude was here," I said wistfully.

The couple concluded their business, and Amarantha exited the gazebo. The person inside lingered for a few moments longer.

"Come on, come on," I whispered.

"Shall I follow Amarantha?" Gabriel said.

"No," I replied. "Call J.B. and tell him where she is."

"Which is what I wanted to do in the first place," Gabriel muttered.

The figure in the gazebo stirred just as Gabriel concluded his call to J.B. Amarantha had resumed her slow drifting down Lincoln, and there didn't seem to be any urgency in chasing after her now.

The clouds shifted, and the moon, which was three-quarters full, was revealed. A shaft of light fell across the person who had met with Amarantha.

It was Nathaniel.

"I'll kill him," I snarled, and shot forward. I had no real plan in mind other than grinding Nathaniel into tiny pieces.

Gabriel snatched me out of the air and pulled me back to him, both arms around my middle.

Nathaniel left the gazebo with a furtive look and crossed to the northwestern side of the park, disappearing into shadow.

"I'll kill him," I repeated. "That dirty sneaking *scumbag*!"

"Wait," Gabriel soothed. "Wait. You can gain nothing by killing him now."

"I can gain the satisfaction that comes from knowing I have squashed a poisonous bug," I said angrily, thrashing in Gabriel's arms. "This is what he was talking about when I overheard him on the phone at Amarantha's castle. I figured it had to be some stupid angelic shit. I didn't think he had the balls to kill humans and participate in rebellion right under Azazel's nose."

"Think," Gabriel said. "Just think. We already have enough difficulties with the Grigori. If you murder Zerachiel's son in cold blood, then it will cause additional problems."

"My blood is not cold right now," I growled. "Jude was right. Nathaniel helped kidnap the cubs. He helped take away their memories. Little kids. And they were nothing to him—just another means to an end. Like me."

"What are you really angry about?" Gabriel said.

"I didn't love him, if that's what you're asking," I said. "I never loved him. But he used his relationship with me as a cover for his extracurriculars. I'm sure that as long as Azazel thought everything was humming along nicely on the betrothal front, he didn't bother to question Nathaniel too closely. And his position as negotiator with the faerie court gave him leave to meet with Amarantha multiple times over."

"We must inform Lord Lucifer," Gabriel said.

"You mean inform Lucifer's voice mailbox?" I said bitterly. "What's to say that he'll rush back from wherever he's been holed up to deal with Nathaniel? We've got to do it ourselves, before any more people are captured."

Gabriel looked at me steadily. "If I release you, do you promise not to act rashly?"

"Define 'rashly,'" I said.

"Rushing after Nathaniel and taking his head off with Lucifer's sword," Gabriel replied.

"So if I do anything less than that, it won't be considered rash? What if I rush after him, jump on him and beat him until his face is mangled?"

"I do not want you touching Nathaniel. You might catch something," Gabriel said solemnly.

I laughed, and Gabriel relaxed, releasing me. I took his hand.

"I'll call Lucifer. I'll let him know what's going on. But then I'm going in," I said. "I won't have Nathaniel running around doing more damage."

"Fine," Gabriel said. "We will collect our allies, and then we will confront him."

"You know where he'll be," I said grimly.

"Azazel's court."

Maybe now Azazel would see just what kind of man he'd tried to force me to marry. Even Azazel couldn't overlook his favorite undermining Lucifer's kingdom by consorting with vampires.

"I'm guessing Daddy won't be happy to see me."

A couple of hours later the usual suspects were assembled at my house—Jude, Wade, J.B., Samiel, Gabriel and, of course, Beezle, who seemed to have completely given up on the idea that he was supposed to be a home guardian.

"So, what's the plan?" Beezle said, rubbing his hands together.

"The plan is we go to Azazel's court, get Nathaniel and

get out of there," I said grimly. "Let's try to limit casualties if possible."

"I do not know if Azazel will allow us to limit casualties," Gabriel said. "He will likely take offense at your presence."

"I'm prepared for that," I said.

"I told you that Nathaniel was involved," Jude growled.

"And I told you that I would get Wade back," I snapped. "Everyone's right, so can we dispense with the I-told-you-so's?"

Gabriel put a restraining hand on my shoulder. Wade mirrored his action with Jude. Jude was having a lot of trouble with the idea that he had to be grateful to a descendant of Lucifer.

"When we go through the portal there may be soldiers waiting for us," I said. Azazel would know who had generated the portal in his castle and would likely interpret my impending arrival as an act of aggression. "If we're lucky, Azazel won't notice our arrival."

"You have no such luck," Beezle said.

"There's no point in standing around talking about it," J.B. said. "Let's go."

We all filed into the yard and huddled in a half circle. Beezle climbed down to the inside pocket of my jacket.

"Go team," he said, and disappeared under my lapel.

"I'll wake you when it's over," I said. "I'm going first."

There was a general rumbling of male disagreement.

"I'm going first," I repeated. "Azazel may interpret my presence as an attempt at contrition, and if they notice our arrival immediately, then that may save us. But if the lot of you come through before me loaded for bear, then it could get ugly really fast."

I could tell Gabriel did not like this at all. His innate

need to throw himself before any possible threat to me was warring with his common sense.

"Trust that I can take care of myself," I said softly.

"I do," he said.

"Then show me."

He nodded reluctantly, and turned away to open the portal. A moment later I stepped through.

There was the familiar disorientation, the sensation of my brain being squeezed, my ears popping, and then I was through. I landed in the hallway outside Azazel's throne room, as usual, and even managed to land on my feet for a change. I drew Lucifer's sword immediately and spun in a circle, looking for the threat that I was sure would be there.

The hall was empty. The doors to the throne room were closed, and the sounds of a loud and raucous party drifted out.

So Azazel was likely too distracted by his guests to notice my arrival. Good.

"Although that seems like a pretty big security hole," I muttered. "Not that it's my problem, but still . . ."

Gabriel came through a second later, followed by J.B., Samiel, Jude and Wade. They all had their battle faces on and seemed as surprised as I was that no one was waiting for us.

We didn't speak. We all understood what was about to happen. It was not very likely that Azazel would allow us to quietly take Nathaniel away.

I pushed open the doors to Azazel's throne room for the second time that week, and the others arranged themselves around me.

A slow wave of ceased conversation started from the individuals closest to the door until everyone in the room had stopped what they were doing and turned to stare. Several angels cleared a path out of my way, leaving a direct line between my father and me.

Azazel stared. Nathaniel stood beside him, looking haggard. I didn't feel in the least bit sorry for him.

I stalked forward. Azazel made a motion at a couple of his bodyguards, who moved to block my way. They were both quite a bit taller than me, but I looked between their shoulders at my father.

I ignored them, addressing Azazel. "We have come for Nathaniel ap Zerachiel, to charge him with the crime of stealing humans' memories and selling them to vampires."

Nathaniel started next to Azazel. It was small, it was subtle, but it was there. That was all the confirmation I needed.

Azazel gave Nathaniel a sideways glance. It was hard to read.

"You have evidence of this?" he said.

"Yes," I said. "He was witnessed speaking with the ghost of Amarantha, the faerie Queen."

"And was he simply witnessed in her company?" Azazel asked. "There may be many perfectly innocent reasons why Nathaniel was speaking with her. He has long been an associate of Amarantha's, serving as a trusted negotiator on behalf of Lord Lucifer."

"So what if no one actually heard Nathaniel plotting?" I said. "He was consorting with a known traitor to Lucifer's kingdom."

There. I said it. The *T* word. Azazel surely wouldn't want the taint of rebellion on his court.

Nathaniel assumed a familiar expression of arrogance. "How dare you enter Lord Azazel's court and cast aspersions on my character? You should not even be permitted in this place. You have behaved shamefully toward your father."

"Don't try to wriggle your way out of this one. I'm not afraid of you." I looked up at the two lunkheads blocking my way. "If you don't get out of my way, I will blast you into the next millennium. And don't think that you're faster than me. You're not."

I don't know if my reputation preceded me or if Azazel's bodyguards are just that cowardly, but they both stepped aside. I strode forward until I was within a few feet of Azazel. The shiny pink mark from Lucifer's sword marred his handsome face.

"Nice scar," I said.

Gabriel gave an almost inaudible sigh next to me.

Azazel's mouth tightened. "One day someone will teach you to respect your betters."

"You're not better than me," I said. "And this scumbag is definitely not. Now, we're taking Nathaniel, and you can either cooperate, or you can suffer the consequences."

I really had to stop throwing the gauntlet down in front of these immortals.

"Guards!" Azazel roared.

There was a flurry of activity from the sides of the room. Several of the partygoers jammed toward the exit. Everyone in my group quickly turned around so that we formed a loose circle, back-to-back.

"I thought we were going to try to limit casualties," J.B. said. "Why do you have to provoke everyone you meet, Maddy?"

Azazel smirked as about three dozen soldier-angels surrounded us.

"Now, what was that about suffering the consequences?" Azazel said to me, and then addressed his guards. "Take the thrall first. Whoever kills him will be rewarded."

"Apparently you haven't learned your lesson," I said to Azazel. "I'll raze the whole building before I let you harm my husband."

"She will, too," Beezle said from inside my jacket. "Do not underestimate Maddy's ability to destroy real estate."

The soldiers inched closer. A winding coil of tension built in my stomach. No one wanted to make the first move.

I was heartily sick of fighting. I'd done more than enough of it in the past week to last me until the end of my days. But I would not allow Nathaniel to roam free, and I would not let Azazel harm Gabriel. So my options were fight, or surrender.

I don't surrender well.

I felt the shimmering of magic on the air that meant that Jude and Wade had turned into wolves. I didn't turn to look behind me, but kept my eyes on Azazel and Nathaniel. The others would take care of the soldiers. These two were mine.

To my left, one of the soldiers feinted forward with a blade that looked like it was made of lightning bolts. J.B. blasted the guy with his stave, something red and sizzling.

And just like that, it had begun.

I moved forward to engage Azazel for the second time, but Nathaniel stepped in front of my father, blocking my sword with a blade of his own. Azazel perched on the edge of his throne like a child enjoying an entertainment prepared just for him.

"Fine," I snarled. "You're the one I came for, anyway."

I thrust upward, aiming for his throat. He deftly parried the stroke and swung back at me, lightning-quick. I barely had time to block him before he attacked again.

I had two distinct disadvantages. One was that Nathaniel was a little more than a foot taller than me, and thus his reach was longer. He could slash at me all day long and effectively keep me blocked from reaching him.

The second disadvantage was that I was only half-angel,

and Nathaniel didn't have my mortal weaknesses. I would tire a lot quicker than he would, so the faster I took care of him, the better.

Even with the unnatural boost that I got from Lucifer's tattoo, I was a far inferior swordswoman. Nathaniel slashed and parried with the elegance of a dancer. I could feel my anger rising as sweat dripped in my eyes and made my fingers slick on the hilt of the sword. He was toying with me.

Well, there was no law that said I had to play fair.

Nathaniel obviously expected me to fight him sword to sword. He didn't expect me to blast him in the face with nightfire.

He threw up his arms and flew backward, landing on his butt. Behind me I heard the cries of angels, the howls of the wolves, and the crackle of magic flying everywhere. I couldn't check to see if everyone was all right. I had to make sure Nathaniel didn't wriggle off the hook.

I threw nightfire at him again, but he blocked it with the sword and the spell came flying back at me. I ducked, the nightfire singeing my hair. I sincerely hoped I did not have a reverse Mohawk now.

I didn't wait for him to start generating magic of his own. I pushed the fire spell through my heartstone and sent it singing along Lucifer's sword so that it focused the fire in a long stream at Nathaniel.

Nathaniel dove out of the way and the fire blasted into some of Azazel's Baroque furniture.

Beezle poked his head out of the jacket. "I smelled smoke. What are you burning now?"

"Stay *down*!"

I shoved him back inside as Nathaniel loosed a fiery ball of what looked like lava at me. I ducked to the side, but not quick enough to keep the stuff from grazing my shoulder.

My jacket ignited from the heat. Rather than mess around with a flaming coat I tore it off, shouting at Beezle.

"Get out, get out!"

"Stay down, get out—choose, why don't you?" he shouted back.

Beezle clung to my T-shirt as I flung the coat away from me and blocked another flaming lava-thing Nathaniel shot at me. The shot hit the sword and bounced off, but the edges of it sprayed back onto my cheeks and chin and I screamed. My face burned where it touched. I could almost feel the skin melting.

To the left of me Gabriel dueled with two soldiers. He was handling them easily, and several more were already on the ground. Jude leapt toward the neck of another soldier. I didn't stop to see what happened, because Nathaniel was stalking toward me again.

"Get high," I said to Beezle, and he flew off.

I ran at Nathaniel, sword upraised, attacking furiously. He blocked my blows, but as I grew angrier and angrier it seemed he was having more difficulty keeping me away. His arrogant mask slipped and for the first time there was a trace of alarm in his eyes.

I pressed forward, sensing weakness. Nathaniel stumbled backward. I slipped the blade into an opening and it slid into his shoulder.

There was no time or chance for mercy. I ripped upward with all of my strength, and Nathaniel howled. The cut exposed muscle from his collarbone to the shoulder joint, and blood spread everywhere, staining his white wings. He dropped his own weapon and staggered backward, snarling at me.

"You are hell's own bitch," he said, his face white.

"Thanks. I hate you, too," I said, and blasted him in the face with nightfire.

He fell to the ground, out cold.

"That's one problem taken care of," I said.

I nudged his ankle with the toe of my boot to see if he was playing dead. He didn't move. I picked up his sword, which was a lot longer and heavier than mine and felt significantly less friendly in the hand.

I turned back to the battle to see my little band of brothers finishing off the last of Azazel's soldiers.

We were bloodied and bruised and burned. Samiel bled from a gash in his forehead. Both wolves had small cuts and burns in their fur. Gabriel looked pretty good except that several of his feathers had been torn from his right wing, giving him a slightly lopsided appearance.

I rubbed my hand over my face, felt the long, tender marks where the lava had burned my skin.

We turned as one toward Azazel's throne.

He wasn't there.

17

"THAT SNEAKY COWARD," I SWORE.

Beezle fluttered down from his vantage point near the ceiling. "He snuck out when it became obvious that you were going to win. He went in there."

Beezle pointed to a back door behind the throne room. I knew that there was a kind of parlor back there, and doors to other parts of the castle.

I started toward the door, but Gabriel grabbed me around the wrist.

"There is no point in pursuing Azazel through the castle," Gabriel said. "He knows this place far better than you do."

"Besides, we came for Nathaniel," J.B. said.

We all looked toward Nathaniel's still form.

"I guess we're going to have to carry him out of here," I said.

That was when the room exploded.

The windows crashed in, glass flying everywhere. Gabriel pulled me toward him, sheltering my face as hundreds of charcarion demons came pouring in like clicking beetles, over the walls, up to the ceiling, and surrounding us. Everyone assumed the back-to-back position again, protecting one another. Wade snarled at the demons as they came closer. I brandished the two swords in front of me.

The demons circled us, careful not to come within reach of a blade or a wolf's jaws. J.B., Samiel and Gabriel seemed to be holding their spells back, waiting to see if the demons attacked.

There was the sound of applause from near the main doors, and a path materialized in the horde of demons.

Azazel stood there, and beside him—Antares and Focalor.

"You?" I spluttered. I was well aware of the fact that I sounded like I spoke dialogue from a bad movie. "You and Focalor? You and *Antares*?"

This last was practically a shriek. Antares had tried to kill me more times than I could count, and he'd nearly succeeded twice.

Antares smirked at me from behind his father. Focalor could not hide his delight. The three of them walked toward us, the charcarion demons bowing low as they passed.

"Yes," Azazel said silkily. "A Grigori does not give up his children, no matter what provocation."

"What about me, then?" I said angrily. "You seemed pretty willing to sell me to the highest bidder."

"Antares has demonstrated his loyalty to me time and again," Azazel said. "He has put his own life at risk on numerous occasions as he pretended to be a traitor to the court."

"I thought Focalor was your sworn enemy," I said.

"It has suited us to pretend thus," Azazel replied.

"So it's been you all along," I spat. "You created the

technology. You set up the operation. You sent Nathaniel to recruit Amarantha."

Azazel nodded, as though I were a good pupil.

"Why?" I said, thinking of the cubs, all the humans, who'd lost their memories. "You have broken the laws of Lucifer's kingdom. You've harmed humans for your own gain."

"Do not quote chapter and verse at me," Azazel said. "You, who defy Lord Lucifer and the Grigori at every turn. You, who cleave unto the laws only when it suits your purpose."

"I've never killed an innocent for money," I said. "Don't compare my actions to yours. I thought you were the right hand of Lucifer, his most trusted advisor."

"I have played that role for centuries untold," Azazel acknowledged. "But I have waited, always waited, for my opportunity. And now it has come."

"You're crazy," I breathed. "Open warfare against Lucifer? Do you really think you can seize power?"

"I do not think," Azazel said. "I know. You cannot comprehend how many of the Grigori have longed to be rid of him—his arrogance, his changeability, his cruel whims. We have been at his mercy since time untold. And now we will band together and overthrow him, and a new order will begin."

"A new order in which humans are subservient to angels?" I guessed, and seeing the answer in his eyes I felt anger pushing at my skin. "You would turn humans into nothing more than slaves, to be used by vampires and faeries and demons at will?"

"Yes," Azazel replied. "And even you, Madeline Black, cannot prevent this. All over Lucifer's kingdom the dominoes have begun to fall. And there is no savior to come for you now, no ally that has not sacrificed himself already to stand at your side."

I felt a trickle of dread. Not for myself, but for Beezle and Gabriel and Wade and Samiel and Jude and J.B. I'd thought I'd assembled a pretty badass collection of back-ups, but all I'd really done was gather all my friends in one place so we could be killed together.

"And what of the Morningstar?" I said.

"You may have noticed that Lord Lucifer has been out of touch of late," Azazel said. "Wherever he may be, he is not available to answer your cries for help."

"You think I care about me?" I said furiously. "I'm talking about the complete and total destruction of you and your stupid plans. Lucifer is stronger than all of you put together. He won't allow you to enslave humans."

"You are overestimating Lord Lucifer's strength," Azazel said. "He has survived thus far on cunning and guile, two qualities that he has used to manipulate us against one another for centuries. He has maintained absolute power by playing the Grigori and the other supernatural courts as if we were nothing more than pieces on a chessboard. No more."

"You'll lose," I said with certainty.

"And you will die regardless," Azazel replied. "You shall not leave this court alive."

Beezle tightened his claws on my shoulder. The rest of us pressed together more tightly as the demons inched closer.

"Don't bother trying to fight off the demons," I said to Gabriel in a voice barely a whisper.

I felt rather than saw his nod. I knew he understood.

Azazel and Focalor turned to leave the throne room. Antares gave me a cruel smile.

I blasted him with nightfire and he fell to the ground screaming. The demons descended on us. I dropped Nathaniel's sword and scooped up Wade under one arm before he could attack. Gabriel grabbed Jude, and we all took flight. I passed Wade to Samiel in midair. Several of the charcarion demons that clung to the ceiling released their hold in an attempt to fall on us and knock us to the ground. J.B. blasted them out of the way with his wand.

Azazel and Focalor had stopped and turned to see what was happening. Azazel seemed amused as he looked up at us hanging near the ceiling.

"You will have to come down eventually," Azazel said.

"Everything does," I agreed. I felt the buildup of power inside me, and I dug deeper than I ever had before. I would get only one shot, and I needed it to count. "Gravity is a powerful force."

I blasted the electricity spell out, and it exploded in a torrent of lightning from my hands. But I wasn't aiming for Azazel or Focalor, as much as I would have enjoyed frying them both. I aimed for the ceiling.

There was a terrible crack, and half the ceiling came down.

Electrical wiring sparked, and wooden cross beams ignited.

Charcarion demons cried out as they were crushed. The ones that were not turned into mosquito splats rushed toward the door. Azazel and Focalor shouted at them to stop, blasted the demons for disobeying, but their desire to live overrode their instinct to obey. The two Grigori were overrun by the panicked horde.

Samiel's shoulder was hit by falling debris and he lost his grip on Wade. The wolf tumbled toward the floor, barking and howling.

I shot downward to Wade, heedless of the falling chunks of ceiling, and grabbed him out of midair. The others followed me as I swooped through the room. I aimed for one of the broken windows, thinking it would be safest to get out of the throne room.

I pulled my wings in to fit through the shards of broken glass and discovered that the windows overlooked a giant sweep of landscaped garden. There were beds for flowers and sculptured hedges in the forms of animals, all covered in a heavy blanket of snow. I imagined it was quite magical in the summertime with everything in bloom. I had never actually looked out those windows before. Usually when I was in Azazel's court I was too busy thinking up excuses to leave as soon as possible.

I flew most of the way across the lawn to the place where it bordered a forest, landed heavily in the snow on my knees and put Wade down. He nudged me with his head and I patted him tiredly.

The others came out behind me. Gabriel pulled me to my feet.

"Think we can catch a portal out of here?" I asked hopefully.

Gabriel shook his head. "I already attempted the spell as we flew. Azazel has blocked us from exiting that way as long as we are on his land."

I glanced back at Azazel's mansion. Charcarion demons flowed out the windows and over the lawn toward us, shouting and screeching their battle cries.

"What are the chances, do you think, that his property ends here?" I asked.

Gabriel shook his head. "It does not. Remember, I lived here for many years. Azazel owns acres of land. He desires complete privacy for his court."

"So we either stand and fight, or we run through the

woods being chased by demons for hours on end," J.B. said.

"We could try to fly . . ." I started.

"And carry the wolves for how long?" Beezle asked.

"They can't be any heavier than you," I retorted.

The demons were getting closer.

"I'd rather stand and fight," J.B. said.

The wolves barked in agreement.

Samiel nodded.

Gabriel took my hand. "At least we will die together."

I shook my head and let his fingers drop. "We are not going to die."

The demons poured over the hill, a mass so large that they seemed one giant monster. Where had they all come from? Hadn't I killed most of them?

"Madeline, their numbers . . ."

"Screw their numbers," I said, my face hot and angry.

I'd had *enough*. I was tired of running for my life, fighting monsters, getting blasted by spells. I was tired of worrying about the lives of those whom I loved, lives that were in jeopardy because a bunch of angels wanted power that they would never possess.

From the moment I'd learned I was Azazel's daughter, my life had been an unending battle. The faces of the dead swam before my eyes. Patrick, my best friend, killed by Ramuell. The people slaughtered by the nephilim at Clark and Belmont. The murdered wolves of Wade's pack.

Even the living had not been left unharmed. The victims who screamed in padded rooms at the Agency were proof of that.

All of them had been caught in the cross fire of a battle they hadn't even known of, a battle for supremacy over all creatures. A battle that Lucifer was determined to win, and that his enemies were equally determined he lose.

For the first time the power of the Morningstar came when I called, easily, naturally. I rose up above the others, my wings outspread, the light of the sun moving through me.

The demons covered their eyes, fell to their knees. I raised my arms, hands open, and let the magic in my blood take over. The clearing was filled with light.

When it was over, all the demons were gone.

I fainted.

I woke up in Gabriel's arms, everyone huddled around me at the edge of the forest.

"What?" I croaked. My throat was very dry. I felt like I hadn't felt in a long time—like my magic had run out, and that it would take a good long time for it to come back.

"You fell out of the sky," Beezle said. "For some reason, everyone's concerned."

"I can get up," I said to Gabriel.

"I am not sure that you should," he replied.

"Well, we all know how Maddy feels about what she *should* do," Beezle said.

I pushed to my feet and immediately stumbled. My legs felt like jelly.

"You see how well she listens," Beezle said.

Gabriel put his arm around me. I did not want to admit that the only reason I was upright was because he was holding me there.

The mansion was silent before us. The snow on the lawn had been melted away by my spell. No creatures crawled through the broken windows.

"Do you think I killed them all, or is Azazel just marshaling his forces for another round?" I asked.

"Oh, I'm sure he's more determined to kill you than ever," Beezle said.

"We've got to get out of here," J.B. said.

"Azazel will have closed his lands by now," Gabriel said grimly. "I have seen him do it only a few times, but it is a spell that he has in place to prevent the escape of prisoners. We will not be able to leave by foot or by air. He cannot allow us to leave and notify Lord Lucifer of his plans."

We all looked helplessly at one another. Would we be trapped here like rats running around a maze, fighting until Azazel managed to wear us down?

"Gabriel, there has to be some way of getting out of here. You lived here with Azazel for years. A secret tunnel that leads off the property?" I asked.

Gabriel shook his head. "There is only one way that I know of to leave this place once Azazel has activated the security measures."

"And that is?"

"There is Azazel's personal portal."

"And where is that?" I asked, dreading the answer.

"In Azazel's quarters. The east wing, on the very top floor."

"Well, that's like asking to get caught," Beezle said. "You want us to go back inside? Why do none of you pay attention when we watch horror movies?"

"Because it's hard to hear the narrative when there's a little gargoyle screaming, 'Don't go in there,' at the actors," I said.

"What narrative?" Beezle said. "It's just people making stupid decisions and getting chopped up by a maniac. Like we're going to be when we go back inside Azazel's house and head straight for the only exit."

"You know that he'll expect us to try something like that," J.B. agreed.

"Does anyone else have a better idea?" I demanded. "Or do you want to let Azazel run us ragged on the grounds until we can't run any farther?"

No one answered. We all knew there was only one choice.

"Okay," I said briskly, addressing Gabriel. "I'm assuming if that's the only way out, then Azazel will have those windows on the upper floors well guarded."

"That is a safe assumption, yes," Gabriel said.

"So the best way back in is through the broken windows."

"You could pass through the walls, since you're the Hound of the Hunt," Beezle said.

"I could, but the rest of you couldn't. And my power is temporarily out, anyway," I said. "What's next?"

"Up two flights of stairs and down a long passageway to Azazel's quarters," Gabriel said. "Which are guarded by a phalanx of his most trusted soldiers."

"This might be the dumbest thing we have ever done in a long line of dumb things," Beezle said.

"Much as it pains me to agree with you, you're right," I said. "But I really can't see another option."

Samiel tapped me on the shoulder. *Would the invisibility spell make a difference?*

"Not with Azazel," Gabriel said. "It may protect us from any lesser demons."

"Don't bother," I said. "I'm sure that Azazel will know that we've entered the building."

"Yeah, what with the smashing and the mangling that usually follows in your wake," Beezle said.

We walked slowly over the lawn. I limped, leaning on Gabriel. The wolves trotted ahead, sniffing the air. I was exhausted down to my bones. The house seemed like a giant repository of menace, and I was suddenly afraid for all of us.

J.B. and Samiel flew ahead to check inside the broken windows. Samiel looked back and gave us a thumbs-up.

The bottom sills of the windows were only a few feet off the ground, so the wolves were able to leap through easily. Gabriel lifted me inside, as my wings had disappeared along with my magic.

The throne room was completely destroyed. The fires had been extinguished, but there was a lot of scorched and charred wood everywhere. Three-quarters of the ceiling plaster had come down completely, and the remainder looked like it was going to fall any minute. Bodies of demons and soldier-angels lay everywhere under the rubble. There was nothing stirring, and no sign of Azazel, Antares or Focalor.

"Do you think Nathaniel was smashed underneath the falling ceiling?" I asked hopefully.

"Nah, he's a cockroach like Antares," Beezle said. "And like you, come to think of it. Everyone tries to kill you but you keep popping back up."

"Real nice, Beezle. I'll remember that the next time you're crying for a doughnut," I said.

"Perhaps the two of you would like to cease your bickering until we manage to get out of mortal peril?" Gabriel asked.

We picked our way over the debris until we reached the doors at the back of the throne room.

"This way," Gabriel said, and led us through into a hallway. A number of other doors opened off the hall, and at the end of it was a wide staircase.

Everything was silent and still. I'd expected more activity—that Azazel would be gathering troops and making plans to destroy us. But there was no noise behind all of the doors that we passed, and there was no movement in the hall.

Gabriel still had his arm slung around me, propping me up. I was so tired I could barely lift my feet. Beezle made a concession to my extreme exhaustion by letting Samiel carry him instead. The wolves scouted ahead. J.B. and Samiel brought up the rear.

Wade and Jude stopped at the bottom of the stairs and waited for us to catch up. I looked up the flight, and then at Gabriel, and saw that he was thinking what I was thinking.

If we got caught on the stairs, we were dead.

"I had better carry you," he said.

He put his arms under my shoulders and knees and held me like a baby. It was pretty much impossible to piggyback on an angel. The wings get in the way.

The wolves bounded up quickly, lightly, skipping steps. Gabriel extended his wings as far as he could and flew, carrying me with him. Behind us J.B. and Samiel followed suit.

We landed at the top and faced another long hallway with doors leading off it.

"This is just like Amarantha's castle," I muttered. "What does he need all these rooms for?"

"His projects," Gabriel said. He put me down. The hallway was too narrow for him to carry me.

"What projects?" I asked.

"I was never told," Gabriel said. "I was a thrall. But I assume that at least one of the projects was the creation of the memory-extraction technology."

I stared at the doors, sorely tempted.

"No," said J.B. "We don't have time."

"Gods know what he's got behind there," I pleaded. "We could destroy his research, stop him from unleashing some other horrible thing on the general population."

"We don't have time," J.B. repeated. "I'd like to go home to my cat tonight."

"I didn't know you had a cat," I said.

"There are a lot of things you don't know about me," J.B. muttered.

He was right. It seemed that whenever we talked it was always about me—the problems I had, the family politics, the monsters trying to kill me.

"I haven't been a very good friend, have I?" I asked.

"Why do you feel compelled to have a heart-to-heart when we are in danger of losing our lives at any moment?" Beezle snapped.

"Because I'm human," I said angrily. "And I'm trying to remember that I'm more than just some monster-killing machine."

The wolves stopped abruptly, whining, at the end of the passage.

"Gods above and below," I said. "What now?"

I hurried forward as quickly as I could on my unresponsive legs. Gabriel cursed softly and ran after me, catching me just as my right ankle buckled and my leg folded underneath my body.

I stared up the second flight of stairs. The wolves growled, their hackles raised.

Two creatures stood on the steps, one behind the other. Both of them were more than seven feet tall, with the raw red skin of exposed muscle, wicked-looking claws and protruding fangs.

I couldn't believe my eyes.

They were nephilim.

18

"MEAT," THE FIRST ONE CROONED.

My mind went blank with terror. I had no magic with which to fight these creatures. And the last time I'd faced a nephilim, I'd died. I'd managed to come back, but it was a traumatizing experience nonetheless.

"Azazel loosed the nephilim?" Beezle said. "He's totally lost it. He can't control those monsters. No one can."

"Meeeeeeat," the second one said.

All of the nephilim had been locked up in the Forbidden Lands for centuries. The cages that bound them were magically enspelled so that when the nephilim touched the bars, they would be burned or shocked. The cages were just small enough that there was no place for the nephilim to go to find relief, no way to avoid the magic that bound the cage together. Essentially, the nephilim had been tortured for almost the entirety of their existence. It had made already cruel creatures even crueler, and rather single-minded.

"Meeeat," they said together.

I pulled Lucifer's sword from the scabbard.

"Do not even think about attempting it," Gabriel hissed. "Let Samiel and me manage them."

"I'm not helpless," I said.

"You are doing an excellent impression of it," he replied.

There was a clatter of leather and armor in the hall. I turned to see several soldier-angels filling the gap behind our party.

"Now it doesn't matter," I said grimly.

We were trapped at the end of the corridor with the nephilim above us and the soldiers behind us and only about ten or fifteen feet with which to maneuver. The tight quarters meant it would be difficult for Azazel's troops to fight as well, but that wasn't going to be much comfort when the nephilim tore our heads off.

J.B. and Samiel engaged the soldiers. Spells shot everywhere in the hallway, bouncing off walls and doorknobs.

Wade and Jude howled and bounded forward toward the nephilim. Gabriel cursed aloud and followed after them. I chased after him, alarmed. I knew that he didn't want to throw spells that might accidentally harm the wolves, but what was he going to do without magic? Engage the nephilim in hand-to-hand combat?

The wolves reached the first nephilim. Jude leapt for the monster's neck, jaws open. The nephilim swatted him aside with one giant hand, but Jude seemed to expect this. He went boneless and twisted in midair, landing on his paws.

Jude's purpose had been to serve as a distraction for his alpha. Wade closed his fangs around the nephilim as the creature was absorbed with Jude. The nephilim screamed as Wade tore a giant chunk of flesh from its side.

Gabriel reached the first nephilim and blasted it in the face with white fire. The monster lashed out with its fists, blinded by the blast but not particularly hurt. Nephilim are very resilient, and every nephilim responds to the same magical spell differently. What is fatal to one can be nothing more than an itch to another.

The white fire that represented Gabriel's nephilim magic had barely harmed this one, but Gabriel was already ducking underneath its elbows to go after the second creature.

Jude leapt into the fray again, latching onto the nephilim's arm and clamping it between his jaws. The nephilim smashed him repeatedly against the wall to try to dislodge him, but the wolf held on.

Wade sprung into the air, slashing the monster across the face with his claws. It felt like it was intruding on the functioning of a well-oiled machine, but I figured the sooner the nephilim were brought down, the better.

"Wade!" I shouted.

The alpha seemed to understand immediately. He squeezed between the nephilim's leg and the wall and moved on to help Gabriel. Jude released the creature's arm as I raised the sword high and plunged it into the nephilim's chest.

The monster screamed. Then, rather horribly, he just kind of . . . disintegrated. Blood and bone and muscle seemed to melt into long sticky strands that flowed over the steps and made my boots hard to lift. Jude whined and slipped around the mess to help Wade and Gabriel.

Beezle landed on my shoulder. "That is disgusting. That's even grosser than the spider goop."

"Like I needed you to rank the quality of monster fluid,"

I said. I lifted my boots out of the muck and ran up the stairs as fast as I could, which was not very fast. The nephilim's remains were hardening quickly and it was even more difficult to get through them as they changed consistency.

"J.B. and Samiel aren't getting a break back there," Beezle said. "For every soldier they kill, Azazel sends three more."

I didn't have to look to know that. I could tell by the unrelenting pitch of battle that things hadn't eased up. "We've got to get rid of the other nephilim. Then we can help them."

I reached the top of the stairs. Gabriel, Jude and Wade had managed to back the second nephilim into the hallway. This one wielded some kind of magic that looked like purple paintballs, but wherever it splattered, the walls were cut through as if by lasers.

"If that stuff touches any of them, it will take off their limbs," I said to Beezle.

Worse, the nephilim seemed entirely unfazed by either the attacks of the wolves or Gabriel's spells. Gabriel's shoulders were set in grim determination, and both the wolves panted from the effort, but they were getting nowhere.

"I've got a plan," Beezle said.

"Really," I said, looking for an opening.

"Really," Beezle insisted. He quickly outlined it to me.

"If this works, you get all the doughnuts you want for the next month, no questions asked," I said with a lightness I did not feel. Beezle was an old gargoyle, and the place I usually liked him to be was somewhere safe, away from battle.

He flew toward the nephilim, but close to the ceiling so as to avoid detection. Beezle is so small that the monster could hardly have perceived him as a threat, even when he landed on the nephilim's head. He clung to the back of the monster's skull with his legs like a tiny demented monkey.

Then he jammed his claws into the nephilim's eyes. The nephilim screamed and reached to grab Beezle, but my clever gargoyle had already let go and flown up to the ceiling with the monster's eyeballs sticking off the ends of his claws like some grisly cocktail snack.

I ran into the fray and tackled the nephilim to the ground. It still screamed and thrashed. I gagged from the smell of sulfur coming off its body, then pushed away to my feet and beheaded the thing.

It stopped screaming immediately.

Beezle flicked the eyeballs off his claws and then flew down to Gabriel's shoulder. He's learned to tolerate Gabriel, but my husband is still not his favorite person, so I was surprised. At least, I was surprised until Beezle used Gabriel's coat as a napkin to clean the gore off his fingernails.

Gabriel shook his head in resignation.

"Let's help the other two," I said, and we backtracked down the passage to the stairs.

J.B. and Samiel were holding on, but barely. They had been pushed up the stairwell by the steadily increasing throng.

"Where the hell does Azazel keep all these soldiers?" I asked incredulously.

"Have you seen how big this house is?" Beezle said. "He could store them in the basement and never even know they were there."

We grimly reentered the battle, but it was quickly apparent that all we were doing was tiring ourselves out.

"We need to distract them and make a break for it," I told Gabriel.

"I have something appropriate," he said.

He threw another blast of what looked like nightfire, but actually was a gigantic cloud of sulfurous smoke. The passage quickly filled up and everyone was coughing and groping.

Gabriel grabbed my hand and pushed at Samiel, and we all ran up the stairs. A couple of soldiers followed us but J.B. leveled them before they had the chance to get too far.

Gabriel was the only one who knew where Azazel's quarters were, and he led us unerringly down the hall to the room at the very end.

The door was unlocked, and we poured in, slamming the door shut behind us.

I half expected Azazel to be waiting there, but there was no one.

The portal spun in the corner. It was inside a glass case to protect the room from the constant force of suction that was generated.

Bodies crashed into the door outside.

"No time to celebrate," I said to the others. "Let's go."

I strode to the portal, pulling open the glass case. Lucifer's tattoo wriggled in warning.

"Yes, I know we're in danger," I said to my hand. "Thanks for the update."

Gabriel nudged me aside. "I will go first."

"We're going home," I said. "What difference can it possibly make?"

"I will not take chances with your safety," Gabriel said.

"Will the two of you just hold hands and jump together so that we can get out of here already?" Beezle said. He'd switched to Samiel again.

I took Gabriel's hand firmly, thought of my backyard covered in snow, and we went through. I hoped the others would follow quickly.

Gabriel squeezed my hand tight as we emerged into the early-winter night.

I turned my head to smile up at him, and that was when I saw the sword protruding from his chest, and Azazel standing behind Gabriel with a look of malicious glee on his face.

Gabriel released my hand and fell forward into the snow.

"NOOOOOOOOOOOOOOOOOOOOO!" I screamed, and I turned on my father with a fury I had never felt before.

I slashed at him with Lucifer's sword, and a long cut formed across his chest. He narrowed his eyes and swiped back at me, the longer reach of his sword slicing into my arm. Blood flowed down the sleeve of my shirt—my jacket was long gone, caught on fire and discarded in the throne room.

I didn't care. I didn't care about anything except killing this monster called my father. My magic still lay quiet inside me, and I knew it would not wake. I had depleted myself too thoroughly at Azazel's.

I swiped at his face with the sword and gave him a cut to match the one on his other cheek. I felt numb inside, a machine with no purpose except to destroy this man. He seemed to realize this, and in any event he'd gotten what he came for—Gabriel.

Azazel swung with his fist and punched me in the face. I saw stars and blackness spinning before me. I tried to hold myself up, tried to keep fighting. But my body was half-mortal, and it betrayed me.

I fell to my knees, shaking my head, and when I looked up, Azazel was gone.

He'd flown away like the coward he was, and because my power was gone I couldn't follow him.

I screamed his name into the darkness.

There was nothing but the emptiness of night, and the flashing lights of airplanes blinking across the sky.

"Know this," I said to the darkness. "I am Lucifer's Hound of the Hunt, and there is no place you can hide from me. I will hunt you to the end of your days. You will never know peace. You will never know rest. I will destroy you utterly, and the last face you see before you leave this Earth will be mine."

I stood wearily, using the sword as a staff to push me up, and turned to face that which I did not want to see.

A pool of dark blood stained the snow around his body. Samiel, Beezle and the wolves, changed back into humans, stood beside him.

"Where's J.B.?" I asked.

"He took Gabriel," Beezle said. There were tears glittering on his cheeks.

I looked again at the body, the thing that could not be Gabriel, and then back up at Beezle.

"Took him?"

"To the Door," Beezle said.

"The Door," I said. "No. No. Gabriel wouldn't choose the Door. He wouldn't leave me. He knows I can see him. He would stay. He wouldn't leave me."

"Maddy . . ." Beezle began.

"No," I said angrily, swiping at the tears that were falling now, falling so hard I could barely see. "I told you once before, when he was kidnapped. Gabriel would not leave me. He would stay with me. J.B. must have made him go. You know how J.B. feels about ghosts and paperwork."

I was babbling. I knew I was babbling. But it couldn't be right. It couldn't. Gabriel could not be dead, killed by

Azazel, a maggot that had somehow crawled free. It should be Azazel who was dead, not Gabriel. Not my husband.

My husband, I thought, and I broke.

I screamed my pain and grief to the sky, a black howl that had no beginning and no end.

19

SAMIEL TRIED TO PICK ME UP, TO TAKE ME AWAY.

"No," I said, and when he tried to make me move anyway I hit him in the mouth.

He looked shocked and hurt, and somewhere under all the pain I was sorry for it, but not sorry enough to let him take me from Gabriel.

"No," I repeated. "Just leave me with him."

"Come on, Samiel," Beezle said softly.

They went away, but I didn't care. I just wanted to be alone with Gabriel. I crawled through the snow to him and laid my head on his back. I hardly felt the cold and the wet through my jeans.

He was still warm. His coat smelled of him, apple pie baking in the oven. Tears leaked from my eyes.

"Madeline," a voice growled, and there was a gentle

hand in my hair. Someone crouched beside me, someone who smelled of wolf.

"Go away," I said. "Just leave me here."

"Madeline," Jude repeated. "You can't stay here in the snow."

"Why not?" I said.

I had seen an incomprehensible amount of death in my life. I had fought against Death with all the power I had within me, and still it had triumphed. It had taken the only person who made me want to keep living.

"Gabriel would not want to see you this way," Jude said.

"Don't tell me what Gabriel would want or not want," I said furiously, raising my head to glare at him. "Gabriel's not here, and you didn't know him."

"That's the Madeline Black I know," Jude said. "Stand up. Stand up and fight. If you stay here, you will fall into grief that you will never overcome."

"I don't care," I said, the fire that had lit me momentarily going out. "I want him back. I want to be where he is."

"I know," Judas said.

The pain in his voice drew me back from the darkness that threatened to swallow me, a pain so old and so familiar to him that he hardly knew he carried it most of the time.

I came to my knees, my hands on my thighs, staring at Jude. His blue eyes shimmered with unshed tears in the streetlights.

"Samiel needs you," he said. "And your gargoyle."

"Yes," I said. It was hard to keep my head above the blackness that rose up inside, the blackness that tried to pull me under again.

"And you have a promise to keep, Lucifer's child," Jude said, but there was a gentleness that had never been there before.

"Azazel," I said, and inside me a shard of ice pierced the darkness.

"Azazel," Jude agreed.

He held his hand out to me, and I took it, and we rose together. He gripped my fingers urgently.

"From this day henceforth, I am your ally. When you hunt for Azazel I will be by your side, and I will hold him to the ground as you swing the sword to take his life."

"Jude," I said uncertainly, looking at Wade, who looked unsurprised by this proclamation. The ways of the alpha are certainly mysterious.

"I swear," he said, and energy passed between our hands. I knew then that we were bound in some magical way, and that Jude would keep his promise no matter what the cost.

"Let us take Gabriel's body," Wade said.

I looked down at the ground in panic. They couldn't take him. I wasn't ready to say good-bye.

"You cannot bury him here, not without attracting the attention of the authorities. We will take him to a place near where our pack summers. No one will find him there," Wade said.

He lay in the snow, facedown, with the dark stain around him, and this would be the last time I saw him.

But I knew Jude was right. I couldn't lie in the snow beside him forever. I had promises to keep.

"Okay," I said.

I knelt beside him for the last time, and Jude and Wade helped me roll Gabriel to his back. I tenderly wiped the snow from his face with my sleeve and closed his eyes.

For the last time, I pressed my lips against his, and then I let them take him away.

I stood and watched Jude and Wade disappear into the

alley with the body of my husband. I was still standing there, staring at the place they'd gone, when J.B. returned.

He landed a few feet away from me. We watched each other without speaking for a few moments.

"Did you know?" I asked.

"Maddy, I'm so sorry . . ." he began.

"Did you know?" I repeated. "You're the regional supervisor. Every fated death in this city goes across your desk. Did you know that this was going to happen?"

He stared at me for a minute, then finally said, "Yes."

It was like the blow had come down all over again, and for a few seconds I couldn't breathe.

"How could you?" I shouted. "How could you not say anything, not do anything? You knew that Gabriel would die on this night, in my own backyard, and you stood by and let it happen?"

"You know the rules as well as I do," J.B. said angrily. "We are duty bound not to interfere, no matter what the circumstances. What could you have done if I told you?"

"I wouldn't have let Gabriel go through that thrice-bedamned portal first!" I screamed. "I would have gone through myself."

"And left him grieving for you the way you're grieving for him? Is that really a better option? Besides, there is nothing I can do once it was written down. You should know that better than anyone."

"Always duty. Always Death," I said, throwing Amarantha's words back at him.

J.B.'s jaw tightened. "You should be grateful to me. I volunteered to take this one personally. Otherwise somebody else would have offered him the choice."

"He didn't need a choice!" I screamed. Everything that was holding me together was unraveling again. "He was supposed to stay with me! You shouldn't have taken him to the Door at all!"

"Maddy," J.B. said, his face shocked. "You can't mean that. Every soul has the right to a choice."

"He should have stayed with me," I said, and my voice cracked. "He should have chosen *me*."

J.B. closed the space between us, put his arms around me. All I could think was that there was something not quite right about his embrace. He wasn't Gabriel.

After a few moments I pushed away. "Go home, J.B."

"So that's it?" he said. "After everything we've been through this week, all I get is a 'go home, J.B.'?"

"I'm sorry I'm ungrateful," I said dully. Ice was closing in on my heart, covering that beating sunstone, making it numb. "I'm sorry I killed your mother, and destroyed your family home. I'm sorry I made you risk your life in a fruitless venture in Azazel's court that gained us nothing. I'm sorry."

"Wade is going to bring the cubs in tomorrow," J.B. said. "Will you be there?"

"Don't count on me," I said, and turned away.

He said nothing else. After a few moments I looked back. He was gone, and I was alone with a dark stain in the snow.

I went to bed, but I didn't sleep. I couldn't. The sheets smelled of Gabriel. His clothes were hanging in the closet. His spare dress shoes were underneath the chair in the hallway. There were two coffee cups drying in the dish rack.

I lay awake in bed, staring at the ceiling. I wanted to cry. Crying would be a release. But all I could think of was ice, and revenge.

When the sun came up Beezle appeared in the doorway. He hovered there, tentative, unsure of his welcome.

"J.B. called this morning," Beezle said. "He said that Wade was bringing the cubs into the Agency."

"Yeah, I know," I said. I rolled to one side so that I wouldn't have to see Beezle.

"Don't you want to see if Chloe's spell will restore their memories?" Beezle asked. "You were the one who found the cubs. You were the one who thought to bring the machines back. Without you, there would be no way to cure them."

"Yeah," I said. It was hard to remember why I had cared so much, why I had fought so hard for everything.

There was a flutter of wings and then I felt Beezle's hands yanking me roughly to face him.

"Get up, Maddy," Beezle said, and he smacked my cheek with his little hand.

I covered the place where he had hit, shocked.

"This is not you. You don't lie down and go to sleep. You get up and fight."

"That's what Jude said, too."

"Well, if that redneck werewolf can recognize it, then it must be true."

I laughed involuntarily at his categorization of Jude as a "redneck werewolf"; then I stopped. It didn't seem right to laugh.

Beezle looked at me tenderly. All the love that had bound us together for all the years of my life was there in his face. "Life goes on, Maddy. You know that better than anyone. It might be a cliché, but it's true. You're still alive. And Gabriel is alive inside you."

My cell phone rang. I looked at the caller ID. It was Jude, and I knew what he would want from me.

I clicked on and without saying hello I said, "I'll be there."

"I knew you would," he growled.

* * *

Since there were so many cubs, we couldn't meet in Chloe's underground laboratory. J.B. made special arrangements for Wade, Jude, and the mothers of all of the children to enter the Agency through the loading dock. They still had to be checked by security, though. No one was taking chances.

I waited outside the large conference room where Chloe had arranged all of the machines in a long row. When the pack came trooping down the hall I caught my breath. I didn't know what to say to these women, to these mothers.

I didn't know how to tell them how sorry I was that it was my father, my kin, who had torn their children's minds away from them and left them broken.

I didn't know how to tell them that this might not work, despite the fact that progress with the restored adults had been positive. Children's brains were different. They were still developing. There could be permanent damage, even if Chloe did manage to restore their memories.

I felt the weight of all my failings crushing me as Wade strode up to me. He held hands with a formidable-looking African American woman who wore a denim vest over jeans and a flannel shirt, much like her husband. In her arms I recognized the small toddler I'd carried through the caves—their daughter.

"Madeline Black, this is my wife, Roxie Wade. Roxie, this is Madeline Black."

I held my hand out to her, unsure if she would take it.

Her face crumpled suddenly and she threw her arm around me. The toddler was crushed between us as Roxie sobbed into my shoulder. I looked at Wade in panic.

He gently extracted their daughter from between the two

of us. Roxie put her other arm around me and tried to speak through her tears.

"Th-th-th-thank . . . you . . . so . . . much," she managed. "Thank you for bringing my baby back to me."

"Uh. Of course," I said. I didn't know what to do with this woman. She shouldn't be thanking me. She should be hitting me for bringing her daughter back in such a state.

Chloe peeked her head out of the room. "I'm ready."

I patted Roxie's back awkwardly. "Ma'am? Mrs. Wade? They're ready for us now."

"Y-y-yes. Of course." She lifted her head and wiped her face, and then she smiled brilliantly. "I know this is going to work. I feel it in my bones."

I wished I were as confident as she was, but I didn't say so. I indicated that she should enter first, and I let everyone file in ahead of me. Jude and J.B. were last, at the end of the line. I tried to give them both a watery half smile but wasn't sure I succeeded. They waited for me to go into the room before them. Jude squeezed my shoulder once before dropping his hand.

Chloe was talking to the mothers, determining which child should be positioned in which chair. The children were the same perfect little automatons that they had been in the woods after I'd started ordering them around.

"Wade has instructed the children to do exactly as their mothers say," Jude whispered. "The power of the alpha."

I looked at Wade, so strong and compassionate and wise. His pack was lucky to have an alpha like him. What happened in packs where the alpha held so much power and used it cruelly, to subjugate those beneath him?

I wondered briefly if that was the greater purpose for which Amarantha and Focalor had been holding Wade.

They'd never tried to extract his memories. Perhaps Azazel had been working on a machine to draw on the power of the alpha, that all-powerful word. I regretted not destroying Azazel's workshops when I'd had the chance.

I had discovered that I regretted a lot of things.

The children sat obediently in the chairs, and Chloe went down the line turning on the machines. As each cub's eye was scanned by the laser, the child would go rigid. A few mothers stepped toward their children, as though wanting to pull them away.

"You have to wait," I said, and they turned to look at me. "I know it's hard. I know they look like they're suffering. But we can't stop the process once it's begun."

A couple of the mothers whimpered, but most of them took their cue from Roxie Wade, who nodded regally at me. She watched, unflinching, as her toddler stared into the eye of the camera.

Since some of the children were so young and had correspondingly short memory lives, the cubs did not reach the crisis moment all at the same time.

The first to cry out was Wade's daughter, and that was the only time I thought Roxie would break.

"Mama!" the little girl shouted, and her voice was so plaintive that I almost ran to her myself.

"This is the hardest part," I murmured like a mantra. "Don't give in. Wait it out."

Some of the other children also cried out for their mothers, and Chloe had to restrain one woman who would not listen to admonitions to wait.

It was unbearable, almost as bad as listening to the children scream when we'd taken them off the machines in the caves.

One of them began to wail, a cry of pain so piercing that it broke the ice that encased my heart. All the grief I'd suppressed the night before rose up in my throat, and tears overflowed. Roxie took my hand and gripped it tight. And we waited.

One by one, the cubs fainted in their chairs.

"You can take them now," Chloe said.

Roxie and Wade rushed to their daughter. Wade scooped her up and rested her head on his shoulder.

"Papa?" the little girl said sleepily.

Someone had put a little pink barrette in her dark hair, and the barrette stood out in bright relief against Wade's vest. She opened her eyes to half-mast, as if to affirm that it was indeed her father who held her. Then she laid her head back on his shoulder and began to snore.

Roxie laughed and cried at the same time, her hand over her mouth. Wade just gave me a long look, and in that look was all the gratitude that he wanted to say but couldn't speak because of the lump in his throat.

I only nodded, and left the room. My work here was done. I had something else to do now. I was done with the living. Death was coming for Azazel, and I was going to deliver it.

J.B. followed me into the hallway, grabbed my hand so I would face him.

"Maddy," he said. "If you need anything . . ."

"I know," I said. "And the same goes for you. I think I should try harder to be a better friend."

"I might need a shoulder to cry on," J.B. said. "I'm king now, you know."

I stared at him. Somehow the implications of his mother's death hadn't really set in.

"King of Amarantha's court," I said. "How are you going to manage that and your Agency duties?"

"How are you going to be the Hound of the Hunt and an Agent?" J.B. shrugged. "I'll manage. Same as you."

"I'll have something else to do besides act as Hound of the Hunt, I'm sure," I said. "If Lucifer ever returns my phone calls, he'll probably want some assistance with quashing this rebellion of Azazel's."

"I can help with that, too," J.B. said. "My mother was a part of it. She was perfectly happy to enslave humans. I should do something to make up for that."

"You already have," I said quietly.

He rubbed his hands through his hair, and the gesture was so familiar and so dear that I smiled.

"I don't think I'll ever be able to do enough," he said. "We found over eighty ghosts that had been damaged and killed by the machines. There may still be more out there that we never found."

Those lost souls would haunt him, as they would haunt me.

"We can only do as much as we can," I said. "We saved the cubs. We saved the people in the warehouse. We can't save everyone."

"But we should be able to," he said, brooding.

I knew he was thinking of Gabriel, but I wasn't ready to talk about that. Part of me resented J.B. for not warning me, for not helping me avert Gabriel's death. I didn't want that tiny part to fester and grow. I knew why J.B. had made his choices.

I went home. I slept a lot more than I normally did for the next few days. I didn't miss a soul pickup. I watched movies with Beezle and Samiel when they wanted to try to cheer me up, and sometimes I even allowed myself to be cheered for a moment.

I cried when I thought they couldn't see. I wouldn't take the two coffee mugs out of the dish rack. At night I slept in

Gabriel's shirt so that it felt like I was sleeping in his embrace again.

On the fifth day after Azazel had killed my first and only love, Lucifer rang my doorbell.

I knew it was him at the bottom of the stairs. I can feel his presence, the call of blood to blood. Funny how I'd never felt that way about Azazel.

I threw a sweater over my shirt and went down to answer the door. Lucifer stood on the porch, looking solemn. I'd never invited him inside.

I opened the outside door and leaned in the jamb. "Back from Aruba, are you?"

"Will you come out and speak with me?" he said.

"Sorry—all my coats were destroyed suppressing the rebellion," I said, anger rising up at the sight of him standing there. All this could be laid at his door, every bit of it.

Lucifer sighed impatiently and snapped his fingers. A black wool overcoat appeared, much like the one that Gabriel used to wear except that it was smaller and cut for a woman. It was also a lot more expensive than anything I could have afforded for myself.

"Will you come out, please? I would speak with you about Gabriel."

I stepped out of the doorway and took the coat. "What do you want to say?"

"I am sorry," he said. "I am sorry that you lost Gabriel. I am sorry that I was not there to assist you."

"I find that very hard to believe," I said coldly. "The best chance you had of finding out who was plotting against you was to disappear."

"Yes," he admitted.

"So you did take yourself out on purpose. I thought as much," I said. "Can you see the future?"

Lucifer looked as though he wasn't certain whether he should answer that question.

"Can you?" I persisted.

"I cannot see the future the way you may imagine. I can see . . . possibilities. Implications."

"So you knew there was a *possibility* that Gabriel would die," I said. "But you never thought it necessary to mention it to me. Why? Why did you give him to me only to take him away?"

Lucifer put his arm around me. It felt like the comforting of a parent, a parent I'd always wanted—a father. The air filled with the scent of cinnamon. It reminded me so strongly of Gabriel that the tears that always hovered beneath the surface spilled over.

Lucifer said nothing, only held me as I wept. After a long while, it felt like there were no more tears to be cried. I lifted my head and saw Lucifer watching me with great compassion in his eyes.

"If there is one human emotion I truly comprehend, it is grief," Lucifer said. "I lost Evangeline and my children so long ago, and I never stopped grieving for them."

"So it doesn't stop hurting, then," I said dully.

"The pain becomes, perhaps, not quite so sharp. In the future, you may find that days may pass when you do not think of him at all, but when you do there will be a tenderness there, like a bruise that has never healed."

I didn't need Lucifer to tell me that. A piece of me had been taken forever when Gabriel died. You can't replace the missing parts of your heart.

Lucifer released me. I felt lost again, empty, except for

the flame that burned bright with anger at the thought of Azazel. He would not be able to run far enough.

"Still, all is not lost. Gabriel lives on inside you," Lucifer said.

"Yes, I've heard all the clichés." I sighed. Beezle and Samiel had been repeating them ad nauseam.

"No, I mean Gabriel really does live on inside you," Lucifer said. "Here."

He put his hand on my abdomen, and I looked up in shock.

Far below, deep inside, I felt it.

The beating of tiny wings.

An Agent of death should know when her time is up.

FROM
CHRISTINA HENRY

BLACK NIGHT

A BLACK WINGS NOVEL

If obstinate dead people were all that Maddy had to worry about, life would be much easier. But the best-laid plans of Agents and fallen angels often go awry. Deaths are occurring contrary to the natural order, Maddy's being stalked by foes inside and outside of her family, and her two loves—her bodyguard, Gabriel, and her doughnut-loving gargoyle, Beezle—have disappeared. But because Maddy is Lucifer's granddaughter, things are expected of her, things like delicate diplomatic missions to other realms.

She's an Agent of death who really needs to get a life.

FROM
CHRISTINA HENRY

BLACK WINGS

As an Agent of death, Madeline Black is responsible for escorting the souls of the dearly departed to the afterlife. It's a 24/7 job with a lousy benefits package. Sure, the position may come with magical abilities and an impressive wingspan, but it doesn't pay the bills. Things start looking up, though, when tall, dark, and handsome Gabriel Angeloscuro agrees to rent the empty apartment in Maddy's building. It's probably just a coincidence that as soon as he moves in, demons appear on the front lawn. But when an unholy monster is unleashed upon the streets of Chicago, Maddy discovers powers she never knew she possessed. Powers linked to a family legacy of tarnished halos. Powers that place her directly between the light of Heaven and the fires of Hell . . .

penguin.com
facebook.com/ProjectParanormalBooks

M975T0911